FIRE
IN THE
BLOOD

A NOVEL

PERRY O'BRIEN

RANDOM HOUSE

NEW YORK

Fire in the Blood is a work of fiction. Names, characters, places, and incidents either are the product of the author's imagination or are used fictitiously. Any resemblance to actual persons, living or dead, events, or locales is entirely coincidental.

Copyright © 2020 by Perry O'Brien

All rights reserved.

Published in the United States by Random House, an imprint of the Random House Publishing Group, a division of Penguin Random House LLC, New York.

RANDOM HOUSE and the HOUSE colophon are registered trademarks of Penguin Random House LLC.

LIBRARY OF CONGRESS CATALOGING-IN-PUBLICATION DATA
Names: O'Brien, Perry Edmond, author.
Title: Fire in the blood : a novel / Perry O'Brien.
Description: First edition. | New York : Random House, [2020]
Identifiers: LCCN 2019038390 (print) | LCCN 2019038391 (ebook) |
ISBN 9780812988581 (hardcover) | ISBN 9780812988598 (ebook)
Subjects: GSAFD: Suspense fiction.
Classification: LCC PS3615.B765 F57 2020 (print) |
LCC PS3615.B765 (ebook) | DDC 813/.6—dc23
LC record available at https://lccn.loc.gov/2019038390
LC ebook record available at https://lccn.loc.gov/2019038391

Printed in the United States of America

randomhousebooks.com

2 4 6 8 9 7 5 3 1

First Edition

Book design by Victoria Wong

To Evans, who was the best of us.

FIRE IN THE BLOOD

CHAPTER ONE

Piles of garbage lay heaped and frozen along the sidewalk of Valentine Avenue. Kosta sidestepped the jutting wing of a flayed umbrella so as to avoid catching his coat, barely slowing as he threaded his way between the mounds of snow, hopping over runnels of mud and ice. He had come to know cities as places of battle, and his momentum was dictated by a soldier's code—always stay alert, never linger—as if the Bronx were an enemy land.

Turning onto the next block, Kosta found himself halted by the sight of a new black truck: a Denali, with chrome headlights and a cheese grater grille. The vehicle was enormous, big as the armored NATO transports he'd ambushed, back in Albania.

A voice crackled in his ear.

"I'm at corner now," said Buqa. Next he heard Zameer join the line.

"So we are ready, or what? My asses are freezing for real."

Kosta checked them both with a low hiss.

He peered into the truck's window, allowing himself a moment to admire it. Leather upholstery and wood grain paneling, glowing with richness and warmth. Kosta hungered for a refined interior such as this. For a second he thought to simply take the truck, but already he could hear the scolding voice of Luzhim. "Stop thinking like a Gheg," the old man would say. "You're not in the mountains anymore."

Put differently: first came the grind, then the come up.

"On my way," said Kosta.

Framing the tenement's doorway was a tangle of buzzers and exposed wiring. Kosta mashed the buttons with his fist, and after a few seconds the door opened with an electric squawk. The entryway was colder than the street outside. Squatting in the dim light was a fat kid on a stool.

"Who're you?" said the fat kid.

Kosta closed the door with his foot, casting the entryway into orange darkness. Now he could smell the place: the unmistakable reek of human waste. Kosta looked casually around the lobby, ignoring the chubby sentry. A narrow staircase dripped with graffiti. Under the stairs was the gaping mouth of an abandoned elevator.

"Man, I said who are you?" From his back pocket the kid slung out a long gym sock, weighted at one end. He jiggled the sock against his leg with a heavy clink.

Kosta angled himself in the darkness. "So they pay you, sit down here?" he said.

The kid nodded.

"Anyone you don't recognize, you supposed to jack them?"

The kid didn't respond, but curled his fingers tighter around the sock.

Kosta nodded thoughtfully. Then he moved, a quick two-step, closing the distance as the kid flicked back his arm. But not fast enough. Now Kosta stood too close, blocking a good swing. He smiled widely, let the kid see his perfect teeth.

"They pay you enough?"

Coming up the stairs Kosta passed an old man wearing a fuzzy blue electric blanket. The corded prong hung behind him like a tail as he ambled his way down, skittering on every step.

Kosta came to the fourth floor and prowled down the hallway. Most of the rooms were closed up, except one where a pregnant girl leaned against the doorway, smoking a cigarette and wearing a Burger King crown.

"Get the fuck out of here," said Kosta to the girl.

She blinked at him and kept smoking.

Kosta snatched the cardboard crown off her head and sent it gliding down the stairwell. The girl threw her cigarette at him and closed herself behind her door.

"Okay," said Kosta, into his microphone. "Buqa, come up."

Less than a minute later she came bouncing up the stairs in her dayglo trainers. Buqa was Kosta's age but had the wide face of a child, with black-button eyes and hair pulled back too tight.

"Sorry I take so long," she breathed, a little winded from the stairs.

Together they went to the door marked 4G.

They knocked and waited, each of them looking down the hallway. When there was no answer, Buqa took a small crowbar from her jacket. The doorframe showed wounds from old pryings, and she quickly popped the bolt.

The room was empty. A bare space with a mattress on the floor and few belongings. Stacks of cardboard packages climbed one wall, the boxes filled with black Maximo spray cans and Krink markers. No sign anywhere of the missing package. Probably cut up and resold, Kosta figured; dust floating back into the ether.

He paced the room. Then went to the window, which opened to a snow-covered fire escape. Forty feet down through the ironwork was the figure of Zameer, crouched in the trash-strewn alley, using an old length of pipe to draw angry X's in the snow.

Kosta whistled.

Zameer looked up but didn't wave. "We doing this now or what?" he said, into Kosta's ear. "It's fucking cold, is reason I make the question."

Kosta shut the window and looked around the room again. Whatever might happen, he didn't want it happening here. Risk-wise, drug addicts were easy to lowball. They tended to come off compliant, even friendly, but you never knew when one of them would turn. It was how they had lost Leke, a roofer from Tirana who'd worked part-time as a soldier for Luzhim. Leke was on a collection job when out of nowhere a half-dead teenage girl had gotten up from the floor and stuck Leke in the calf with a dirty syringe. The crew kicked her to pieces, but it didn't help Leke; three days later he died at Montefiore from septic thrombosis. So no excitement inside the den, if possible.

Kosta went up another set of stairs and prowled the hallway until he came across an unoccupied room. He was working to free the swollen window frame when Zameer reported from the street.

"Hey, shit, here comes the guy."

Kosta popped the window and clambered out, tucking his head against a chilly blast of air. He crouched on the rusty scaffolding and took a moment to gain his balance, the fire escape dropping crookedly below. All around was the frozen Bronx. Skyscrapers ridged the horizon where a gash of purple light spread across the morning haze. Nearby was a church under construction, its spire wrapped in a cocoon of reconstructive mesh.

Kosta spoke into his hoodie, covering the mic with one hand to be heard above the wind.

"Okay, here's what we do."

A few minutes of quiet passed. A car went by and Kosta felt the rhythmic pulse of low-sonic dub.

There came a banging from below. Buqa in the hallway outside Sean's apartment, her knuckles going cop-loud against the door. Kosta pictured how things would go: Sean jumping to his feet, looking frantically around the small apartment. Maybe he'd risk a glance through the keyhole before realizing there was only one exit.

The knocking continued. Then came the scrape of Sean's window being opened.

Kosta drew a canister from his pocket. In the survival catalogs it was sold as "bear mace," a highly concentrated pepper spray approved for hunters and outdoor enthusiasts. Multiple labels warned that it should never be used on humans. Kosta snapped off the can's plastic safety. The fire escape trembled with new weight, and here was Sean crawling out his window, a skinny black kid in a Godzilla T-shirt, breathing hard as he climbed out into the cold, his jacket bundled under one arm.

Sean had been one of Kosta's best dealers. The kid had connects with a whole network of art-type students living in Brooklyn, a market to which Kosta would never otherwise have gained access. Which made it all the more disappointing when Sean missed their last meeting and hadn't shown up since to pay the dividends he owed.

Kosta whistled. Sean looked up and actually managed to pull off a smile, as if he was going to offer an explanation. Kosta fired the canister, discharging a whooshing cone of white fog into Sean's face.

For an instant Sean was lost in the blast, but as it cleared Kosta saw the kid's face, dark and broken by violent sobs. Sean put a hand to his eyes, taking it away from the ladder, and his body weight swung him out over the drop. He snatched himself back to the fire escape with both hands. He began to retch. His feet kicked out. He gurgled and clung for life.

Kosta leaned down, close to Sean's weeping face. "What's the deal, playboy?"

A few minutes later Kosta and Sean came downstairs, the kid's face purple and slimy. Buqa trailed behind, walking backward to cover their rear, just in case Sean had any friends in the building who might get bad ideas.

"Come around front. Check the street," said Kosta into the earphone. They waited in the entryway, where the fat kid seemed to have abandoned his post. Then came word from Zameer: no sign of police, no neighbors screaming. They decided to take Sean's wheels, a shitty old Volvo parked on the curb. Reminiscent of the cars back home, thought Kosta: stitched together from cannibalized parts and repainted in gray primer. He shoved Sean into the cramped backseat, where stuffing bloomed from gashes in the upholstery, and once again Kosta felt a longing for the Denali.

Buqa took the driver's seat, Kosta sat shotgun, and Zameer went in back with the kid. Kosta turned on the radio, found a song he liked. The beats came through as a racket of thuds on the bootleg system, but he kept up the volume in case Sean starting yelling.

The Volvo pulled off toward the Grand Concourse. He saw Buqa nodding along to the music, her relief visible. Even Zameer seemed happy.

Kosta twisted in his seat. "So," he said to Sean. "You been busy?"

Sean just squinted at him.

"A month ago I give you a package of eight bundles. Supposedly you're stinging for forty-five each, right? Except, funny thing, you don't bring nothing back. And now you don't answer your phone?"

Sean put his head down. The car slowed at an intersection.

"Which way?" said Buqa.

Kosta began to give Buqa directions when he heard a metal snap from the backseat. He turned to find Zameer with his knife out, a little hook-shaped razor, the kind they make for cutting linoleum. Zameer was tickling Sean's earlobe with the blade.

"The fuck are you doing?" said Kosta, switching to Albanian.

Zameer glared back, sticking out his chin.

In a surge of movement Kosta thrust himself between the seats, grabbed Zameer's hand and twisted away the knife.

"You fucking listen to me—" he began.

Something hit the car with a gunshot smack. Kosta whirled around just in time to see a figure slam against the front of the Volvo and fall away, vanishing beneath the wheels.

Buqa stomped the brake and the car skidded through the empty intersection.

Kosta punched off the music. He looked out every window, trying to put together what had just happened. The neighborhood was bright and silent—a weekend morning, he remembered—no one on the street except a crumpled shape in the snow behind them, lying between two arcs of tire track.

"The fuck was that?" said Zameer. He'd stopped searching for the knife and was holding Sean facedown against the backseat.

Behind them, a young woman stood up. In the gray morning light Kosta could see she had a pretty face, even with all the blood. The sun was bright on the snow. She turned toward them and began to spin, arms stretched out for balance, looking around as if getting a full picture of the world. Then she teetered and slumped to the ground.

This time she stayed there, motionless in the churned-up snow.

CHAPTER TWO

Coop made his way down a cracked strip of tar, the only highway in Afghanistan. He walked with his weapon slung at the ready, padding heel-foot, heel-foot, stalking the bright apparition that lay ahead of him: a lone pale horse, quivering in the morning light.

The wind blew cold but still Coop sweltered under the weight of his gear: his kevlar vest, helmet, and demolition pack. He was nervous about the horse and it made the sweating worse. Reels of bomb gossip played through his mind as he walked; stories of dead camels lying along the road with jiggered Russian mortars sewn up inside their bellies. Coop was pretty sure he'd only heard of this done to roadkill, whereas the horse up ahead was clearly alive. But that didn't eliminate the possibility of bioweapons. Recent briefings had stressed the possibility that Iraq had armed the Taliban with WMDs. Could the horse be infected with one of Saddam's plagues?

His radio crackled, and out came a blare of mariachi trumpets. Coop twitched at the sudden noise, fumbling with the handheld as a voice came over the music.

"Hey Specialist, that horse is like a quarter-klik out, hooah?"

Private Greely, The Fucking New Guy.

"Roger that," said Coop.

"Sergeant Anaya says maybe his morning PT ain't sufficient, you have all this energy for walking."

Coop took a knee, pointing his M4 carbine toward the dirt, and swiveled back the way he'd come. A few hundred meters down the blacktop sat his team's humvee, where Greely and Anaya were waiting. Coop keyed his radio.

"Private Greely, do me a favor and inform Sergeant Anaya that his ethnic music is compromising my stealth."

Now Coop heard Anaya's faraway voice.

"What'd he say? Give me that," and the transmission cut out for a second, Coop clearly picturing the sergeant wrestling the radio from Greely.

"Hey Specialist Cooper," said Anaya, coming on the radio, his voice full of mock authority. "Listen, Greely's calling you out. He bets his Skittles you won't ride that horse."

Coop looked at the animal in the distance. Then back at the humvee. "Ride the fucking horse," said Coop.

"Into the sunset," said the sergeant. "Greely says his Skittles for a *month*."

"And if the horse goes boom, I get what?" said Coop.

"The unending admiration of a grateful nation."

"What about my Skittles?"

"Coop, I will personally present them to your widow."

"Fuck her," said Coop. "I want the Skittles buried with me."

Over the radio came a burst of cackles. Coop reholstered the handheld in his MOLLE harness, the squawks of laughter making him aware of his own unsmiling face. *I'm sorry,* he thought, looking down at his boots, cold grit blowing against his face. *I didn't mean that thing about fuck you.*

"Drive on, hero, drive on," said the radio. "And here's some shit for your listening enjoyment."

Coop sniffed and headed off again, the mariachi music blaring around him.

They'd sighted the horse at dawn, only minutes after

Coop's convoy left FOB Snakebite. There were no towns within miles of the base. Just empty ruins, sketched under the shadows of the Sulaiman Mountains, whose vast and gauzy angles reminded Coop of a crumpled poncho. Martian desert spread endlessly west, bisected by a thin scrape of highway heading up-country to Bagram, along which the convoy would soon be traveling. And tied up along this same road, the mysterious horse. The wind had been picking up since dawn, and now the mission was on hold, waiting for a weather report. In the meantime, Captain Lee, the convoy leader, had suggested that the sapper team—consisting of Anaya, Coop, and Greely— might go investigate the animal and determine whether it constituted a mission-critical threat.

Coop had volunteered for the long walk. His solo approach was loosely informed by tactical dogma (avoid scenarios where more than one sapper could get killed in the same blast), but mostly he'd wanted a few moments to himself, away from the others. Only now Coop found his desire for solitude fading with every step.

All around him the earth had been burrowed and turned over, as if packs of wild dogs had gone digging for the bones of old wars. The excavations were the work of his colleagues, engineers on route clearance, who went out every day in big armored diggers, tractoring for land mines. If Coop had been a few degrees less hooah, this is how he would have spent the war. Instead he'd been loaned out to the infantry as part of a sapper detachment, his job to find hidden munitions in a country where there were more bombs than people.

As Coop walked he occasionally caught an angry red flare in his periphery; painted rocks flashing at him from the desert. The red rocks were an international warning symbol used for tagging minefields. Coop avoided looking at them. It was like ants on the ground, you noticed one and then suddenly the rest came wriggling into view. There were hundreds of rocks out there and despite his best efforts Coop imagined them swarming, surrounding him, causing an eruption of itchiness under his kevlar vest.

Coop tried to distract himself by making a scene of it, imagining the way he'd describe all this for Kay. The horse, still a figurine in the distance, standing alone on the cracked band of tar, Anaya's music coming out of his radio. And all around him the raw desert permeated with land mines. The last three months he'd found himself doing this: everything he saw and thought and said and felt, it all got processed in terms of how he'd tell it to Kay. It made him feel better, a connection between his present circumstances and the imagined future when he got to see his wife again.

The horse was closer now. Coop could see it was hitched to a post, just standing there, swishing its tail. A few hundred paces and he'd be there, except there was still no way of telling whether the horse was some kind of trap.

The safest thing, he reasoned, would be to go back for his protective MOPP gear. Coop imagined how his teammates would react, laughing their asses off as he got dressed up for a chemical-nuclear apocalypse, all to go check out a horse. But then his imagination countered with a more ominous vision: Greely and Anaya at the Sports USA off Reilly Road, sharing a pitcher, commiserating in their disheveled Class A's after Coop's funeral. Sergeant Anaya would say: "Fucking tragic, man. What was Coop thinking?" And Greely, the FNG, would nod in solemn agreement. "You gotta MOPP up," he'd say, slurping his Budweiser with the affect of a melancholy old-timer. The image made Coop pause on the road. He couldn't abide the notion of his death becoming fodder for the new guy's posturing.

While Coop was considering his options he felt the air began to change. Reflexively he ducked as a crackling wall of noise came tumbling over the floodplain, followed by a cold gust of sand.

"Clouds forming up," said Sergeant Anaya from the radio. "Might want to get back here, you don't want to get wet. Over."

This was the contradiction of his training, that he should cultivate an instinct for hidden ordnance—vessels with enough power to rip a person to pieces and scatter them over hundreds of yards—and then overcome his body's alarms, the chemicals that told him to flee.

"Out," said Coop, and decided, *Fuck it.*

He lumbered forward in a jostle of gear, swimming in his sweat, heat escaping his mouth in rapid breaths, just like the snorting animal in front of him.

Coop had never seen a horse up close before. This one was white with gray and pink splotches. Its eyes stared forward, or to the side; Coop couldn't tell. The horse's ribs heaved massively, suspended in a carriage of muscle.

The two of them were alone together in the desert. Coop came closer and the horse bowed its head toward the ground. Then it charged, shooting out to where the rope snagged, the horse twisting into a circular run while thrashing its head against the leash, one eye aimed wildly at the mountains.

"Whoa there," Coop said, because that's what people in movies said to horses. And now he was trapped in the circumference of its gallop. The rope was closing fast. Coop ducked, but not before it twanged across his kevlar helmet. The horse reared and made another lap, and soon the leash was coming around again. Drawing his bayonet, Coop swashbuckled the line.

The horse broke free but then slowed to a stop, pausing

nearby. Coop put away the knife, panting. He felt he could smell the hot life of the animal, its big, blood-filled heart. Left out along the road like an offering. He wanted to cross the distance between himself and the horse, wanted to put a hand to its dusty flank; not for himself and definitely not for Greely or Anaya or any quantity of Skittles, but for Kay; so this moment could be part of the story he'd tell her. Coop liked to think she would be moved by the danger of this place, the gentle courage he showed while navigating the bomb-strewn terrain. The way he did little things, like saving this fucking horse. And through the story Kay would know the goodness within him, and that would matter more to her than their fights, more than the constant lure of her family, more than the wars and all the other forces that had pulled them apart.

Coop took a step forward and the horse turned its head, regarding him with a single black eye. Coop stopped in place, feeling suddenly like a trespasser. He began to take another step but found himself deeply unnerved, as if there was some force of judgment contained in the animal's flat gaze; a reflection in which Coop saw his own fraudulent heart. The horse seemed to know the truth. Even if they were reunited, Coop would never tell Kay everything he had seen and done.

The wind came up and Coop found himself suddenly aware of his own smallness under the great billowing clouds. He started to fall back, creeping in reverse until his boots hit the highway. The horse studied his retreat with glassy indifference, a look both ominous and serene.

Thunder boomed again over the plain as Coop returned to the humvee and slung himself into the driver's seat. Anaya was on the radio, the receiver cradled between the sergeant's shoulder and his squat turtle head. Mariachi music was still playing from a small boom box.

"Horse ran off," said Coop.

Anaya gave him the thumbs-up. "Chemist Three-Three, roger, we have determined, ah, no threat to the convoy operation, over."

"You didn't ride it," said Greely from the back.

"Bullshit I didn't ride it," said Coop. "We galloped across the plains. Horse and man became one."

"Roger roger," said Sergeant Anaya into the radio, "what is the mission status, over?"

"Why'd you cut it loose?" said Greely. "It's just standing there."

"Any news on the mission?" said Coop. Anaya held up his hand for silence.

Somewhere back at the staging ground, Captain White would be consulting with Bagram, getting a report from the weather combat team, whose pressure sensors might register a dip in the atmosphere; a forewarning of sudden rainfall that could flood the valley and wash their convoy from the road. Coop hoped the mission wouldn't be canceled. There had been a lot of recent gossip about a Big Operation coming down the pike. That very morning, before they went off to inspect the horse, Greely had spotted two boonie-capped civilians in a powwow with Captain White. "Don't get too riled," Anaya had warned when Greely made this report. "CIA don't automatically make it a high-speed mission, hooah?"

Rumors of The Big Op had started with PFC Tosker, a Bravo mechanic from Philadelphia whose Italian-speaking girlfriend sent him a clipping from *Il Messaggero* profiling a local paratrooper. According to the article, this Roman was "currently deployed to a remote Southeastern base, assisting US Forces with the ongoing hunt for Abdul Razaq, former Minister of the Treasury under the Taliban." As others had excitedly observed, there were Italian forces stationed at FOB

Snakebite, so when a convoy operation was announced a few days after Tosker got the article, gossip shifted heavily toward this Razaq guy being the target. It was more information than they ever got from Command, and it was enough for Coop to get excited. His unit had arrived in the wake of Operation Anaconda, a monthlong pummeling of the fighters who'd hunkered in the eastern mountains. President Karzai kept saying that Bin Laden was most likely dead, and in the first weeks of his deployment Coop had begun to worry he'd missed the war. But now, after seven months of missions, his new fear was that he hadn't done anything in Afghanistan he could truly be proud of. Certainly he had done things he regretted.

"No word yet," said Anaya, cradling the handset.

"You know what I'll bet happens to that horse?" said Greely, still talking from the backseat. "Prolly gets eaten by mountain dogs."

A line of gun trucks were arranged along the sloped ridge just down the road from FOB Snakebite, and Coop parked the truck alongside this formation. Overhead the sun had come up but the sky was still darkening toward storm.

"Be back, I'm checking with Command," said Anaya as he dismounted. Coop opted to stay behind and make some final inspections on the vehicle. He watched the sergeant and Greely head downhill toward the staging area, a garden of crooked olive trees and rubble where the infantry sat back-to-back in pairs on the ground, tearing open their morning MREs. Haggling over chow had just begun.

"Cheese spread for cinnamon drink, y'all."

"Peanut butter! Who wants some motherfucking peanut butter?"

Coop turned his attention to the truck. Their humvee was

an eighties-era tactical clunker; basically a plus-sized doorless jeep, still painted green for jungle warfare. For extra armor the floor of the truck had been packed down with several layers of sandbags. According to the official explanation, this protective barrier would help deaden the impact of a land mine or IED, though Coop suspected the result would just be extra sand in your corpse.

"Pound cake?" said Greely, suddenly standing behind him. Coop hadn't heard the private come back up the hill.

"I can't shit for days, I eat one of these," said Greely, holding out a brown foil rectangle.

Coop waved the package away.

"You don't wanna come down and eat with the others?" said Greely.

"I'm good," said Coop. "Gonna resecure these tarps, case it keeps breezing up like this."

"Hooah, hooah," said Greely, lingering by the truck. Coop found himself irritated by the FNG's presence. His kevlar helmet was tilted crookedly, with the chin strap undone, and Greely wore a pair of wraparound polychromatic shades that always reminded Coop of rich-kid snowboarders and highway cops. In the Army they called people like him "ate-up," but it was more than just sloppiness. *Gaumy,* that's what he was, a good old Maine word. Working the tie-downs, Coop contemplated a renaming: Private Gaumy the FNG. He wondered if he could pitch the new nickname to Anaya.

"Chaplain will be here soon," said Greely. He jerked his thumb back to where the grunts were assembled.

"Think I'm good," said Coop.

"You miss the prayer, maybe God lets us drive over a mine. Then that tarp ain't gonna do shit, right?"

Coop turned around to face Greely. He pointed to the far

mountains. "Tell me, Greely, the Taliban fighters living up there in the caves, with nothing but their old Russian weapons and raw onions to eat—you really think any of us are praying harder than them?"

"Joke's on them," said Greely. "Praying to the wrong God."

Coop assumed a grim smile. He knew Greely was just playing his role in the banter. But still the conversation somehow made him angry.

"Hell, Greely, you ever read the Bible? This is the place where your God got invented."

Then Coop turned back to the truck and pretended to make a few more adjustments with the tie-downs until he heard Greely shuffle away. He looked back and watched Greely join the other soldiers as they finished breakfast, leaving their rucksacks and gear in little hillocks throughout the ruins. The grunts began to thicken, standing together without helmets or BDU jackets, bare arms showing tattoos of barbed wire, sugar skulls, and Jump Wings bearing gothic proclamations like "Death from Above."

The gathering provoked a thin sense of longing in Coop. He marveled at the grunts' ability to freely answer the call to come together, to join with your fellows; a shared goodness to which Coop no longer felt he had any claim. But still it pulled at him, and after watching a few more minutes Coop found himself venturing down the hill.

Soon the chaplain arrived, coming weaponless into the disorderly pack. He was lean and bowed like a rusted lumber blade and seemed to belong elsewhere, not to the soldiers and their coarse slackness but to the bare desert and the sky that shadowed them all. The chaplain wore Special Forces and Ranger tabs on both shoulders, and on his right lapel an embroidered crucifix. At his arrival the other soldiers quieted, put out their cigarettes, scooped chaw from their lips and flicked it on the ground.

"Gather round, troops," said the chaplain. "Gather round." Coop hung at the periphery. He imagined the farther he was from the center of the group, the less his misgivings would contaminate the ritual.

"What is this gaggle?" barked the chaplain. "Come around now, everyone link arms."

The grunts became a dense wall of human camouflage. Coop saw Greely grinning within the press, wearing those ridiculous sunglasses. The chaplain began to speak:

"Now, troops, this is a nondenominational prayer. There's no litmus test for faith in my Army, men. You can be a Christian, pagan, Satanist, Jedi, whatever you may feel. I'm going to say some words about my God, and all I ask is you consider who exactly you're appealing to for protection on this blessed morning. You wouldn't kick down a door without knowing who had your six, hooah?"

"Hooah," the circle responded.

The chaplain lowered his head and began to pray.

Almighty God, I ask for your blessing.
These are humble creatures before You,
this congregation of infantry.
Pay no attention to their ferocity,
for though they are made of sand and steel,
these men are fragile and require your favor.
These are killers, God, but they are *your* killers.

"Hooah, amen," said the grunts, and they began to release one another. But the chaplain let forth with a second movement. His voice lost its bark and took on a low, quivering quality, a seizured crooning—*like a Pentecostal Elvis,* Coop thought.

There are IEDs out there, Oh Lord, and forces
of the devil who would do them harm!
You, Lord, who cast out the serpent,
help us destroy the enemies of salvation!
Save your mercy for these men.
I beg for their protection from wickedness
so they may enjoy each other's camaraderie
and the fruits of this world for one more day.
Amen.

Coming back up the hill Coop heard the roar of truck engines, the mechanical swiveling of turrets, the *thwunk*ing of rucks being loaded into the bed of humvees. Anaya stood by their truck wearing a big grin.

"Fuck the rain," he said. "Mission's a go. You ready to mount up?"

The sun shone hard over the battered desert. Coop drove with one hand raised in salute, trying to block the glare while his foot fluttered rapidly between gas and brake. The team's sapper vehicle was next to last in the order of march, and all day the convoy had stretched and collapsed like an accordion, a constant flashing of red brake lights. Several times they became lost and were forced to execute tactical halts and turnarounds until it was discovered that some of the vehicles had different versions of the same Soviet map.

At dusk the convoy chugged down a narrow mountain pass, slowing to ease around a series of switchbacks.

"Ahoy," said Greely, pointing to a cluster of flat-roofed buildings huddled beneath a hogback ridge. Coop heard a *whump* of displaced air and looked up to see three black Kiowas taking the lead. Coop leaned on the accelerator, speeding them toward the enemy.

"Easy," said Anaya, patting the air with a cautionary glove. "Slow is smooth, smooth is fast."

The convoy snaked toward a gap in the village wall. By the time Coop brought their truck to a halt, teams of infantry had already dismounted. Anaya gave the radio a "hooah" and an "over-out," then presented Greely and Coop each with a gloved fist.

"All right, engineers, let's bump it. C'mon Coop, bump it!"

Coop dropped from the humvee. Using the door as cover he squatted down to take up a firing position, cushioning his cheek against the plastic stock of his M4.

The village was made up of about forty buildings, each an angular mound of clay. There wasn't a body in sight: no one in the tapered alleys, nothing moving in the square. Engines idled. Radios scoffed with tactical gossip. Outside the perimeter Coop heard the intermittent shouts of infantry across the dusty courtyard, and over their heads, the steady hum of the Kiowas.

From the top hatch of the command vehicle Coop saw Bill pop out with a megaphone. Bill was the unit's hired interpreter, a stumpy Afghan wearing glasses and an oversized helmet. He lifted the megaphone to his mouth, cleared his throat, and coughed out a tirade of back-throated Pashto, the voice echoing off the clay walls. Coop understood the gist of it: *Come out with your hands up.* For added effect one of the Kiowas performed a low buzz, tracing the dusty architecture with its spotlight.

As if they had been waiting for this courtesy, men began to emerge from the village huts. They came a few at a time, palms raised, robes blowing around them, squinting into the weapon lights. Their mouths moved emphatically, as if trying to reason with Bill and his megaphone, the soldiers, helicopters, and all their millions of rounds of ammunition, held in suspense.

As the men began to show themselves, grunt teams swept forward to clear the village. Raids were conducted in three stages. First came the infantry, bounding like a pack of pit bulls, sizing up the villagers for signs of a fight and then happily and viciously barking off. After the infantry came the MP shepherds, pulling everyone from their homes, separating men from women, corralling them in the village square. Finally, Coop and the other sappers, bloodhounds with their snouts to the ground.

The buildings of the village were of the usual construction; flat-roofed huts of mud and clay, with doors framed by raw timber or pallet wood. Standing in Coop's first hut was a woman he recognized: Corporal McKenzie, an admin clerk he knew from Airborne School. McKenzie had been drafted for door busting by the Military Police, who never had sufficient female recruits to search all the Afghan women they detained. She stood over a blue ghost crouched on the floor of the hut, a woman in a burqa, struggling to pull clothes on a shivering little boy. The boy's eyes jumped between soldier and veiled mother, and in the flashlight Coop saw the kid's snot-crusted nose, his turquoise pajamas with cheap gold embroidery, and the outline of murmuring lips as the woman made shushing sounds from behind the ornate screen.

"I know, I know," McKenzie was saying, "but you gotta hurry it up, Mama." Then she saw Coop and grinned, punching him playfully on the arm.

"Hey there, jump buddy," she said. "I'll be clear in a sec."

McKenzie cracked and shook a chemlight before dropping it on the clay floor, signifying the hut had been cleared of civilians. Her freckles glowed in the blue light. "All yours," she said, and gave Coop a wink.

"Okay, Mama, *gzi gzi*," she said to the woman, ushering her out of her tiny home.

There wasn't much to search. Two dusty rugs lay on the ground, the weaving undone and dangling. Coop lifted the rugs, tossed over a lumpy sleeping mat, shook dust from a mound of bedding. Besides the rugs and the mat, the entire contents of the hut were the following: two handmade pots, three food cans with Arabic labels, a single blackened onion, two cloth bags of long-grain rice, one aluminum can containing rusty nails, a roll of tape, and a single ink pen decorated with glued-on fragments of indigo glass. Coop stood in the small, cold room, letting his weapon hang from the sling. One hut down and he could already feel it: There was nothing in the village. No Taliban chief, no arms cache, nothing but dust.

Coop cracked a red chemlight and left the hut. The far sky had deepened to a purple band on the horizon, and through a wide alley between the huts Coop could see the main square, brightened by spotlights to an unnatural clarity that reminded Coop of night construction. The captive Afghan men lay facedown and spread-eagled while military police patted them down. At the periphery the women and kids were cordoned together, a brightly colored band of blowing veils and crying children. Coop looked for the child in the turquoise pajamas but couldn't pick him out from the crowd.

Turning from the square, Coop drifted back to the village periphery. Under the mountain's shadow it had turned to complete night, with just the glow of red and blue chemlights emanating from the mouths of old clay huts, and the occasional flashlight beam swimming through the dark. Absently Coop wandered into another hut, giving the sparse quarters just a few quick glances under his flashlight before he threw down one of the red chemlights from his cargo pocket. When he came out he saw Greely leaving a nearby hut, the private's weapon slung low as he drifted toward the darkened cluster of ruins at the back end of the village.

Coop was working on his third hut when Greely came running up, pale-faced, his mouth working silently before he coughed out the words.

"I found some crazy shit."

Lying in the shadows with its dented fins, the bomb seemed ready to swim away. Eight feet long, and easily a five-hundred-pounder, Coop estimated. An old Russian blockbuster. And tattooed across every inch of the shell were running tigers, a huge mystical eye, oasis scenes, beautiful flowing script.

Sergeant Anaya came in shortly after Coop. He crouched, took off his helmet, and stroked one hand across the painted bomb.

"Look at you," he said in a low, intimate voice. "You could kill us all."

The sergeant stood and wiped off his palms. "All right, I'm going to find the commander, see if the terp can hook me up with an old-timer, maybe figure out what the deal is with this monster. You two set up the lights and gear, hooah?"

"Hooah," Greely practically yelled, manic with the importance of his discovery.

Anaya headed out, turned back at the door. "And Coop, you wanna get me a collateral estimate? Probably want to round up."

Coop went outside to take the measurements. On his waterproof green notebook he did some field-expedient math, adding the approximate explosive weight of the aerial bomb to the initiating C4, plus some guesswork to get a sense of the blast damage. From the edge of the hut he performed a pace count, walking out to where he guessed the initial detonation would reach. He whistled. Checked the pad again. Felt a small tic in his heart. Remeasured, looked up, used his arm to indicate the blast angle. Even in the best scenario, there were seven homes he could figure being vaporized by the explosion. One of them was the first hut he'd searched, home of the kid in the turquoise pajamas.

Back inside, the hut was filled with buzzing light. Greely had finished angling the tripods, big battery-powered bulbs that made the bomb seem even more enormous in the cramped clay dwelling. Dust spilled through the hot white air and over the unrolled wire reel with fifty feet of detonation cord, the MDI kit, a galvanometer, and a pair of lineman's pliers. Then Greely came up licking his lips. Looking weirdly anxious.

"What is it?" said Coop.

"Specialist," said Greely, out of breath. "You have to let me put my dick on this bomb."

Coop stared at him.

"You're fucking with me."

"Please, Coop."

Ever since they invaded Afghanistan, photos had been circulating within engineer units. Grainy shots of guys exposing themselves to unexploded ordnance, dicks hovering over mortars and piles of grenades, and though Coop hadn't seen it, there was an alleged photo of their first sergeant with a grenade hanging off his cock.

"I'll give you three minutes," Coop said, turning away to study the rubble that had been piled against the opposite wall.

"Coop? One more thing. Like, a big favor."

"Not a chance."

The private lifted his arms toward the smashed-in roof. "But who's gonna take the picture?"

As Coop walked out of the hut, he heard Greely mutter

"Okay, Jesus" and unbuckle his gear. He put his eyes back on the notepad, hoping somehow to magic the calculations. Change it so the kid's house would get spared.

Anaya returned from the square wearing a slightly stunned expression. "What the fuck?" he said, looking into the hut, then jumped back out.

"Jesus Goddam Christ," he said. "Fucking new guy."

"Fucking new guy," Coop agreed. "What say the council of elders?"

Anaya shook his head. "Total goatfuck. Afghans are telling Bill and the CIA guy that we were just here last week."

"Wait, our guys already raided this town?"

"Not us, I don't think. But the old hajji says the soldiers wore our camo," said Anaya. He tugged on Coop's sleeve in monkeyish imitation. "Like this, they were saying. Same uniform."

"That's fucked," said Coop.

"Captain White was confused as hell, he went out to radio with HQ. Thing is, they said these other soldiers *took* some people."

"What do you mean they took people?"

"Arrested them, supposedly. Bill said it was probably a local warlord looking for ransoms, but the CIA guy says no way, all the chiefs in this region are on the payroll."

"Wait," said Greely, coming out of the hut. "What's up with the CIA? Did you tell them about the bomb we found?"

"So what are we gonna do?" said Coop. Anaya shrugged.

"Mr. CIA says we give these folks money and destroy any weapons we find. So let's boom this bitch."

"Listen, Sergeant," said Coop. "I'm wondering, any way we can try moving this thing instead?"

Anaya looked at him incredulously. "Sure, I'll just put it on my back, hump it back to the FOB."

"The collateral is bad," said Coop.

"Sucks to be hajji," said Anaya with a shrug. "First Sergeant says twenty minutes until rollout. Maybe you want to go in there, play red wire, blue wire?"

They began to lay the explosives. While they worked, a few MPs showed up with an assortment of other confiscated weapons: a handful of curved daggers, some cans of gasoline-smelling sludge, and a bolt-action hunting rifle with a busted stock. These were arranged around the bomb like offerings, all wound together with loops of det-cord.

"Hell of an arms cache," said Greely.

CHAPTER THREE

Greely drove for the return trip, leaving Coop in the backseat, alone with his misgivings. He kept thinking about the upturned faces of the Afghans, watching as fireworks replaced the sky over their village.

They were almost back to FOB Snakebite when a call came in over the radio.

"Pyro Two, this is Black Cat Three-Three, over."

"Roger, this is Pyro Two," said Anaya.

"Once you guys arrive, have Specialist Cooper report to the TOC. Captain wants to see him, over? It's urgent."

Coop sat up. The sweat went cold on his neck. "What was that, Sergeant?"

"Roger," said Anaya, into the radio. "We'll be there, maybe twenty mikes. Pyro Two out."

"Why's the captain want to see *me*?" said Coop, coming forward between the seats.

The sergeant yawned and patted his face. "How should I know?"

Greely revved the humvee up a steep incline, and Coop slid back into the rear compartment, the engine rumbling in his guts. *Wants to see me urgently*, he thought. Coop looked to the dusty road ahead, where shadows jumped away from the light, and his mind traveled back to October. He saw an ancient chimney rising up from the sand, surrounded by rubble and red-painted rocks.

Coop rubbed at his eyes and looked around the humvee. In the rearview mirror he caught sight of a pale, stricken face; his own reflection. *They caught me,* he thought. *Somehow they caught me.*

Once inside the FOB they left Coop at the edge of tent city. He watched the humvee putter away, imagining the mission's conclusion: Anaya would circle up with the noncoms while Greely ghosted the motor pool, trying to steal a drip pan so he could log out the vehicle. Then Coop's teammates would be free. They'd hit the DFAC for hot chow, possibly grab a shower, then head off to the sleep tent, where, swaddled in Gore-Tex cloaks, they'd finally get to rack out while the rest of camp began its morning. Staring down the crooked path of sand that led to the TOC, Coop feared he was facing a different kind of day.

It was almost 0500 Zulu, twenty hours since Coop and the others had left the base. Lone grunts were starting to slip from their sleep tents, and from the blue-dark morning came the first formations of runners, each gang led by a private carrying their unit's guidon, the pennants bobbing over the shoe-kicked dust. The soldiers sang cadence as they ran, and Coop caught snatches from the nearest group:

Mama mama can't you see,
what this Army's done to me?

Continuing down the path, he tried to keep his mind on the soreness of his sleep-starved joints. Overhead the camp lights were seething in a fury of insects.

Every step carried Coop closer to the unavoidable conclusion that his lie from October had been uncovered. He knew what would happen next. They'd take him off Anaya's team to spend the rest of deployment washing dishes with the crazies. Like Private Linklater from construction platoon, who'd gotten bad news from his wife and tried swigging a canteen full of ammonia. Or that grunt Figueroa, busted for locking and loading on a fellow soldier after accusing him of stealing a *Sex and the City* DVD. Rather than sending these lunatics home, Command threw them on kitchen patrol, and Coop expected he'd end up there, too, at least until he was court-martialed.

He eyed the glinting razor-wire fence, felt the immense presence of the Conex storage containers. The sun had set and Coop began to smell the reek of smoke from the burn pit, where hajji contractors worked all night feeding refuse to the fire.

The Tactical Operations Center was a collection of three newly fabricated B-huts shrouded under a tent of camouflage netting. A long ramp led to the swinging double doors of the main building, and muraled over this threshold was a big-chested woman in robes. Saint Barbara, the patron mother of demolitionists. In one hand she held a cartoon bomb, and in the other a fistful of jagged lightning. Rather than trespass under her image, Coop instead chose to circle around the perimeter of the TOC. At the rear of the complex was a smoking pit—currently occupied. Coop watched from under the meshwork canopy. A figure was perched in one of the lawn chairs arranged around the ash pail, a smoldering cherry poised between two fingers. Coop sniffed; the air was spiced with the smell of clove cigarettes. Then the ember brightened, and Coop recognized the freckled cheeks of his jump buddy, Corporal McKenzie. She was already cleaned up from the mission, wearing a fresh uniform and good boots, her hair still wet from a shower. But something was wrong. Her eyes were wet and she shuddered a little between drags.

It occurred to Coop that McKenzie, being a clerk, might know something about his summons, and more than anyone else, she might be willing to help.

"Coop!" McKenzie said, wiping her eyes as he stepped from behind the camo net.

Abruptly she was hugging him. "Oh Jesus Coop, I am so fucking sorry."

Coop went rigid. His heart hit an irregular pulse as she cried against the dusty shoulder of his gear, and he watched in surprise as his own arms floated up to return the embrace. He felt a slackening of his nerves. Since October the guilt had coiled and grown in his intestines. But now the secret had been taken from him. McKenzie knew.

"It's fucking unfair," McKenzie said.

Coop pulled her closer, getting dust all over her clean clothes and showered skin. He shivered with the notion that somehow, even knowing what he'd done, McKenzie was still able to like him.

"They told you everything?" he said.

"Just that it happened yesterday. I'm so, so sorry."

Coop fell back from her, shook his head. "Yesterday? Wait."

They looked at each other for a moment, and McKenzie's tear-streaked face assumed a sudden panic.

"Oh, god . . . oh god," she said, and looked around the tented yard as if seeking cover.

"Hey," Coop said, his fingers tightening on her arms. "McKenzie."

"I can't, I can't . . ." She shook her head. "Oh, fuck, Coop, you need to talk to the chaplain. Go inside, please."

"What did you hear? Are they here for me?"

A creak. Both of them turned toward the unhinging of the TOC's back door. Standing on the deck was one of the junior clerks, taking in the scene with a raised eyebrow. "Oh," he said. "Sorry to interrupt."

"Wait," said McKenzie. "Private, go back inside." She turned her eyes back to Coop, said again with a frantic whisper: "The chaplain. Talk to him."

"Corporal," the clerk continued, impatiently, "Captain told me to give you the heads-up. That engineer whose wife got killed, he's on his way over."

"Get the fuck back inside!" said McKenzie. But her eyes stayed on Coop.

Coop started blinking. First at the clerk, then at McKenzie. He didn't understand.

"Hooah," muttered the clerk, and banged back into the operations center.

"What did you say?" Coop managed. He was trying to follow these impressions down a new, darkened path. Everything was starting to buzz, and Coop turned his back on McKenzie. He put his hands on his helmet. There was a moment of pure relief, the thrill of amnesty. Then came the acid, gushing up from his bowels in a caustic wave. Coop bent forward and spit up his stomach on the gravel. He sank forward and stayed there until he was lifted away.

Coop sat alone in the commander's office, a bottle of water shaking in his hand. The office had a single small window, shaded by sandbags, and a fluorescent light bolted to the ceiling. A large map of Afghanistan bristled with pushpins. Captain White's only other wall decorations were a Celtic cross soldered from bullet shells and concertina wire, and a hand-painted plaque that read BE POLITE. BE PROFESSIONAL. BUT HAVE A PLAN TO KILL EVERYONE YOU MEET.

On the captain's desk was a short stack of folders held down by a glass paperweight. Trapped inside the glass was a rearing camel spider. Coop tried counting the tiny hairs on the spider's legs. Then he looked back at the map, avoiding the gaze of the chaplain, who sat across from him, his face a crinkled frown.

"It was a real mess-up," the chaplain said, "you finding out the way you did."

Coop risked a look into the chaplain's gray eyes and instantly shifted his gaze away. In these early minutes of grief he was beginning to learn there were consequences for allowing his mind to stray.

"I won't presume to know your sufferings, right now," the chaplain continued. "But son, I need to ask, are you a person of faith? Because you're being tested very seriously."

Coop yawned. He couldn't help it; he needed to flex his jaw, as if some suffocating thing was crawling up from his throat.

"Now listen, we're gonna get you home, Cooper. Captain's already talking to Brigade. Give you a break, you can go to the funeral, sort some things out."

Finally, this got Coop's attention. Going home.

"There's just one hang-up, Specialist, so bear with me. Do you remember signing your wife up with DEERS?"

The chaplain went on to explain there had been some bureaucratic confusion. The emergency Red Cross message had clearly identified the late Katherine Bellante as Coop's wife, married in the state of North Carolina, but the Defense Enrollment system didn't have Kay registered as Coop's dependent. Until they could get things sorted, Brigade wouldn't be able to cut orders for emergency leave.

"I've already talked with your commander, and what we're gonna do is get you to K2 while we sort this out, so you can be on the first plane home. Okay, Coop? You listening?"

Coop stood up. His helmet rolled from his lap and hit the floor with a bony crack. He left his rifle leaning against the wall and walked out of the captain's room and into the TOC's main chamber, past the computer clickers and map scanners and book counters, outside across the empty road and into the city of tents. Coop unbuckled his Kevlar armor, let it slump off his back. His body trembled with nervous energy.

Overhead came a volley of cackling birds. Coop tracked them as they flew west to hunt the desert floor.

Then, suddenly, he could smell her. Dandelions and bug spray, the perfume of Kay's body, this smell of home rising up from the crust of the desert. All he had to do was go to her. Behind him Coop heard footsteps, the slow crunch of gravel. Someone scooped up his vest. He ignored them and followed Kay's smell through rows of giant Conex containers. She was there somewhere, hiding.

He went faster now, running over rubber cables and humming air units. Onto the airfield and across the tarmac, where Chinooks lay like upended windmills, and beyond, to a short stretch of scrub grass and windblown litter. Wading through the grass Coop collected a tangle of plastic fibers around one leg, trailing like unspooled innards. He stopped by the final boundary between camp and desert, a high fence of coiled razors. She was out there, Coop felt, just past the concertina, her scent drifting up from the pores of the desert. All he needed to do was hurdle the wire, slice his palms, find her in the hollow of sand beneath a red-painted rock.

Coop started toward the wire. Behind him came a quick murmur of boots.

His collar tightened and he was tugged backward, strangled, the smell of his wife flashing like gasoline as Coop toppled backward into the grabbing hands, riding them toward the ground. He saw it was Greely flailing underneath him, and with a growl Coop put a forearm across the private's neck. Abruptly the earth slammed into his back. Gravity had turned on him, and now a hunched mass straddled his chest, stealing the air from his lungs. Coop growled and stabbed his hands into Anaya's belly, trying to wriggle away. One leg kicked free and he hooked it around Anaya's neck. But the sergeant keeled sideways with cunning momentum, pivoting in the hard scratch, and Coop had barely drawn breath before a new force filled the space under his chin.

Black flies congregated at the periphery of Coop's vision. Just before going unconscious he thought he saw the chaplain, a wicker figure against the firelight, watching Coop get choked unconscious. Then smoke and shadow pressed in on him, blooms of fire in the infinite black.

CHAPTER FOUR

Kafe Skanderbeg was empty but for the three saints, gathered as usual around their television in the corner. Kosta stood on the sidewalk, spying through a frosted window. On the big television screen was a scrambling of black and white soccer uniforms, KF Tirana at Belarus. The three old men were in midritual, as if conducting the game, a pantomime of finger-jabbing obscenity and vigorous supplication.

The saints turned as Kosta entered. They watched him shed his fine wool topcoat and shake away the snow. Underneath he wore his tailored black suit and a chunky, onyx-colored Bulgari. The watch was fake but it was a good fake. He hung the coat among the pillowy jackets of the old men and took a table at the other end of the room.

The sounds of the game mingled with turbo-folk coming from the kitchen—a pandemonium of violins and synth beats—and under this landscape of noise Kosta could make out whispery tunnels of gossip. One of the old men stared at him with hard eyes and spat into his cup.

"Coffee," said Kosta, as one of Luzhim's runners came over to his table. "And tell him I'm here."

Kosta waited for his drink and tried to ignore the old men's curses. Normally he would wear their judgments proudly, the same way he wore his clothes. But tonight he felt a chill on his hackles; the last breaths of the girl they'd left dying in the snow.

The coffee arrived. Surreptitiously Kosta lifted the cup and held it suspended a hair's width from the saucer. He heard a slight clink of porcelain. His hand was shaking. Kosta continued to grip the cup, the muscles in his forearm straining, and gradually the clicking took on a menacing, hungry quality, like the pincers of crabs.

The runner returned from the kitchen and Kosta swallowed the remainder of his drink in a scalding chug.

"What?" said Kosta.

"He's ready for you."

The door to Luzhim's office was on the second floor of the Kafe. Kosta knew the protocol. From inside a tin box next to the door he retrieved a pouch made of antistatic mesh, the kind they used to ship computer components. He placed his cellphone inside this envelope and returned it to the tin container, then knocked.

"Come in," replied a low, croaking voice.

The lights were off, but street glow illuminated the room. Luzhim sat with his feet propped up on a battered aluminum desk, a wiry old geezer with a full beard and military buzz-cut, sipping *rakia* from a china teacup.

"Sit down, sit down," said Luzhim. He offered Kosta a bottle from his desk drawer, sloshing it around. A glass was poured and they toasted.

"*Gezuar.*"

The *rakia* tasted of apples and gasoline.

"The three saints," said Luzhim, sipping from his cup, "they give you a hard time?"

Kosta shrugged.

"Old fuckers," growled Luzhim. "For them it's football, football, football." He held up a finger. "It has nothing do with a man's country."

"Luzhim, we need to talk—" Kosta paused. He was eager to report on the run-over girl, but didn't want to sound panicked, as if the situation was out of control.

"Of course, of course," said Luzhim. "But first a matter of business."

From a drawer Luzhim produced an old metal device that looked like an intercom. While he fiddled with the knobs, the old man's other hand scratched at the gray hair on his throat, where just beneath the beard was an angry rupture of scar tissue. Kosta found himself staring at this raised asterisk of flesh. The old wound a visual echo to the red star of Communism, a symbol featured prominently on the walls. All round Luzhim's office hung awards from the Sigurimi, Albania's long-disbanded secret police, these certificates displayed alongside plaques of recognition for his humanitarian efforts. Luzhim's official job was director of Rebuild the Homeland, a charity whose ostensible mission was fundraising for reconstruction efforts in Kosova.

Luzhim finished tinkering with the box, and a low, steady hiss filled the room.

"Okay, business," said Luzhim, clapping his hands together. "The boat arrives this morning, and for you I have a quarter key, high-cut."

"A quarter. You need, eh . . ." Kosta was preoccupied, he struggled with the math. "So, eighteen five?"

Luzhim shook his head. "For this I'm thinking twenty-two. And remember, Kosta, you still owe me eighteen five from the last—"

"I know, I know," said Kosta, waving away the conversation. As if his debts to the old man could be so easily banished. "Look, my guys, they couldn't sell the last batch for more than forty-five per ticket. You feel me?"

The smile vanished from Luzhim's face. He set down his

teacup and put his palms together. "Kosta," he said. "Why must you talk like a nigger?"

Kosta stared. What he wanted to do was grab the old man by his beard and smash his face through the window. Instead he lowered his voice and, switching to Albanian, said: "We killed a girl yesterday."

Kosta watched the flicker of shock in Luzhim's eyes. Luzhim lifted his chin and began urgently scratching at the red scar. "It's bad timing, Kosta."

"I know."

"I'm leaving tomorrow on important business."

Kosta nodded. One of Luzhim's regular trips to Macedonia, though Kosta hadn't been told the purpose. This was one of his grievances with Luzhim, how little information was shared. He couldn't be sure if this secrecy was the man's paranoia, or just paternal disdain. *I'm your father figure,* Luzhim had said, once, when he was very drunk. *Figura patrona.* The expression always made Kosta think of the church ruins near his old village, back in the mountains. All those headless statues.

"Okay," said Luzhim, pressing his temples. "So this girl, she was business?"

Kosta shook his head. "Just something stupid."

"What's your liability?"

"One of our street-level associates, he saw the thing. But we've got him."

Luzhim nodded. "At least there's that. Where are you keeping him? Not at the duplex?"

"Of course not," Kosta lied.

Luzhim sat back, sipping his *rakia.* "Why don't you tell me. What would you do if I had already left?"

Fuck, thought Kosta. He hated coming for advice, hated reporting a mistake to this man.

"That's why I come here," said Kosta. "To get your advice."

"And that's why I make the question. Walk me through. What next?"

Kosta sucked air through his nose. "We already got rid of the car," he muttered.

They'd taken the Volvo to the junk-filled swamp under the Port Morris tunnels, then discharged three cans of oven cleaner into the interior to scour away any incriminating residues.

"As for our associate," Kosta continued, "I figure we have to let him go."

Luzhim held up a finger. Fuck. Kosta knew he'd stumbled.

"Even though someone might be looking for him?" said Luzhim. "His family, maybe? Or what about his clients, a whole tribe of monkeys needing their fix."

"He's an artist, lives alone. Makes drawings on the wall."

"So maybe he's a faggot, with a faggot boyfriend who goes to the police."

Kosta sat back. He looked out the window, wanting to crawl out there and bury himself under all that freezing slush. He could sense, overhead, those vast meteors—*consequences*—and all their gravity, ready for collision.

"This associate," said Luzhim. "You can sit on him for a while?"

Kosta nodded. He could see Luzhim's gray eyes working in the darkness.

"Keep him junked. Hang on to his phone, see who calls. Watch the news. A few weeks pass and you don't hear nothing, it's maybe safe."

"A few *weeks*?"

"In the meantime I'll give you something. A formula. Something the Czechs used to make."

Luzhim stood from his chair and consulted the bureau again.

Kosta felt a bad taste in his mouth. *The formula.* Something from the old days, a toxic mix of brain fryers and hallucinogens, developed to neutralize the People's Enemies. A potion to inflict hell.

Luzhim returned from the storeroom and placed the rectangular metal container on the desk. A Russian snakebite kit. Gingerly he opened the tin, revealing three glass ampules packed in sawdust.

"You give your dealer the formula, understand?" Luzhim rasped. "Play the angles with me. Worst case, the police come looking, but when they find him, what? He's crazy. A fucking junkie, they're all crazy.

"But let's say nobody comes looking," he continued. "Then disposal becomes a confident matter, and easier, because he's—" Luzhim's throat seemed to seize up, he coughed raspily, opened his mouth, coughed again. Giving up, he twirled his finger around near his temple to indicate insanity.

"Got it," said Kosta. "Super."

"Super, yes, indeed," said Luzhim. "Now, about the girl. Who was she?"

Kosta shrugged, and Luzhim lowered his head again, in disappointment.

"Kosta, you know what I went through, for you to get your papers? Check the obituaries. And don't fuck this up."

Kosta stood up. "You don't need to worry."

Luzhim sat back. He nodded to himself, clearly satisfied at his role in repairing the crisis.

"Good luck in Macedonia," said Kosta.

"Of course." Luzhim grinned. "And about the other thing?"

"I'll get your twenty."

CHAPTER FIVE

Dusk came down over Karshi-Khanabad Airbase, the last pit stop before the war. Falling from the orange horizon came an endless procession of aircraft, big planes landing on the pitted runway, discharging their load, then returning to the sky. Coop tracked the planes as he drifted through the commotion of the airbase. All around were jib cranes and flashing lights. Forklifts scurried past like giant ants, freight clutched in their jaws, going out to the supply yard where towering monuments of cargo were erected and torn apart.

Out in the distance was a bright orange lace among the foothills. Wildfires. Coop had seen them every night of the last week, ever since he'd been marooned at K2. Moko had explained the phenomenon of the wildfires: "What happens is, these Uzbek hunters load up with old Russian tracer rounds, they hit the dry brush, and whoosh." Even from the great distance, Coop imagined he could smell the stench, wood-char mingling with the tang of jet fuel.

Arriving at the terminal, Coop was confronted by an unexpected silence. Usually the station clamored with voices, the nonstop bullshitting of transient grunts. But now it was quiet as a church. Frozen in the doorway, Coop heard a single, broken voice:

"—*the whole kitchen was rocking, then I saw this jaggedy smoke trail—*"

On a nearby television screen, white-hot fragments cut

across the sky. Like shrapnel from an explosion in heaven. Coop stood for a moment in the dilapidated Soviet-built airport, trying to make sense of what he saw. Now one half of the screen was replaced by a red-faced woman:

"—and something fell back there in the thicket, up in them piney woods—"

"What's happening?" Coop said to the nearest group of soldiers. Nobody seemed to hear him. He looked back at the television. The headline proclaimed MULTIPLE TARGETS STREAK-ING OVER PALESTINE, TX, which only confused Coop further. Then the banner changed again and Coop understood that a U.S. space shuttle had exploded.

The news struck him with a funny kind of irritation, and soon he couldn't stand to look anymore. The same contrails through the same empty sky.

He scanned the heads of the crowd and found Moko, a skinny guy wearing big glasses and a ridiculous uniform of blue tiger-stripes, some experimental pattern the Air Force was testing. Coop made his way across the terminal floor. Soldiers were everywhere, waiting their turn to fly, their gear spread all across the airport, a maze of rucksacks, poncho liners, and sleeping bags. Coop thought about the Russians who built this place, what they'd think seeing their airport turned into a hobo camp for American soldiers.

"During reentry you have some major heat buildup," explained a NASA technician as Coop crossed the terminal.

"You believe this shit?" said Moko, leaning in to bump shoulders with Coop, never taking his eyes from the television screen.

They watched together for a little while in silence.

Over the last week Moko had assumed a battle-buddy intimacy with Coop, driven by his discovery that they were both Mainers. It was a lucky friendship; while Moko was technically a midlevel NCO, his status at K2 was closer to that of a minor warlord.

Now the televisions showed a pretty young correspondent in the newsroom. She had sharp blue eyes the same color as the Texas sky into which the *Columbia* had vanished. The same color as Kay's. Coop rubbed at his chest, where he felt a hot pain growing. It was like this, anytime something called up her memory. A tender stab, like a stinger slipped in between his ribs.

Ask him now, Coop thought. The blue eyes of the reporter were an intrusion against his resolve, and he worried that if he was too keenly reminded of why he needed to approach Moko, he might lose the courage to do it at all.

"No way," said Moko, out of nowhere. "I'm not gonna suck your dick."

"What'd you say?" said Coop, looking around, seeing other grunts looking.

Moko grinned. "Just fucking with you, man. You look so nervous." Then he lowered his voice and leaned in. "So what you need?"

Coop felt his face go red. "Maybe we can talk outside?"

"Okay, but hang on," said Moko, distracted again by the screen. "I want to see this."

Now a correspondent stood in a Nacogdoches field, one finger held to his ear, answering questions from the reporter.

Coop tried to stay patient. He looked around, checked the button of his cargo pocket, where he'd put $1,200 in an envelope, along with a printed copy of his emergency message from the Red Cross.

"*Rick, I want to ask you a question on the minds of many Americans,*" the newswoman was saying. Her face assumed a grim intensity. "*Is it possible that we're looking at some kind of terrorist attack?*"

Several soldiers in the airport made guffaws and fart sounds with their mouths, but Rick on television bobbed his head with utmost seriousness and waited a few beats before responding.

"Great question, Janet. Authorities are telling me there's nothing, at this time, to suggest terrorist involvement in the destruction of the space shuttle *Columbia*. But it's probably too early to know anything for sure."

"Terrorists in space, you imagine that?" said Moko. He scooped up his poncho. "Let's go."

Leaving the terminal, Moko and Coop came to a covered marketplace of tarpaulin roofs and ramshackle stores, each operated by an impoverished-looking Uzbek local. Mostly they sold PX crap, backpacks and commemorative coins and camouflage teddy bears. Moko stopped under one of the tarps to light a Black and Mild. He smoked the plastic-tipped cigar with one hand cupping the ember, and Coop couldn't help a flash of judgment: this pogue rear-echelon flyboy, smoking like he was worried about snipers.

"So what you need," said Moko. "Calling cards? Pills?"

"That other thing we talked about," said Coop, keeping his voice low. "The orders. I'm ready to go."

Moko blinked and stared at him. Just then a colossal shadow moved across the tarmac, and they both turned to look. A C-17 Globemaster, gliding after a tiny airman waving neon batons.

"You hear me?" said Coop.

Moko took the cigar from his mouth and threw it into the gravel. "You're really ready to pull chocks?"

"You said you could do it," said Coop.

Moko looked back at the horizon. "Understand," he said, "if you get caught, I will categorically deny any kind of arrangement between us."

"Sure," said Coop.

"Hang on, I'm fucking serious. Do you doubt I'll be able to produce witnesses on my behalf, who will all swear I never helped your ass in any way?"

"Not at all," said Coop, noting how fast the same-state camaraderie had faded, now that they were talking business.

Moko studied him. "And you understand I'd need a thousand dollars."

Coop patted his cargo pocket. "We can do it now?"

Moko's office at K2 was a giant shipping container perched on the gravelly shore of a water-filled depression. Someone had removed several odd-angled sections from the hull and bolted sheets of Plexiglas in their place to make windows, complete with drapes of camouflage netting. The hot, rust-filled gloom overflowed with cardboard boxes, supply crates, and ammunition canisters.

Moko stooped toward a miniature fridge. "Would you care for a nonalcoholic malt beverage?" he said.

"No thanks," said Coop.

"All we can get out here, thanks to Wesley Clark. The fucker."

Moko seated himself in an ergonomic black leather chair with a backrest of octagonal mesh, the undercarriage sprouting a complex system of chrome adjustment levers.

"You like that?" said Moko, tracking Coop's gaze. "When I first got here I sent a query to Command Supply about our budget. Got back a fax with, what's it called, one of those loopy sideways eights?"

"The infinity symbol," said Coop.

"Yeah man. Un-fucking-limited."

While Moko's computer booted up, Coop peered around at the stacks of boxes. Many were open. Cartons of Mefloquin and Ambien. Flashlights, velcro pouches, ballistic sunglasses, and all manner of gear mounts, sprockets, and weapon attachments. He picked up a box of frame-lock Striders with coyote-colored grips.

"You like those knives?" said Moko. "Give you one for a hundred bucks. That's like eighty percent off the asking."

"Nice operation you have going," Coop said, surveying the hoarded equipment. Thinking how back in Afghanistan there were guys still waiting on armor plates for their vests.

"Shit, I'm small-time," said Moko. "You should see what the contractors have going. Talk about a bunch of gear queers. Not to mention they got hash, porn, real booze, whatever you want. Outside the wire I hear they even have a hooch full of girls."

"Huh," said Coop. "So how do we do this?"

"Pure fucking magic, that's how," said Moko, turning back to his laptop. He hit more keys, cycling through a series of menus and forms. "Okay, I've got Kandahar as your point of embarkation. Where you going?"

"New York."

"You want JFK, LaGuardia, or Newark?"

"The Bronx, whatever's closest."

"LaGuardia it is," he said, and began flipping through a spiral-bound book. "Hang on, I gotta call up the movement designator code."

Moko made some entries into the computer.

"And how long you plan on being gone?"

"Just a few days."

"All right," said Moko, "you know the deal, right? Forty-eight hours until you're technically AWOL. And this provisional pass I'm cutting, it'll only exist on paper. Someone looks you up in the system, you're out of luck."

"They do that?"

"Unlikely. MILPER is all dicked up these days because of restructuring. Plenty of guys traveling outside the system."

"Wait, what happens if they do look me up?"

Moko sighed dramatically. "Lemme make this Army-proof: Don't give anyone a reason."

Coop flexed his jaw. *Six days,* he thought. Six days he'd been stuck in bureaucratic limbo, waiting for the Army to un-fuck itself and green-light his emergency leave. And now Kay's funeral was just a few days away, leaving Coop with no other choice but to pay off this computer gnome, to break the first rule of military service: Never abandon your duty station without orders.

Coop took one of the Striders from the box. He felt the heft of the blade in his palm. Then, while Moko was focused on the screen, Coop transferred the knife to his back pocket.

Meanwhile the printer chugged out three sheets of paper: blue, yellow, and white. Moko crumpled the blue and yellow forms and hucked them into a burn barrel, then set the white form down and signed a squiggle over the signature line marked "Adjutant General." He handed Coop the forged orders.

Coop looked them over. "How do I get back?"

"At the airport, tell them your duty station, and that you lost your papers. They'll issue a Form 460."

Coop folded the orders gently and put them in his pocket. "That's it?"

"That's it. You're on the manifest for a flight leaving at 0340 Zulu, connecting in Dublin."

From his cargo pocket Coop dug out the money and slapped the envelope on Moko's desk. It represented one-fifth of his total savings from the war.

Moko toasted with his nonalcoholic beer. "*Sláinte*, mother-fucker. Don't get caught."

Back in the transition tent, Coop packed up his gear, preparing for his flight, still seven hours off. He knew he wouldn't be able to sleep, so he clipped his tactical light to a loop of cord hanging over his cot while he played with his new knife, oiling the mechanism so he could flip it open with one hand. Then he reread one of Kay's postcards. All of them were handmade, with illustrations from an old book of fifteenth-century religious prints ("Maybe it's unhealthy," Kay had written in her first correspondence, "sending portraits of doomed martyrs to my overseas soldier man").

The image on the back of the card he'd selected was titled "Madonna and Child in a Glory." The woodcut showed a red-robed woman wearing a crown of stars. In the sky over the Madonna's head was a crescent moon, and at the bottom of the postcard was a quote by someone named Jorgius: "As the Moon rules the tides, so Mary by her prayers helps those who are tossed on the bitter surges of the world."

Coop flipped the card over and read, even though he knew the words by heart:

Hello My Husband,

I hope you get this, I know you said they're still working out the kinks in the mail. Hope you don't mind these postcards. Some triple-p (pervy postal private, I just made that up) will probably be reading my innermost thoughts, but I figured the Patriot Act lets them read your mail anyway, right? I really hope you're safe over there. I tell myself you are OK. This distance is so cruel, Coop. Do you know how much your baby misses you?

It was one of the postcards from the early months of deployment, when things had still been good between them. And now nothing. Nothing more.

Two days ago Coop had waited in line for the chance to use one of K2's sat-phones. Each booth was a plywood cubicle, the walls covered in dirty carvings, a knife-marked collage of tits and pussies and spurting cocks. Coop dialed in the code for Pope Air Force Base, where an operator bounced his call to the New York Police Department. He was hoping to get more information about what had happened to Kay, about how it had happened at all. But the NYPD operator told him she couldn't say anything over the phone, he'd need to come to the precinct in person and be prepared to offer proof of his relationship with the deceased. In response Coop informed the operator he was in the middle of fucking Uzbekistan and wondered if she could make an exception. She thanked him for his service but said that being a military man he should appreciate there are rules people have to follow.

Coop slipped the card back inside the envelope and with great care returned it to the stack, which he kept in a Ziploc at the bottom of his duffel bag.

I'm a widower, Coop thought.

Widower. The word sounded like a title for someone who makes widows for a living.

The wind picked up outside. Coop imagined the wildfires stoked into new fury, flames spreading across the foothills. He lay awake the rest of the night, listening to the tent walls relax and go taut, like the lung sounds of a giant animal.

CHAPTER SIX

Red light glowed from the tip of one wing, and Coop watched it flicker against the onrush of frozen clouds. He was thinking of Kay's heartbeat, the wiry throb of her pulse. *Don't start,* he told himself. *There's nothing you can do. Focus on your surroundings.* The felt rainbow on the back of the airplane chair, a hot cup of coffee in an eco-friendly polystyrene cup. Across the aisle, a suited man in heavy sleep. Coop imagined flies buzzing around his open mouth.

In the seat next to him there was a woman knitting. A ropy trail of purple yarn wound off the folding tray and into her lap, and in the darkened cabin the needles made an insect clicking. Coop found himself studying her fingerwork. Click, swoop, click, swoop, a private cadence, mangled by the words from the Red Cross message: hit and run, hit and run, click, swoop, hit and run.

"It's for my brother," said the woman. Coop blinked at her. Doughy face but still pretty, flashing him with big friendly teeth. A small gold crucifix hung between her breasts.

"The scarf," she said.

"Oh," said Coop, and he turned back toward the window.

"So, are you just coming back?" said the woman.

Coop nodded.

"Wow," she said. "I can't even imagine."

Coop scratched at a rash on his elbow. While waiting for

his flight in Dublin he'd become convinced that his uniform was still carrying particles of Afghan sand.

"Well," she said, a little more tentatively, "your wife must be happy you're coming home."

"Goddamn," Coop said loudly, shaking his burned hand. Hot coffee dripped down the rim of his crushed cup. "Excuse me, ma'am."

"Oh no," said the woman, making room for him to slip into the aisle.

In the bathroom he stooped to run water over his scalded hand, the skin raw and pink against the dull gold sheen of his wedding ring. During his last night in K2 he'd retrieved the band from the Ziploc at the bottom of his duffel bag, a talisman for his rogue journey. Now he regretted it.

A few minutes later he was back in his seat. Out of the limbo rose New York City, a kingdom of orange lights. The plane banked toward the glowing coast. The pilot thanked everyone for flying and said he wanted to offer a particular thanks to the soldier in the twenty-seventh row. The lady with the scarf beamed. The pilot went on saying how proud everyone was of our men and women in uniform. Coop stared down at his lap during the scattered applause. Across the aisle, the man in the suit came awake in a fit of blinking annoyance, trying to make sense of the disruption.

Coop's first priority after arriving in New York was to use a real toilet. For seven months he'd been stuck with the claustrophobic reek of Port-a-Johns, where you had to control your gag reflex for any latrine trip lasting longer than thirty seconds. Now he sat in the men's room of LaGuardia's USO lounge, a private stall with crisp rolls of toilet paper and white-tiled floors. He listened to the murmur of ventilation in the walls. Afterward, Coop had just returned to the terminal when he felt a panicked, diagonal nakedness across the fat of his back. He hurried back to the lounge, banging on the doors of the bathroom stalls, then putting his hands on his head when he found them empty.

"Something the matter, sweetheart?" said a frowning, middle-aged USO worker as Coop rooted through cushions in the sitting area, looking for his M4, and it was then he remembered he hadn't lost his weapon. It was back in Afghanistan, racked in the unit armory.

Back in the neon concourse, Coop reeled at the sick-sweet odor of cinnamon buns, the dizzying glare of the lights, and the urgent beeping of a golf cart. Something clipped his shoulder, hard, almost making him drop his duffel bag, and Coop whipped around but it was just a red-faced suit on a cellphone, dragging a wounded piece of luggage. His anxiety worsened as he exited the airport into Ground Transportation: a freezing world of concrete, traffic, and blowing snow. Coop waited shivering beneath a vibrating overpass, trying to figure out where he was supposed to go. There was a long line to get a cab. An Arab guy in a leather jacket came up and whispered "Taxi?" like it was some kind of code word.

Coop shook his head, feeling a sudden itch to move. He shouldered his duffel bag and marched off toward a narrow, snow-covered sidewalk, and soon found himself walking along a congested freeway that led out of the airport. The cars kicked up icy spray as they passed, and quickly his desert boots were saturated with freezing silt from the road.

As he walked, Coop did a slow 360 every minute or so to check his rear, trying to keep it nonchalant. He imagined himself at the center of a geometric flower, direct bullet paths and graceful mortar arcs, vectors of potential attack radiating from a million points of origin: far rooftops, windows, the highway, the airstrip of snow and blue lights. Yet the cars all followed one another in an uninterrupted line, edging together in the imagined safety of their vehicles, not understanding that a bomb of sufficient power would kill them all and mix their pieces together in fire. Coop wondered how they could all be so stupid, especially in this city, where the war had started.

As if convened by these thoughts, three cars ahead of him tried to merge into one lane, and amid the sharp blare of horns Coop found himself scuttling away, a sudden gravity of nerves bringing his body into a low crouch. A Prius swerved around the blocked cars, and through the window Coop caught a disturbed expression on the face of the driver.

Coop got back to his feet and lifted his bag. The cold had soaked his desert-thin uniform, but he was more conscious of a throbbing embarrassment. The problem, he felt, was war movies, where you never saw the tough guys flinch or take cover. But in Coop's experience the best soldiers came off like tweekers, with quivering jaws and eyeballs buzzing in their sockets; signs of a superstitious nervous system. *So excuse me if I flinch,* he thought, glaring after the Prius as it vanished into the river of red lights.

Once outside LaGuardia, Coop picked the first place he saw, a cheap-looking roadside bunker called the Crotona Motel. At the front desk sat a black guy with thick glasses and a cursive tattoo on his neck. His name tag said Denis.

Coop came in expecting attention for the uniform, but the man didn't look up until Coop cleared throat.

"How long you staying?" said Denis, turning his attention to a computer.

"Not sure yet," said Coop.

"Rates are hourly, nightly, or weekly."

"Just tonight."

"Cool. That'll be a buck ten."

"One hundred and ten dollars?"

"And there's no room service," said Denis. "You gotta clean up after yourself. That cool?"

The room smelled like sweat and poisonous chemicals, with a bed squeezed between four peeling walls and a single window. Investigating the bathroom, Coop found a weird scene: a dried-out bunch of centipedes on the floor of the shower, some still squirming, all coiled around a little black cylinder.

Coop used the room phone to call downstairs. "There's a fuck-ton of dead bugs in my shower."

"Sorry man, forgot to mention," said Denis. "What you want to do is take out the poison, let the shower run for a bit. Just remember to throw the canister back when you're done. See, they're attracted to the moisture."

Coop unpacked his gear. Then sat for a while in the tiny room. He took out his wallet, a folding camo pouch he'd picked up at Jump School, and spread it open. Hidden under the laminated ID window was a deteriorated slip of paper, which Coop gently unfolded.

He'd acquired the business card during Basic at Fort Benning, back in 2000. One night, after final formation, his drill sergeant had informed the company that an "old hippie" had been caught on post distributing subversive literature to recruits. Even though no one from Charlie had seen or talked to the man, the drill sergeant seemed personally insulted.

"No need to be secret squirrels about it, men. You want to 'know your rights,' here you go," he said, and slapped down a big stack of cards on the fireguard table. Then he'd left and turned out the barracks lights. By morning the cards were still untouched. Later, while doing a pre-inspection cleaning of the barracks, Coop spotted the cards in a trashcan, mixed among MRE bags and crumpled letters and empty cans of Gold Bond powder. On impulse he decided to snag one, a clandestine treasure, and for the last three years the card had remained in his wallet, tucked behind his ID card.

The card said: *Military Legal Assistance Center: Know Your Rights,* followed by an 800 number. Now, sitting on the edge of his bed in a hotel room outside LaGuardia Airport, Coop picked up the phone and dialed.

It rang twice before someone answered.

"Legal Assistance, this is Jackie," said a woman's voice, surprisingly young-sounding.

"Hi," said Coop, caught off guard. He'd expected some kind of automated system. "Um, I had some questions."

"That's why we're here," she said. "First off, can you tell me if you're military, or calling on someone's behalf?"

"I'm Army."

"Great, that answers my next question—hang on."

Coop heard the clicking of a keyboard.

"Are you taking notes?" said Coop. "I don't want a record of this."

"Relax, it's confidential," said Jackie, in a brisk tone that Coop felt bordered on the dismissive. "So what's going on?"

Coop hesitated.

"Still there?" said Jackie.

"Yeah," said Coop. "I had questions about being someplace I'm not supposed to be."

"Did you miss a major troop movement?" said Jackie.

"No, it was just a transitional thing. I was waiting for orders, but I left before getting them."

"Got it." Coop heard more clicking. "How long have you been absent without leave?"

"Whoa, hang on," said Coop. He stood up from the bed. "I thought that was only if you're gone more than forty-eight hours."

"False," said Jackie.

"What?"

"That's false. You've been given bad information. A service member can be designated AWOL as soon as they abandon their duty station."

"I didn't *abandon* . . . that can't be true," said Coop. "We had this one guy who was gone for a whole weekend—"

"So here's the confusion," said Jackie, cutting him off. "A lot of this is under your commander's discretion. But technically, based on what you're telling me, you are in fact AWOL and you could be prosecuted accordingly."

No sympathy in her voice, barely a professional consolation. Coop had assumed these people were on his side.

"Okay," said Coop, his head racing. "Now listen, are you a hundred percent sure about that? I mean, have you dealt with other cases—"

"Look man, I'm an L-3 at Berkeley," said Jackie. "Want me to quote you the UCMJ?"

Coop whipped the phone cord over the bed so he could pace the room. *Jesus,* he thought, *I'm AWOL.* A designation reserved for shitbags, pogues, and shammers, the Army's lowest forms of life.

"Motherfucking Moko," Coop whispered.

"What's that now?" said Jackie.

"Nothing."

"So how long have you been gone?" said Jackie.

"Just since yesterday. And I'll be back tomorrow, but here's the thing," said Coop, "see the paperwork for my leave got all fucked up—"

"I'm sorry, but you don't have to convince me. It's up to your commander's discretion, but you should know he could put you in for an Article 15, or even go for a court-martial."

Coop lowered his head, feeling a surge of nervous rage, the

legal clusterfuck only highlighting the larger, cosmic betrayal of Kay's vanishing.

"Can I ask something?" said Jackie. "What's so important you'd go AWOL for seventy-two hours?"

"My wife's funeral," said Coop, and before Jackie could respond, he marched across the room and slammed down the receiver.

CHAPTER SEVEN

Kosta sat at his kitchen table watching a kid named Edi peel surgical tape from a mummified canister. Edi was one of Luzhim's runners, another migrant growing up soft under the old man's protective wing. The kid worked at a slow, methodical pace, a cigarette pinned between his lips, brow knitted with concentration.

"You're not done yet?" It made Kosta nervous to have anyone in the duplex.

"I like your watch," said Edi as he tugged away another layer.

The property belonged to Luzhim, but the old man had invited Kosta to stay here, rent free, ever since arranging for his emigration from Albania. Only one condition: the property should never be used for storing product, weapons, or anything else that might attract attention. Which made it stressful, having one of Luzhim's kids here when just down the hall Kosta was keeping a prisoner.

During the chaos following the accident, when they'd hit the girl, this was first safe place Kosta had thought of to bring Sean. They'd put him in a spare room and kept the kid sedated, feeding him a steady dose of Olanzapine wafers.

And now Edi had arrived at Kosta's door, saying Luzhim wanted to talk. All the way from his business trip in Macedonia, a rare occurrence. Meaning it was something important. But first Kosta would have to play the old man's spy games.

Finally Edi made it through the last layer of tape. He eased the blade around the rim of what appeared to be an old rusted coffee tin, and extended it toward Kosta. The tin was packed full of small brown paper envelopes.

"We're supposed to close our eyes," said Edi.

Kosta sighed and stuck his fingers into the tin, snagging an envelope and opening it while Edi dutifully looked away.

There were two cards inside the envelope. The first had the words "Belmont Tobacco" carefully handwritten on it. The second card Kosta pulled out was cut from heavy black stock, with the words *Crypto Dial* embossed over a skeleton key logo. Under the key was a long series of numbers.

"The greatest method of countersurveillance is unpredictability," Luzhim liked to say, though sometimes Kosta wondered if this was more about superstition than tradecraft. Putting the two cards in his pocket, he rose to get his coat.

"You mind?" said Edi, holding up the cigarette.

"Please," said Kosta, through his teeth. He jerked open the window over the sink and waited as Edi took a last, measured drag of his cigarette, then dropped the ember into the tin of paper, setting it alight.

An ancient Dominican man sat in the front room of Belmont Tobacco, rolling cigars on a rolltop desk. He had an empty tip jar on the table in front of him, along with several ribbon-wrapped bundles of torpedoes. The man didn't look up from his work as Kosta walked past him toward the back of the shop, into an empty lounge with a tiled floor, a few scattered tables and chairs, and a pay phone.

Now Kosta entered the string of digits from the Crypto Dial card and waited, listening to clicks and beeps.

His eyes flicked around the room while he waited for a connection. The floor and walls of the lounge were decorated in a slightly crooked mosaic, the kind one saw throughout the older institutions of Arthur Avenue. As Luzhim had once explained, these artworks were built in the early 1900s by Italian immigrants, workers who had tunneled the original subway lines. The men had been prisoners of the *padroni* bosses, an arrangement of municipal serfdom (which, according to Luzhim, still existed in America, though in slightly modified form), and as a small rebellion against the killing conditions and low wages, these Italians would bring home materials from their underground worksites, smuggling a few precious tiles at a time. And over many years, sometimes even generations, they managed to assemble these complex mosaics, illuminating their homes with scraps of stolen marble.

While he waited for the connection, Kosta wondered if there had been an agenda behind this parable; if Luzhim's stories of the slow, plodding climb of fellow immigrants were in fact another method for him to assert his authority, each tidbit of knowledge designed in some way to remind Kosta of his station.

Without warning Luzhim joined the call, his voice clawing through the payphone static. "Have you seen the newspaper?" he said.

Not even a hello, and *fuck,* Kosta realized, he'd forgotten to check the obituaries.

"Yes, I saw," said Kosta.

"Good, good," said Luzhim. His tone sounded urgent. "So you know what we need to do?"

"Well . . ." Kosta faltered. "Yes, I had an idea, but then I thought, better to ask you first. To be sure."

"Obviously you need to say goodbye to your associate," said Luzhim. "Immediately."

"Okay, sure, that's what I figured," Kosta improvised.

The old man wanted him to kill Sean. What Kosta didn't understand was *why*.

"So the family, you recognized them?" said Luzhim.

Kosta didn't respond. He was staring across the lounge, where crumpled beneath one of the tables he'd spotted a gray sheaf of newsprint.

"What?" said Kosta. "I think the connection is bad." Gently he left the receiver to hang, then quickly crossed the room and snatched up the newspaper.

"Hello?" Luzhim was saying, when he picked up the receiver again.

"Okay, it's better now," said Kosta, flipping through the soiled pages. "I hear you. You were telling me about the family?"

Kosta rapidly scanned each headline, trying to make sense of the paper's order.

Luzhim was quiet on the other end.

"Hello?" said Kosta.

"Is something the matter?" said Luzhim, his voice careful now. A sharpness of suspicion.

"All good," Kosta murmured. He had found the article. Not even an obituary, the girl's death had made the news.

Bronx Hit-and-Run Kills Daughter
of Prominent Banking Family

Katherine Bellante, a 24-year-old social worker and daughter of Elizabeth Bellante, was killed in a hit-and-run incident in Tremont. Paramedics were called to the intersection of Valentine Ave. and E. 177th St. at roughly 7:20 a.m. She was pronounced dead at Montefiore Medical Center. The vehicle and driver have not been identified. Police are urging anyone with information about this incident to contact the NYPD's Bronx Traffic Division immediately.

"The family," said Kosta. He spoke softly and deliberately, gripping the paper in front of him, his head awash. "You were telling me about the girl's family."

Another long pause on the line. Finally Luzhim spoke.

"It's like the Falconaras, Kosta. *The Falconaras*. You understand?"

"Yes," said Kosta, though he didn't. The name registered as something from before; from Albania, during the time of the uprising.

"Don't waste any time," said Luzhim. "And stay low. We'll talk more when I get back."

Kosta nodded to himself, his mind working.

"When do you get back?" he asked. Too late. Luzhim was gone.

CHAPTER EIGHT

Sean waited in the low darkness of his captivity. He sat on a thin pad of foam, his hands fastened in front of him with zip-ties. Not that he needed the restraints. They'd given him something, a mighty benzo, Sean guessed, and the drug had knocked him from the orbit of coherent fear and into a spinning oblivion. Which he guessed he should be thankful for, except that for the last three months he'd been sober, and now he was deep-sixing again. Waiting through the gloom for his next high.

The building was full of sounds, uncertain and muted through the cinder-block walls. Sometimes he heard voices, a man yelling, and Sean imagined he could hear whole conversations, only to wonder if he'd invented them.

He didn't want to be afraid about the future because there was nothing he could do about it. At first he'd been scared the Albanians would kill him, had even tried to get up and explore the outer dimensions of his prison, trying to devise a means of escape. But the drugs and injuries compounded each other and now he rested in a half coma of misery and paralysis.

Sean didn't hear or see the door open. He looked over and there was Kosta. Just standing there, looking in.

"What?" said Sean.

Kosta didn't respond, just kept staring. A mountainous shadow in the doorway. Even doped up, just a glimpse at Kosta's eyes reminded Sean of those moments hanging from the fire escape, and he felt the instinct to push himself backward, crabwalk toward the opposite corner of his prison.

"Hey, listen," said Sean. "Please, I know I fucked up. Just let me explain."

Kosta stared a bit longer, then replaced himself with the door.

The kid wasn't looking too good, and Kosta was surprised by his own sense of concern. Sean was weak, an addict, but also a loner; solitary and hungry, attributes Kosta could identify with. Except Sean was fixated on his wall drawings, the photographs and spray cans, things Kosta couldn't make sense of. He intuited it was a kind of religion, like Buqa and her Bektashi pamphlets—except for Sean, all that mystery and power seemed self-contained, a thing he owned for himself.

It was unfortunate, because things were going to end badly for Sean. No way around it.

Kosta went back down the hall to the kitchen, where Zameer and Buqa sat at a small folding table covered in takeout detritus: Styrofoam containers, plastic cups of Russian dressing, crumpled balls of foil.

"Your boy, he's alive?" said Zameer, talking through one side of his mouth as he ripped off a hunk of lamb kebab.

"I got you the chicken," said Buqa, using both hands to push the container toward Kosta.

Kosta pulled out a chair, used his hand to sweep away a clear spot. "You were right," he said to Zameer. "Olanzapine is working good."

Zameer grinned, then took on a mock formal tone. "So, what you're saying, the subject is not a flight risk?"

Buqa chuckled, as if it were much of a joke. Probably another stupid thing Zameer had heard in a movie. Kosta looked back and forth between his teammates, Zameer gnawing on his kebab like a starved dog, Buqa with her face smeared in oil. He hadn't told them his new plan yet. The idea had come like lightning; he still felt it trembling through his nerves.

"I have something I want you to deliver," said Kosta, looking at Zameer.

"A package?"

"No, something else. It goes to a funeral."

"A church," said Zameer with a grimace. He pulled a string of fat from his teeth.

Buqa stopped chewing for a second, closed her eyes, and raised one finger. "Go not to the mosque," she began, quoting from one of her little dervish devotionals, "but to the house of idols, with faithfulness, and attach your heart to God."

"You're not going," said Kosta. He turned to Zameer. "You have a suit?"

"And with God rise," Buqa finished, opening her eyes.

"Fucking churches," said Zameer.

Kosta fished in his pants, unfolded a wad of cash, and counted out a thin stack of twenty-dollar bills, which he placed on a bare spot on the table. "Get yourself a nice suit. Black, you know?"

Zameer glared at the money, his jaw working. He opened his mouth, then closed it.

"Get Vadik to fit it for you. Your shit is too baggy."

"Why me?" said Zameer, eyes still aimed at the table. "Reason I make the question is Buqa was driving, she's the one who hit the girl . . ."

Kosta leaned slowly forward, resting his arms on the table. The weight shifted, and an overturned yogurt container rolled past Kosta, who ignored it. Finally Zameer looked up to meet the stare, leaning back with his bare arms crossed, undershirt hanging off his thin frame.

Kosta stared level into the black of Zameer's eye. *So long as you can break a man's stare, you will always have power over him.* Another of Luzhim's lessons. The trick was, if you looked close enough within the eye's inner dark, you saw your own reflection.

"Fuck all this," Zameer said. "Right?" He looked to Buqa, but her eyes were elsewhere.

"You have any nice shirts?" said Kosta, still staring through the space where Zameer had been. "A tie, maybe?"

CHAPTER NINE

Coop came awake panting in the dark, keenly aware that he was being watched. Tossing aside the covers he crawled from the small bed, moving to the window. Across from the motel there was an abandoned shipping depot, and frantically Coop scanned the scarred brick facade, checking each broken window for a shape of greater darkness.

Finally Coop sank down to sit on the floor. The red digits of his bedside clock read 4:00.

It was the morning of Kay's funeral.

Sucking air through his nose, Coop tried to calm himself. He hadn't known that grief could feel so much like the death-fear of combat: the hurried heartbeat, the pale sweating. A superstition against movement competed with the sudden feeling that he needed to shit.

There was no chance of getting back to sleep, so Coop turned on the lights and began to prepare his Class A's. He settled into the ritual with a grim concentration, losing himself to the hot steam from the iron, the smell of Brasso, the prick of steel grommets against his fingertips. After smoothing the creases in his shirt, pants, and jacket, he began to polish his Sta-Brite skill badges, starting with the billowing chrome parachute of his Jump Wings and then moving to the laurel-wrapped Expert Marksman's cross. Next he fetched his jump boots, attacking any scuff marks with his wood-handled brush, then using a lighter to heat up a can of black Kiwi. With two rag-wrapped fingers he buffed the leather until it shone like volcanic glass.

Coop hoped the uniform would make up for the raw, blistered pink of his sunburned face. Even worse were the fight signs; a dark crescent below his left eye, and under his neck, the collar of bruises from when Anaya choked him out.

Coop called for a taxi and waited outside the hotel. It was a bitter, bright morning. An icy wind came gusting off the nearby bay, stinging his freshly shaved jaw.

In the taxi Coop found his mind drifting toward an image from his childhood: the harpooned man. The man was shot in black-and-white, an old photograph another kid had torn from a magazine and carried to Coop's one-classroom school, where it was passed from desk to desk, triggering a slow wave of wide eyes and uneasy, stifled giggles. The photograph showed a man sitting on an exam table. His torso was bare, except for the bandages. Pinned through his chest was a crooked iron rod. The photo was shot so you could see both ends of the bar. The length of metal protruding from his chest ended in a dull cap, whereas the piece sticking out his back had a broad, jagged head. The man was fully conscious, his face clenched in a look of exasperation, like he was annoyed to still be alive.

The traffic was bad, and Coop felt his heart beat faster with each lurch of the car. Three years he and Kay had been married, but they'd never met each other's families—it was something they had in common, a proud and willful rootlessness—so the Bellantes had always existed for him as an idea, a storm cloud of power and gloom. He knew only a basic assortment of facts. Her father had died when she was five, there had been no other children, and Mother (as Kay had always called her) had never remarried. While the immediate family was just the two of them, Kay had grown up surrounded by friends, distant relations, and business associates of her father, all of them immersed in the financial world. Hence Kay's nickname for this network: the Black Magic Money Club.

In Coop's mind it was a fitting epithet, because money was his only real experience with the Bellantes. The checks came in regularly, monthly deposits of $2,000. "My mother's insurance against remorse," Kay had once called the allowance. "This way, if something bad happens to me down here in Army Land, she gets to say she was doing her very best to provide."

The money was more than Coop's base salary, and combined with Army marriage benefits—healthcare, a house on post with free utilities, and an extra living stipend—the payments had made it possible for Kay and him to plan numerous escapes from Fort Bragg, at least whenever Coop managed to get a weekend pass. But even when he couldn't leave, Kay would always find ways to vanish the money. She seemed afraid to let her bank account grow, as if this would represent an accumulation of her mother's influence. Once Coop had returned from a weekend of field exercises to find that Kay had donated her allowance to a Florida-based snake rescue group. Soon after Kay made her contribution they began to receive thank-you cards in the mail, each featuring a photo of an exotic python and signed with names like Mojo and Cleopatra. The postcards were probably still coming, Coop realized. He imagined going back to the house on Honeycutt Road and standing ankle-deep in a squirming pile of glossy postcards.

"The Whitestone, it's all backed up," said the taxi driver. "I'm gonna take the 295."

"Sure," said Coop.

"Okay, okay," said the driver, licking his lips as he angled toward the right lane.

Coop was clueless as to what this might mean for the journey. He'd purchased a pocket map of New York at the airport, but found it head-poundingly intricate. He was accustomed to grid maps of wide-open terrain, the desert's concentric geography interrupted by singular roads and the occasional minefield.

Now the taxi vaulted up onto a wide suspension bridge. Coop caught glances of hazy towers to the west, the skyline flashing between the bridge cables. City of all cities; the wounded capital of the war. Even at this great distance Manhattan seemed to perch on the world like a crown, looming over the river and the huddled docks and port yards along the river. Then the cab sank down onto a web of concrete highways spanning a canal of frozen mud before dropping into the Bronx, where they drove past delis, municipal offices, and low-roofed housing blocks. As the cab pulled off East Tremont the cathedral seemed to rear up from nowhere, a gray fortress flanked by two stone towers.

Around the church were snow-covered grounds with a few trees, surrounded by a low black metal fence topped in spaded prongs, and as they pulled closer Coop saw the towers were slotted with narrow windows, as if ready for medieval archers to take aim. Alongside the church stretched a long line of black luxury vehicles. Floating free from the cars came a steady parade of funeral guests wearing scarves and long dark coats. They collected in a throng, helping one another across the frozen parking lot, and as Coop exited his cab he saw several heads turn in his direction.

Since there was no point in trying to blend in, he made his way toward the oxblood-painted door that marked the church entrance. Here he joined the other guests, all of whom were dressed in rich black wools. Standing among them Coop became increasingly self-conscious of the coarse nylon of his uniform, the gaudiness of his tin medals. Even his wedding ring felt cheap against the tailored finery of those around him. He drew back his shoulders, but the posture felt forced, and the harder he tried to stand proud, the more he felt a rising anger of deficiency.

The line moved forward toward the main cathedral. At the end of the hallway each guest was being greeted by a small, black-shawled woman: Kay's mother. Inadvertently Coop slowed his march, struck by the narrow figure and sharp eyes of this woman he'd only seen in photographs, the Bellante matron who'd exercised such phantom power over his wife.

Coop remembered the vacation he and Kay had taken together to Wrightsville beach, the trip coming back to him as desolate stretches of sand and the frantic light from bonfires. They had rented a cottage with weathered shingles and big windows looking out on the sea, and every night they went down under the concrete fishing pier and sat together in the cooling sand, watching the ocean crash in green sprays against the weather-stained pylons. On the last day of their vacation Coop had found Kay in the backyard behind their cottage, sitting with her legs up in a rusty lawn chair and crying. Wild marsh weeds sprouted around her, and insects careened through the hot salty air. At first Coop felt a spike of worry, the tight-chested apprehension of things unraveling, and quickly he tried to guess what he'd done wrong and how he might fix it. But then he saw the true culprit, a cordless phone lying in the dented grass.

"Your mother?" Coop asked, kneeling down next to her. Kay's shoulders trembled, and when she turned to look at him her face was ruddy and wet. She had a strong, almost manly definition to her jaw, and now she stuck her chin at him, in defiance of the tears running down her face.

"One of these days you should let me to talk to her," he said, staring hard at the phone.

Kay wiped her eyes. She looked up at him and smiled.

"My mother would destroy you."

Then she unfolded herself from the chair, and in a few short steps Kay vanished into the afternoon darkness of the beach house.

The line in the church had flowed steadily forward, and now there were only a few guests left between himself and Mrs. Bellante. Coop was struck with a fresh panic: What if they didn't let him in? Then the guests ahead of him parted, and Coop found himself standing before his mother-in-law.

Up close Mrs. Bellante was surprisingly young, with bright eyes and just a few crackles at the corner of her lips. Her skin was deeply tanned, so dark it was easy to remember Italians had once been considered a different race. Coop watched as her eyes ticked across his uniform, his name tag, and finally, up to his face.

"Oh good," she said. "Mr. Cooper." Breathing his name as if relieved to see him. Before he could respond she leaned forward and placed her arms around him, bringing him into the folds of her black shawl, which he now saw was ornamented with a subtle arabesque of darker black. She's hugging me, Coop tried to process. Other than McKenzie's embrace back at the FOB, it was the second time in nine months he'd been this close to a woman.

"We're just so grateful you could join us," said Kay's mother, her voice breaking a little as she projected over his shoulder.

Coop brought up his arms to return the embrace, surprised by the jolt of bodily recognition; same small breasts, same corrugation of ribs over a plumper, sloping waist—he flashed to memories of undressing this woman's daughter, kissing each other sloppily, laughing as Coop fingered the top copper button of Kay's fancy corduroys. Mrs. Bellante gently leaned back, beginning to release her arms, and Coop felt his grip tighten.

Pressing her toward him with the barest exhale of breath. Abruptly she withdrew, blinking, but left a hand on Coop's shoulder—a sign of affection, but also a point of leverage, keeping him at a certain distance.

"Mr. Cooper, I want you to meet Katherine's cousin," she said, indicating a young man at her right, dressed in a three-piece of charcoal pinstripe.

"Theo," said the man. Coop hadn't noticed him before but now he stepped forward as if coming onto a stage, reaching out to squeeze Coop's hand. "So great to meet you," said Theo. "So great."

"Theo will show you to your seat," said Mrs. Bellante, and Theo nodded at her before turning back to Coop, his smile artificially eager. Coop had the strange intuition that this had been rehearsed.

"And we'll have plenty of time to talk later," murmured Mrs. Bellante, her arms already spreading open to pull in the next guest. Theo's hand replaced hers on Coop's shoulder. He found himself being steered through another set of doors opening into a cavernous hall, where vast columns rose up like giant ribs toward a vaulted ceiling. Arched windows of stained glass provided the only illumination, scenes of martyrdom burning with jeweled light.

The church nave was thickly congested. Theo parted the wall of guests with handshakes and back pats, and it quickly became clear to Coop that Kay's cousin was *somebody* within the Money Club. He had the proud, easy shoulders of a senior officer, someone who expected to be important, and Coop noticed he began every encounter with a preemptive, disarming smile, anticipating the respects that were inevitably paid so he could instantly deflect them ("No, Signora, thank you for being here").

And now that he stood at Theo's side, Coop understood

that he'd been folded into his aura of respect, no longer inspected or scrutinized but lightly appraised, as if he'd become an auxiliary member to this secret club.

They made their way up the aisle, pausing every few rows to give older folks time to lower themselves into the old wooden pews. "It's a beautiful tribute," Coop heard someone say, and his eyes were drawn toward the front of the hall, where a lectern stood half obscured by a massive arrangement of red and white flowers. Coop angled his head to get a better look. And then he understood why the crowd had become so thick here. Frankincense burned in his nostrils. He stood in place, transfixed at the sudden reality of the bronze casket that lay beneath the floral altar.

Now Theo was pulling him away by the shoulder.

"Listen, I know it's a little chaotic in here. But I wanted to say something," said Kay's cousin. Coop let himself be maneuvered toward his designated seat, his eyes still focused on the coffin.

"Thank you. Sincerely. For everything you're doing for our country, everything you're sacrificing."

"Sure," said Coop. The scents and crowd were working on him and he felt increasingly lightheaded.

"We're just so honored you'd come all this way."

Coop turned on him, blinking. *Of course I came, you fucking idiot. She was my wife.* He looked down at the nearest empty pew. "I'm over here?"

"That's right," said Theo, and Coop moved toward his seat, feeling the eyes of Kay's cousin still tracking him.

The church organ moaned to life just as Coop settled himself into a pew, and an elderly man in white vestments appeared behind the altar. The lights were lowered and the priest began to chant. From Coop's vantage he could see the priest's hands shaking over the pages of a massive Bible. His head kept bobbing, a penitent tic, and though he delivered the sermon in a voice just louder than a whisper, his voice seemed to exercise a feeble magic over the gathering. There was no movement or noise in the chapel beyond the flickering of the Easter candle, which Coop found himself watching as it dripped globs of wax onto a fat bronze shrine.

Finally the old man finished, and Coop was surprised to see Theo replace him at the altar.

"Thank you, Father," said Theo, his eyes darting over the congregation.

"And thank you all for coming this evening. We're so blessed to be joined on this day by so many family members and friends.

"Although," said Theo, showing the barest of smiles, "for those of you who were close to Katherine, you know she would have hated all this attention."

A murmur of knowing laughter. Theo tried to repeat the joke in Italian, stumbling a little—"*Questo è un giorno, uh, tragico*"—and the laughter increased.

Coop looked around at the mourners, these clucking bankers with their shiny eyes, nodding knowingly, women dabbing at their eyes, men patting their wives' knees. As if they had understood anything about Kay at all. And still they laughed tearfully.

"We gather on a sad day," said Theo, "having lost someone who was so very special to us all. I'm honored to be introducing this small tribute, something on behalf of my cousin and her brave and beautiful mother, my aunt."

Coop heard a low, mechanical whir. From the ceiling a white screen began descending toward the altar. Theo put his mouth close to the microphone, producing some muffled feedback.

"Memory, after all, is what will keep Katherine with us."

The screen, altar, and casket were suddenly illuminated by a beam of light. Floating in the darkness were millions of dust motes. Coop held his breath.

An image came shimmering to life, words superimposed over a gentle forest canopy: *katherine maria bellante, 1981– 2003*. The text dissolved into a scanned Polaroid, a smiling baby girl with huge blue eyes. Someone in the audience let out a yulp, followed by a few choked sobs half concealed by the soundtrack of chimes and Spanish guitar.

The slideshow continued with Kay's Major Life Stages: lots of baby and toddler photographs, then a big jump to the early teen years. Here was Kay in high school, a sly and skinny teen-ager with red-dyed pigtails to match her Brearley athletic jacket. For the UNC days, the Bellantes had apparently been forced to use a combination of out-of-focus shots taken by friends and promotional photos featuring Kay's nonprofit work. Coop recognized a picture from a Human Rights Center website, and another from Habitat for Humanity. The show concluded with a close-up on Kay's face, a flat look, as if she hadn't wanted her picture taken. And then the projector clicked off and the stage went black.

Sitting in the dark, it occurred to Coop that the reel hadn't included a single picture of him and Kay. He'd been completely eclipsed from her life.

Abruptly the lights came on and the priest shuffled back onstage for a final prayer. Dark suits began rising from the pews as organ music filled the chapel. Coop blinked; his eyes were dry and throbbing.

Theo encouraged everyone to join the family for a recep-tion in an adjoining hall and the guests were ushered out, drift-ing away in black clumps until only Coop was left in the pews, his hands gripping the wooden rail. He couldn't take his eyes off the casket; bronze, inscrutable, cloaked with bright flowers. After waiting a respectful minute, the old priest who'd led the service came hobbling down the aisle and placed a hand on Coop's shoulder, and together they went out to the reception, leaving Kay alone in the dim light of the cathedral.

CHAPTER TEN

Despite all the guests there was a hush over the reception hall, an atmosphere wreathed in low murmurs. Coop heard the clink of porcelain cups and saucers, the occasional thank-you and *grazie* as tuxedoed footmen slipped through the crowd with trays of pistachio cookies.

Coop posted himself against the wall near a full-length window overlooking the churchyard. Outside a group of young Money Clubbers stood beneath a bare tree, their faces lit by cigarettes and phone screens. Looking past them, Coop followed the city's profile as it tapered toward the sky. He felt a shiver, the barest apprehension of a great and unimaginable formlessness: the shape of his new life.

A sudden thump rattled the wall, making Coop spin toward a door as it slammed open and a thin stranger came charging into the reception hall. He looked to be in his thirties but with long hair gone prematurely gray. Like the rest of the Money Club he was dressed in expensive black wool, but the suit was cut too small for his frame, showing pale, bony wrists and a sprouting neck.

The man scanned the room with urgent blue eyes, then reached for the nearest footman.

"Can I help you with something?" said the caterer, a handsome kid with gelled black hair carrying a tray of cups. "Some coffee?"

"Mrs. Bellante," said the stranger. "Where is she?"

"Excuse me?"

"I knew her daughter. The deceased," said the man, lowering his voice. But not so low that Coop couldn't hear.

After getting a helpless frown from the kid, the stranger's head snapped back toward the throng of guests, searching intently. Coop was struck by his total lack of situational awareness; not noticing as the young caterer slipped off, or even how closely Coop, just a few feet away, was now watching him.

Without warning the stranger plunged into the gathering, forcing aside the other guests, a spectacle reminding Coop of seabirds; the Money Club bobbing and murmuring to one another, the newcomer landing among them like a shrieking gull, leaving flutters of disruption in his wake.

Coop tracked the man's trajectory to the far end of the hall, where Mrs. Bellante stood with several mourners beneath a large rose window, the group bathed in a fragment of purple light. Coop ranged around the edge of the crowd, angling to get closer.

The stranger kept on elbowing his way toward Mrs. Bellante, leaving mutters and disapproving glances in his wake. Kay's mother saw him coming, and Coop watched as her eyes flashed up and she began to excuse herself, but the man had already moved into range, flinging himself into the circle of mourners. Mrs. Bellante held up a finger but the newcomer was already speaking, his face both plaintive and intent. Coop wasn't near enough to make out details so he tried easing his way deeper into the crowd. He didn't notice the figure blocking his path until he heard his own name:

"Specialist Cooper?"

Standing in front of him was a heavyset man with a worn face. A crumpled paisley tie hung from his collar, and his charcoal blazer was mismatched with a pair of navy slacks.

"Yeah?" said Coop. He looked toward Mrs. Bellante, but

his eyes were dragged back by the flash of a gold foil shield, Coop's spine going stiff as he read: Detective Melody, 55th Precinct. NYPD.

"It's pronounced Me-*low*-dy," said the stocky cop. "Lotta people mess that up."

Coop took the card. He searched his uniform for a place to put it, his mind running wild. Had someone already reported him missing from K2?

"Very sorry to catch you on this solemn occasion," said Melody. "But I'm wondering if maybe you had some time to talk while you're in town?"

"Talk about what?" said Coop, unable to restrain a tone of alarm.

"Maybe I'm operating on bad information," said Melody. "I took it to understand you called the precinct, a few days back?"

Right. Coop let out an embarrassed breath. During his week at K2 he had tried calling the NYPD to fill in the details left out of the Red Cross message.

"I'm sure you have questions," Melody continued, lowering his voice respectfully. "Given everything you're doing for us over in the sandbox, least I can do is tell you what we know."

"Thanks," said Coop, feeling weirdly moved—here was a deference he'd never gotten from a cop before. Was it the uniform? Or because he was now connected, however thinly, to the Bellante family?

"I have an office up at the Fifty-Fifth, but if you want, we could even talk now."

"Now," Coop repeated, his eyes shifting over the cop's shoulder, where he could just make out Mrs. Bellante huddled with the stranger.

"Sure," said Melody. "I mean, normally we wouldn't do

this kind of thing at a service. But if I were you, I'd want to know what happened."

What happened—the phrase catching Coop in the throat. He looked directly into Melody's face and felt his jaw twitching, fought the desire to flex open his mouth. Of course he wanted to know. He *needed* to know.

"Besides," said Melody, "I can't imagine you're in town for long."

The last sentence sounded more like an order. Coop glanced around at the crowd, caught Theo making his way toward Mrs. Bellante and the stranger. He felt the detective's bulk planted squarely in front of him.

"Sure, let's talk now."

"Okay," said Melody. "Maybe you want to step outside, someplace a little quieter?"

On his way out Coop noticed Theo and the stranger standing close together now, with Mrs. Bellante excusing herself. Theo listening and nodding, but with his eyes pointed at Coop. Watching him leave with the detective.

Coop and Melody went out into the winter air and stood huddled on a plot of frozen lawn in front of the church.

"I saw the thing in the newspaper," Coop began, then stopped. He sniffed loudly, pulling himself together. "I'm wondering if you can spare me the bullshit."

Melody nodded. "Your wife died in the hospital."

Coop felt his jaw begin to work.

"She never regained consciousness after the accident. The car . . ." Melody pointed at his face, indicating an upward angle of force. "It fractured her skull."

Coop found he couldn't stop nodding, his head bobbing like the old priest's.

The formal reality of Kay's death settled upon him. She had

been taken to a hospital, reports had been made. Her death had been *processed*. In his head it was no more real than the funeral, but his body spoke differently; nerves firing, a clenching in his chest, quivers through his lips and around his eyes.

"So who did it?" said Coop. "Who was driving?"

Melody shook his head. "Based on the brake skids, we think it was an accident."

"Right, but I'm asking if you know who *did* it," Coop snapped, surprising himself with the accusatory tone of his voice. He felt powerfully, righteously enraged. It was thrilling to scold a cop.

"Look," said Melody, "all I can say is, the investigation is ongoing, so I'm not at liberty . . ." The detective seemed to catch the red in Coop's eyes. "Mr. Cooper, I understand, but we don't share those kind of details with *anyone* until we know something for certain."

"Can you at least tell me what she was doing up there?" he asked.

"What I gather, it was a house visit. For the clinic."

"The clinic."

"Next Start, the rehab place?" Melody angled his head and gave Coop a long look. Like he was surprised he had to explain.

And Coop saw he'd made a mistake, revealing how little he knew about Kay's apparent job, or anything else having to do with the life she'd made since leaving Fort Bragg. Buried at the bottom of Coop's rucksack was a plastic bag filled with Kay's postcards, but nowhere among these could he recall any mention of a new job.

"That reminds me," said Melody. "A detail I'm hoping you can clear up: You two are married. And you're stationed in North Carolina, right? But she's got an apartment up here, in the Bronx."

"It was complicated," said Coop.

"Sure." Melody put his hands inside his pockets. "Maybe you can help me understand."

Coop crossed his arms, feeling pinpricks of alertness up his spine.

"You know," said Coop, "I think maybe this isn't the best time to talk."

"About what?" said Melody, his eyes narrowing.

Coop avoided the hard, questioning stare. He suddenly felt very stupid. Melody had never seen him as a member of Kay's family. He just saw a clueless grunt; a deviation in the short life of Katherine Bellante. Which made Coop wonder, why had he been brought out here in the first place?

"I'll make sure to call if I have any other questions," said Coop, turning his back on Melody and walking away, he didn't know where.

CHAPTER ELEVEN

The lawn was quiet as Coop made his way around the church. His all-weather black trench coat was still in the reception hall and Coop wondered if he could fetch it without running into any Bellantes. The empty, fatal grandeur of the ceremony had left him drained. He didn't want to say goodbye to Kay's family. It was over.

As he tromped through the snow, Coop thought about Melody's questions. About Kay and why she had left their home on Fort Bragg. In the first months of Coop's deployment, Kay had sent him a postcard almost every week. She was one of those people who had kept a diary since she was a girl, and the postcards were excerpts she chose to share with him. But then came a month when there was no mail from her at all. Coop wasn't worried; if anything the gap in correspondence was a guilty relief, since he rarely found time to write her back. When he finally got mail from her again, it wasn't a decorated postcard but a simple white envelope stuffed with a seven-page letter. The short version: Kay said she was leaving North Carolina and moving back home to New York. She needed to "try and get clear about some things" and wasn't sure what that meant for their relationship, but she knew that she would always love him.

For days Coop stormed around the FOB in a helpless, confused rage. He couldn't make sense of it. They'd always had fights, but now some new distance had risen between them, and for the life of him Coop didn't know how to cross it. Worst of all, there was nothing he could do. He couldn't call Kay and ask what the hell she needed to get clear about, or why she was leaving—the satellite phones at Forward Operating Base Snakebite weren't for personal use.

Twice he sat down to write her back, but never finished the letters. And then, during a furious nighttime walk to the edge of the base, Coop had crumpled Kay's letter and hurled it into the burn pit. He never wrote back to her, and she hadn't sent more letters. Then came the Red Cross message, and the news that he would never see her again.

Coop was so absorbed he almost didn't notice the lone figure standing at the margins of the churchyard. A man in a hooded parka, just outside the fence, his silhouette framed against the ornamental spikes. Something in the man's posture triggered a heightened vigilance in Coop, and he found himself backstepping into shadow.

The man glanced up and down the street, then with both hands grasped the railing of the fence. He vaulted it with a neat little hop.

Now the man crossed the churchyard, his path weaving between panes of light from the reception hall windows. As the man neared the rear steps he drew a long envelope from his pocket. Coop saw that the outside of the envelope was marked in thick black handwriting, but he couldn't read the words. The man bent forward to place the envelope on the steps, then pivoted, moving back toward the fence with a furtiveness that made Coop say: "Hey."

The man took off, kicking up snow.

"Hey!" said Coop again.

Even as he started running Coop knew it was a lost cause. His parade boots had no tread and the dress uniform was too snug for him to find a good pace. But still he slipped and staggered after the hooded figure, who was already at the fence, parka flapping as he neatly cleared the spikes. Coop followed, trying to tuck his legs, but one boot caught the ironwork and he pitched forward, slapping the sidewalk with both hands and skidding before he scrambled back to his feet—only to find the hooded figure was now just a few steps away, facing toward Coop and gripping a small, sickle-shaped knife.

Under the hood Coop saw a pale scrunched face and animal eyes. He heard the man's quick breathing, but he kept looking at the bright metal edge, and with it Coop felt the doom of trespass, the superstition against crossing the wire alone.

The figure stepped toward him and automatically Coop's arms came up into a defensive posture, both palms open, the rear hand guarding his neck. He shuffled in reverse, trying to find distance. The man took another step and Coop scanned the sidewalk, looking for something he could use to defend himself. A remote voice told him he should be more afraid, that he should reason with the man, explain that whatever this situation was, there wasn't any need for a knife. Instead Coop began to bounce on the toes of his parade boots. His gaze quickened, flashing between the knife and the eyes under the hood.

The stranger stood in front of him, nearly motionless, but Coop saw the man's fingers tighten around the hilt of the crooked blade. A look of consideration passed over the man's face, and he bared his teeth. Then he checked the street in both directions and dropped the hand with the knife, concealing the weapon against his thigh, before turning and jogging away. He paused once to shoot back a glance and then rounded a corner and vanished.

. . .

Coop sucked air through his nose while he endeavored to get his shit together. Blood hammered in his ears. He knew he was breathing too fast but couldn't get enough air. Instead of climbing back over the fence Coop decided to take the long way. He found himself limping a little. A new tightness had surfaced behind his left knee, radiating all the way down to the bottom of his foot and up into the muscle of his ass. Worse was the pang of shame arising in his gut. Knife or not, Coop had let the man get away, and he felt a rising, sickly suspicion of his own cowardice. At the same time he began to wonder about a more humiliating possibility: What if he'd made a mistake by chasing the man in the first place? Coop had walked halfway around the church when he suddenly remembered the envelope, but when he came back he found the steps empty. If not for the confusion of footprints in the snow, Coop would have wondered whether the chase had really occurred.

The funeral guests were departing when Coop made it back to the main entrance of the church, and he found himself pushing against the crowd, slowly making his way back toward the chapel. Dimly he registered flickering eyes and frowns of concern. There was a mirror in the entryway and Coop saw his face was bright red and his collar had gone dark with sweat. He rubbed his hands together, freeing the granules of rock salt that were still embedded in his palms. His mind whirled but Coop held to a single imperative: he needed to make a report. Surely someone could make sense of the runner with the envelope and the hooked knife. He considered looking for Detective Melody but decided instead that he should try to find Theo. Coop wasn't sure why, exactly, but he had a sense the Bellantes wouldn't appreciate him going directly to the police.

Back inside the hall Coop found the caterers busy scooping

up porcelain and stray napkins, folding up tables and chairs, and drawing shut the heavy curtains. The Bellantes were nowhere in sight. He went into the altar room and saw that Kay's coffin was gone. Suddenly Coop realized he'd never been informed of the details of his wife's burial.

One of the caterers helped Coop find his coat. He went back outside and watched a line of black cars pulling away from the church. Coop began to shiver and a great fatigue settled over him. The last hour spun through his head, the flashing metal of the messenger's blade and the bronze gleam of Kay's casket, the Bellantes and their secrets, the detective, the thin man with the long gray hair who had said he knew Kay. All of it icy and impenetrable and somehow ancient, like the great stone fortress of the church.

Coop left the churchyard on foot, heading toward the busier area of East Tremont Avenue, where he guessed he'd have better luck waving down a cab. It was the same direction the man with the knife had gone, and despite the stinging cold, Coop kept his hands out of his pockets and at his sides, maintaining a posture of readiness.

He was crossing an intersection at Archer Street when Coop noticed a sleek black car pulled up against the curb, its engine running. The car was a black Maserati coupe, and the dome light was on. Coop halted at the street corner. Sitting behind the wheel of the Maserati was Kay's cousin Theo, and crammed in next to him was Detective Melody.

He began to drift toward the car. Getting close he saw the two men were studying a single sheet of paper. Sitting flat on the dashboard was a long manila envelope marked up in thick black pen.

Theo looked up, and abruptly Coop lost both of them in

the white glare of the Maserati's high beams. He shielded his eyes with one hand. The passenger door opened and a hazy, round-shouldered mass dislodged itself from the vehicle.

"What's going on, chief?" said Detective Melody. His voice was cheerful but Coop saw his head turning left and right, checking the street. A gesture of caution, weirdly reminiscent of the knife man.

"I was just walking," said Coop. His eyeballs throbbed against the harsh xenon lights. Meanwhile Coop's head spun off toward darker places, trying to make sense of what he was sure he'd seen.

Coop pointed north, toward East Tremont. "Am I going the right way? I was hoping to find a cab."

Melody came away from the car, easing the door shut. He approached Coop, stepping into the harsh glow of the head-lights, then turned back toward the Maserati and made down-ward patting motions in the air.

"You trying to blind us out here?"

The high beams went off. Blinking against the floating afterbrights, Coop saw Theo still behind the wheel. He didn't make any motion to leave the vehicle, and in front of him Coop saw the dashboard was now empty. No manila enve-lope.

"Well," said Melody, spreading his hands. "Here we are again, out in the frigging cold."

Coop nodded in mute agreement.

The detective studied him for a second, then took a step closer. "Specialist Cooper, is there something you need to tell me?"

This was straight cop now. All the chumminess was gone. Coop had experience being handled like a suspect. As a teen-ager he'd been questioned by local law enforcement on numer-ous occasions, though rarely for the things he'd actually done.

And while he didn't know what Melody was after, Coop was suddenly sure he needed to be very careful with his words.

"Sorry," said Coop. "Can't think of anything."

"You sure?"

Coop didn't reply. Melody nodded to himself and drew back toward the Maserati, where Theo was waiting. The detective stopped as if he was going to say something, but instead just shook his head, got in, and slammed the door. Coop watched the car pull away, leaving him alone in the street.

He stood for a few minutes at the intersection, his head turning over on itself as he tried to make sense of things. Coop imagined Theo snatching the envelope from the dashboard before he hit the brights, stuffing it someplace out of view.

But he'd been too late. Coop had gotten close enough to read the writing on the manila sleeve, and now the thick black capitals floated in front of him:

FOR K. BELLANTE FAMILY ONLY

And written below that, with two underlines for emphasis, there had just been a single word:

INFORMATION

CHAPTER TWELVE

A sandstorm had hit FOB Snakebite only a day after Coop learned of Kay's death. Cold wind rose up from the valley, and for several days the base had been enveloped, with no planes allowed to fly in or out. In the interim Coop had been moved into the otherwise empty transitional tent, usually occupied by journalists, contractors, and other short-termers.

No one from the unit had come to see him. It wasn't just because of his lunatic walk toward the wire, how he'd forced Sergeant Anaya to choke him out. Instead, Coop got the sense that folks were disturbed by the inauspicious cruelty of his loss. In Afghanistan, no one could afford to be jinxed with that kind of luck.

But on the third day, Anaya showed. Coop had been perched on a berm made of sandbags, and the sergeant waddled up within a few meters before Coop became alert to his presence.

"Specialist," said Anaya.

"What do you want?" said Coop.

"Excuse me?" said Anaya. "'What do you want,' he says, sitting here all ate the fuck up. Like maybe he wants to get choked out again."

Coop looked into Anaya's bulging eyes, then down at his own uniform. His bootlaces were untied and just one button was fixed on his BDU jacket. He scratched at his jaw, feeling three days of stubble. The sergeant was right. Coop had allowed himself to descend into true shitbaggery.

"I'm sorry, Sergeant."

"Damn right," said Anaya. Then the sergeant came forward and sat himself down on the sandbag pile next to Coop. Anaya offered Coop a stubby, hand-wrapped cigar, and they smoked together and watched the sun fall. The dust from the storm had finally dissipated into the atmosphere, and it was the first sunset they'd seen in days.

"So you're going to New York," said Anaya.

"Yeah."

"Where she's from," said Anaya. "But you're a country boy, right? From Canada or something?"

"Maine," said Coop.

Anaya frowned, thinking about it. "You know," he said, "back in Pueblo, my neighborhood? I got popped at more times than we ever did, over here. You believe that?"

"Sure."

Until meeting Sergeant Anaya, Coop hadn't realized there were gangs of any kind in Colorado.

"Listen," said Anaya. "I'm going to tell you something, but keep it to yourself."

"Okay."

The sergeant fingered his cigar in the sunlight. "Thing I'm hearing . . . we're one of the first engineer units headed to Iraq."

Coop raised his eyebrows, genuinely surprised. "No shit," he said.

"Could be early as April. Sandbox number two." Anaya blew a thick cloud of smoke from his mouth. "I'm just saying, over there in New York, you watch your six. Don't leave me stuck with Greely."

Coop shook his head. He found himself smiling weakly.

"I mean, you ever see those pictures he took?" said Anaya. "The man's sick."

They sat a little longer while the cigars burned down.

"Seriously," said Anaya. "Let me tell you something. As fucked up as things are over here, it's no different back home. Maybe worse."

Coop wasn't smoking anymore, just holding the cigar as it burned down. He thought worse might be just what he needed.

After the funeral, Coop lay sprawled under the dim light of his hotel room. From a room nearby he could hear the sounds of a man and woman arguing. Their voices drifted around the room, piping up from the cast iron radiator near the bed.

"We told each other we'd never to do this," said the man.

The woman responded with a sharp, indiscernible noise.

"Embarrassed you?" the man said, his voice growing louder. "I embarrassed *you?*"

While he listened to the voices Coop made halted trapping motions in the air, trying to remember the Combatives technique Anaya had taught him for taking away an opponent's knife. Coop wore a white undershirt and the standard tan camouflage underwear they'd all been issued before deploying to Afghanistan. "How come they give us desert-camo drawers," Greely had once philosophized, "but everything we wear on the outside is bright fucking jungle green?"

His dress uniform and boots were piled in the corner, the uniform soaked in sweat and snowmelt from his chase across the churchyard. Knife or not, Coop couldn't shake the feeling that he'd made a mistake by letting the man with the manila envelope get away. Or better still, he could have ignored the runner and gone straight for the letter he was carrying. INFOR-MATION. The block print lettering was branded on his mind.

. . .

"**I got no** more patience," said the woman from the other room. "And I *definitely* don't have no fucking time." Then came the man's voice, angry and muffled.

Hey man, be nice to her, Coop thought. *You never know what might happen.*

It was supposed to be Coop's last night in America. His plan tomorrow was to check out of the hotel, go back to LaGuardia, and tell the officials he'd misplaced his orders, just like Moko had instructed. If all went well he'd be back in Karshi-Khanabad the same night, then on to Afghanistan, where he could rejoin Anaya and the rest of his unit.

Coop saw himself flying back to the desert, the scene similar to when he'd first landed in Afghanistan. He remembered watching the mouth of the C-17 fall open, the murmurs and shifting of gear from the troops packed in around him, everyone hungry to see this country they were invading. The plane had landed at night, and his first glimpse of Afghanistan was a constellation of red tactical lights, the tarmac of Kandahar airport, and beyond, a barely visible landscape of gravel and low tents.

Now Coop imagined himself on the same plane, except this time he's alone. The ramp drops open. No tarmac on the other side, just a black stretch of starless night. The empty dark and sense of a steep drop makes it feel like he's on a night jump, only there's no roar of wind, no static line gripped in his hand, no parachute weighing him down. Coop sees himself standing at the ramp's edge, staring off into the great abyss beyond the plane.

"Baby, I wasn't trying to fuck with you," said the woman next door. Their tone had changed, the woman talking in a low, throaty cooing. A minute later, from the man: "You just make me crazy, is all."

Then the squeak of bedsprings. Laughter. "Oh yeah?" he heard the woman say, teasingly.

Coop rolled over in bed and grabbed the television remote. He flipped through weather, commercials, a cop show, cartoons. Cop show. Cop show. Baseball. Several more cop shows. And then here was Colin Powell. The general was seated in a crowded hall, speaking into a microphone. In front of him was a placard that said UNITED STATES. Coop liked Powell. On television he always came off soft-mannered and thoughtful, without the usual buzz-cut evangelism you saw with other senior officers. He turned up the volume to listen.

"*This council placed the burden on Iraq to comply and disarm, and not on the inspectors to find that which Iraq has gone out of its way to conceal . . .*"

Powell wore a navy suit with a tiny American flag pin on his lapel. Behind him sat more men in suits, each of them wearing a chunky white receiver over one ear. Captions scrolling below the footage told Coop this was a repeat video from a United Nations speech Powell had given earlier that day.

"*Inspectors are inspectors,*" said Powell. "*They are not detectives.*"

The video jumped forward to the next sound bite.

"*I cannot tell you everything that we know. But what I can share with you, when combined with what all of us have learned over the years, is deeply troubling.*"

Under Powell's voice Coop heard a series of low groans coming from the next room. He heard the breathing, a squeaking voice—like someone talking through a valve that kept opening and shutting.

"*What you will see is an accumulation of facts . . .*"

"Yes, yes . . . oh fuck yes . . ."

"*. . . and disturbing patterns of behavior.*"

Coop put down the remote. For the first time in days he felt the movement of blood through his body. He remembered another hotel room and saw Kay, naked and wet in the shower, paint-chipped nails clawing the wet marble. She had just dyed her hair black, and the product ran in dark streaks down her back, seeping toward him. She turned her head sideways at his reflection in the bathroom mirror, her face screwed up like she was begging, or just about to accuse him of something.

Coop felt the sudden urge to grab himself through his desert camo underwear. He wanted something, wanted *her*, with many months' force of stored-up sexlessness.

"Oh yeah, girl," Coop heard the man in the other room say. "Like that like that like that." The bed squeaking faster.

Coop tried grabbing her hair to pull her closer, but all he got was a handful of black foam, and they both laughed so hard Coop slipped and almost fell in the big shower. The next morning they had to sneak out of the hotel because all the towels and sheets were stained. Later that afternoon, on a woozy drive back to Bragg, Kay suddenly got quiet and sick, remembering she'd put the hotel room on her mother's card.

Now Coop was thinking about the chase across the churchyard, the snow dripping off his parade boots. The man jumping the fence, the envelope left on the steps. The bright curl of the knife he'd waved in Coop's face.

From somewhere came a high-pitched yell and Coop hit the mute button. For a moment all he heard was his own labored breath. Then came another scream, the girl in the nearby room, a crying out for the entire hotel to hear, until suddenly the sound was smothered, like a hand had gone over her mouth. Maybe her face pushed into the pillow.

Coop listened, aware of the humming silence.

He wondered about using his phone to call the front desk, report a disturbance.

Then he heard the man and woman moaning together, and the bed started squeaking again.

He let out a long breath, turned the TV back on. Powell was still talking.

"Our sources tell us that, in some cases, the hard drives of computers at Iraqi weapons facilities were replaced. Who took the hard drives? Where did they go? What's being hidden? Why?"

Coop studied his fist, the glow from the television reflecting off his wedding band. Flashing into his mind came the bright headlights of Theo's Maserati, the envelope Coop had seen on the dashboard. Something was being hidden from him. But why?

CHAPTER THIRTEEN

"Hello," said an unfamiliar voice. "Military Rights Center, this is Craig."

"Oh," said Coop, momentarily thrown off. "Is Jackie there?"

"I'd be happy to assist you, sir. Just need a few secs to look you up in the system. What's the name?"

"Jackie told me I didn't have to give a name."

"That's correct. Can I just get your case designator code?"

"Listen," said Coop, "can I just talk to Jackie?" He lay on the hotel bed, looking up at the cold green shadows thrown on the ceiling by the muted TV.

"I'm going to need that code, sir," said Craig.

"I don't *have* a fucking code."

"Hey Craig?" said a new voice, breaking in on the line. "This is Jackie. I'll take it."

"You sure? I can—"

"Take another call, Craig," said Jackie. "It's fine. Yes . . . yeah, you too."

The line clicked. Coop found himself grinning.

"Is that Mr. AWOL?" said Jackie. Her voice was louder, warmer, less diluted now that Craig was gone.

"I don't like that other guy," said Coop. "And what's this about a code?"

"We're supposed to give anonymous clients a reference

phrase, something easy to remember. You hung up before I could give you one."

"Do I get to pick it?"

"You sure don't," said Jackie. "Believe it or not, we have state-of-the-art software for that purpose. It's like a random word generator, apparently the same thing you guys use for naming military operations. So don't be surprised if you get 'Thundering Eagle' or whatever."

"That would be a major improvement over 'Mr. AWOL.'"

"Okay, hang on a sec . . ."

Coop heard Jackie typing.

"Wow," she said, after a minute. "Oh man."

"What?"

Coop heard Jackie stifling a laugh, then she cleared her throat, assuming a more formal tone.

"Sir, are you absolutely certain you wish to remain anonymous for the purpose of these discussions?"

"Yes," said Coop. "Definitely."

"Okay. Your designator for all future contact is the following—do you have a pen?"

"Sure."

"Fancy Dancer."

"Say again?" said Coop.

"Your code name is Fancy Dancer."

"Do you have a problem with me or something?"

"You know, I have some other clients waiting, so if you called for advice . . ."

"All right, so it looks like I might be gone longer than I thought," said Coop. "There are some things I need to do, to figure out . . ."

Coop trailed off.

"Still there?" said Jackie.

Coop took a deep breath. "If I'm gone longer than the

seventy-two hours, I just want to know what I'm facing, punishment-wise."

"Well," said Jackie, "like I told you, a lot of depends on the disposition of your commander. Assuming they only charge you with AWOL."

"Wait, what else could I get?"

"Desertion."

"What?" said Coop. He sat himself up on the edge of the bed, feet slapping against the floor.

"You hung up before I could explain. Under the UCMJ there's a difference between administrative classifications and disciplinary action. It all comes down to intent."

"But I was supposed to get leave," said Coop, hearing the plaintive pitch in his voice.

"Regardless, the key thing they'd consider is whether you intended to return yourself to military control."

"How do I prove that?"

"Honestly?" said Jackie. "Don't get caught before you have a chance to turn yourself in."

Coop kneaded his scalp, feeling the bristle of new hair. "What if I do get caught?" he said. "What can they do to me?"

"If they charge you with desertion? From a combat theater?"

"Fuck, Jackie," said Coop. He stood up and began pacing the room. "Fuck."

"Don't overreact."

"It's the death penalty, isn't it?"

"Well, technically. But look, nobody's actually been executed for desertion in quite some time . . ."

"I'm hanging up on you again," said Coop.

CHAPTER FOURTEEN

Detective Melody had said Kay was working at a place called Next Start, and sure enough, Coop found a listing for the clinic in the hotel phone book. The next morning he left the hotel and walked to the nearest subway stop. In the underground tunnels Coop pushed his way through a surge of morning commuters, violin music floating over the clamor.

Emerging from the station in the Bronx, he found himself in a neighborhood abandoned to the grip of winter. City buses rumbled down unplowed streets. Snow blew freely through the shattered windows of vacant storefronts, many still decorated with old signage: discount liquor, old time candy, we buy gold, real human hair. Coop headed up Valentine Avenue, following his foldout pocket map of the city. It was only after several minutes of walking that he began to notice the black crosses. There were dozens of them, a cross stuck to every light pole that lined the wide avenue, each made from two slats of cheap wood, with the words "Drugs Crucify" painted along the horizontal slat.

His pace quickened, and at every corner he had the instinct to stop and crouch, his eyes jerking up toward the rising buildings, tracking the rooftops for movement.

Next Start was housed inside a shabby two-story building next to a gated parking lot. The sidewalk in front of the clinic had been hastily shoveled, and chunks of rock salt lay scattered like debris around the entrance. As Coop arrived at the clinic, a man came shuffling out with a steaming cup of coffee. His cheeks bulged, like he was holding his breath. The man poured his coffee into the snow, shaking out the drops, and then leaned over to regurgitate a mouthful of foam into the empty cup. Then he looked up, caught Coop staring.

"Five dollars," he said.

"What?" said Coop.

"Five, man." The guy wiped his mouth with the back of his sleeve. "It's fresh, you just saw me."

"You want me to buy your spit," said Coop. Wondering if this was some weird put-on, a hazing ritual aimed at tourists.

"Man, who the fuck are you? Five is a deal."

Coop opened his mouth to answer, but before he could say anything, the man with the cup arranged the fingers of his other hand into an occult gesture of dismissal.

"Forget your face," he said, and stalked away.

Coop blinked after the man, trying to figure out what he'd done wrong. He'd never been quick with strangers, that was Kay's domain. She had always been so sure of herself, possessed with an honest confidence that Coop sometimes found corny. It was like she had nothing to hide, not even from strangers. Had she still been like that, even after moving back to New York? There was so much he didn't know about her life here. He needed to know what had happened to her. He needed to know if Kay had still been Kay when she died.

Coop continued into the clinic. He passed through a blast of hot air into a small entryway, the rubberized floor puddled with snow and rock salt. Through the glass of a second door he saw a gathering of worn-down faces and cheap coats. In one corner a man was dipped forward at the waist, his head practically touching the floor, while a young black woman with a clipboard tried speaking with him. Everyone in the lobby held a cup of coffee, even the bent-over guy, who was somehow managing to keep it steady.

Pushing his way inside, Coop was immediately stopped by an accusatory voice.

"Sir! Are you here to be admitted?"

It was the woman with the clipboard, walking toward him across the crowded lobby. She wore a turtleneck sweater and a long skirt, and though she couldn't have been more than five or ten years older than Coop, she carried herself with a professional severity that made Coop instantly feel like he'd done something wrong.

"What's your business here?" said the woman, positioning herself squarely in front of Coop. Now everyone was looking in Coop's direction, except the bent-over guy, who was still looking at the floor.

"I'm just looking—" he stuttered.

"Just looking?" the woman repeated. She motioned behind her, toward a cubicle of ballistic glass. A uniformed security guard sat inside, and at her gesture he took up a phone and started dialing.

"I'm just looking for— Wait, who's he calling?" said Coop. "He doesn't have to call anyone."

"Then maybe you want to tell me why you're here, sir?"

"I just had a few questions," said Coop, lowering his voice to a frantic whisper. "About my wife."

Already Coop's mind was spinning out the scenario: police show up, ask for identification, maybe even call his unit to ask why he's in New York and not Afghanistan.

"Your wife?" said the woman.

"I think she worked here. Her name was Kay."

The woman's face transformed: eyes softening, the stern vigilance melting away. One hand went up to wave an okay at the man behind the glass. He hung up the phone, and Coop let out a slow, shuddering breath.

"I'm Eva," said the woman, finally. She reached out to shake hands.

"Coop," said Coop.

Up close he noticed Eva's hair was composed of hundreds of tiny braids, all tied up like a corded tiara.

"Kay and I worked together," said Eva. "What happened . . ." Her voice trailed off. "I'm sorry, maybe you'd like to sit down somewhere?"

"Sure," said Coop. "I appreciate it."

Eva brought him past the barrier of bulletproof glass, toward the back of the building.

"Hey Rodney," she said to the guard in the cubicle, "you got the lobby?"

Rodney buzzed them through a door leading to a long carpeted hallway.

"I'm sorry if I seemed confrontational back there," said Eva. "Unfortunately, not everyone coming through that door is looking for treatment."

"What else would someone come here for?"

Eva didn't answer. They passed a corkboard covered in old flyers, OSHA notices, a calendar featuring quotes from Thich Nhat Hanh.

"Can I ask where you're coming from?"

"Afghanistan, most recently," said Coop.

Eva looked back at him with new curiosity. "What branch?"

"Army."

"Oh yeah? What unit?"

Coop was surprised by the specificity of the question. "Eighty-Second Airborne," he said.

Eva gave him a knowing smile. "So, you jump out of perfectly good airplanes, is that right?" she said.

"That's right," said Coop. It was a tired line—*perfectly good airplanes*—one of those slogans you'd find printed on military kitsch sold by vendors outside the gates of Fort Bragg. Coop wondered how Eva knew the reference, if maybe her boyfriend was a vet.

Before he could ask, Eva opened a door into a small conference room. The walls were covered in scrawled-up sheets of chart paper, and centered on the linoleum floor was a haphazard ring of folding chairs.

"We can sit here," said Eva. "Would you like coffee or anything?"

"Sure," said Coop. He was distracted by the walls. Something pulled at him from the jumble of notes.

"Okay, be right back," said Eva. Coop moved closer to one of the hanging sheets. *I'm THANKFUL for today* was written across the page in purple marker.

Coop stared at the paper, the wide-block capitals and underlined words. It was Kay's handwriting, the same lettering from all the postcards she had sent him during the first months of his deployment. Coop remembered one now. He had memorized the words:

It's SO amazing to think a day will actually come when you're here, back home with me. I'm looking forward to that FIRST moment we lay eyes on each other.

Coop ran his hand over the paper's curling edge, smoothing the crinkles with his palm.

The door opened behind him and Eva stood there with a cup of coffee in each hand. Smiling at him sadly.

Coop yanked away his hand, and as he did, the butcher paper slipped free from the wall, collapsing in folds. Coop bent down to retrieve it, muttering "Sorry" while Eva set down the cups on a small table and came over to help.

"It's okay," she said, and together they got the sheet back

up, smoothing it in place. They both stood for a moment, looking at the paper on the wall. Then Coop turned away, cleared his throat, and went for one of the coffees.

"On my way over here, a guy tried to sell me his spit."

Eva frowned and nodded, as if this oddity, like Kay's death, belonged to a world whose tragedies could be deciphered.

"Spitbacks," she said. "Too many clients were selling their pills, so we started giving methadone in an oral suspension. Now they just cough it back up and try to sell that."

Jesus, Kay, thought Coop. *This is the world you left me for?*

"Anyway," said Eva, "I hope I can answer your questions. We worked in different departments, Katherine and I. She was a case manager, so she was in the field a lot. I'm a resident."

"You live here?"

"I'm a physician," said Eva, a subtle tightness forming in her cheeks.

"You're a doctor?" As soon as Coop heard his own dubious tone, he wanted badly to retract the question. Eva's face became notably fatigued.

"I mean, I didn't realize . . ."

She smiled politely. "I'm a psychiatrist. It's okay, we don't wear the white coats."

He hadn't meant it that way, Coop insisted to himself, though if he was being honest, he *had* been surprised to hear that Eva was a doctor. *It was the coat,* he told himself.

A silence followed. Coop had so many questions, but now he was distracted by an irritating sense of guilt.

"So maybe you were wondering about the work we do?" Eva prompted, obviously making an effort to keep the conversation going. Coop noticed now that her eyes were puffy, and she kept sniffling. Probably she was sick, exhausted, and very much ready to get this conversation over with.

But before he could answer, the door was opened by a man

in a knee-length white smock, a stethoscope coiled around his long neck. Coop was startled to recognize him, a tall skinny doctor with long gray hair. The man who'd burst into the reception after Kay's funeral, demanding to see Mrs. Bellante.

"Dr. Presser," said Eva, looking immediately uncomfortable. The doctor stood regarding them with his hands pressed together, as if in prayer.

"Please, introduce me to our visitor," said Dr. Presser. Coop met the pale blue eyes, the doctor studying him, but without a trace of recognition. Not surprising, Coop thought, given the singlemindedness with which he'd sought Kay's mother at the funeral.

"Doctor, this is Mr. Cooper, on leave from Afghanistan. He's Katherine's husband."

"Husband?" repeated the doctor. Coop didn't like his tone of surprise, but he managed to put on a fake smile and stood up to shake the doctor's hand.

"I'm very sorry for your loss," said Presser.

"I thought you guys didn't wear white coats," replied Coop. Presser frowned.

"Well, unless there's anything else you need . . ." said Eva, standing up. "Dr. Presser, I'm sure you'd be best prepared to answer Mr. Cooper's questions."

Presser looked stumped by Eva's self-dismissal. Coop recognized her maneuver; he used the same trick against officers and NCOs. By asserting your own unimportance, you robbed them of the power to make you feel inferior.

"It was nice to meet you," said Eva, giving Coop a tight-lipped smile before leaving him alone with Presser.

Coop was surprised by how much emptier the room felt with Eva gone. In the two days since he landed in New York, she was the first person he'd met who didn't come off like she was trying to outmaneuver him, and he'd sensed there was more she had wanted to tell him.

"You know," said Presser, "the white coat, it's an important symbol of the profession."

Coop realized the doctor had been staring at him, maybe taking the time to compose this.

"As a man in uniform, I'm sure you understand."

Coop shrugged and kept his mouth shut. He had to remind himself he was here to get information. Pissing off Kay's former employer wasn't going to help.

"It's about respect," continued the doctor. "Not to mention instilling an atmosphere of hygiene."

As if the word—*hygiene*—had reminded him of all the floating, infectious germs of the clinic, Presser turned and paced across the room to a wall dispenser labeled BODY SUBSTANCE ISOLATION. He squeezed a plop of antiseptic foam from the machine and vigorously cleaned his hands.

"So," said Presser, over the wet smack of his hands, the doctor scrubbing with almost frantic energy. "I understand you had some questions?"

"I'm wondering, can you give me a sense of Kay's work?" said Coop. "Like what did she do on a daily basis?"

"She was a case manager. Assigned to outpatient counseling."

"What does a case manager do?"

"Each new client is paired with someone like Katherine. We like to make sure they have a partner to guide them through the process of recovery."

"And these clients, the case manager meets them here?" said Coop, looking around at the room, all the notes on the wall.

"Yes. For group sessions."

"What other kinds of sessions are there?" Coop asked. A motor was going in Coop's brain, he sensed something evasive in the clipped economy of that answer. *She was in the field a lot,* that's what Eva had told him. And something Melody had said at the funeral, something about a house call.

"Case managers also meet with clients on a one-on-one basis," said Presser, still cleaning his hands. The foam was long evaporated, but he continued rubbing his wrist and forearms.

"Where do these one-on-ones happen?"

Presser smiled. "Excuse me, can I ask if there's a particular reason—"

"Do you send people to their homes?" Coop imagined Kay standing on the stoop of a crumbling tenement. Saw her knocking. A door opens, Kay vanishes into the darkness inside the building.

"I can assure you, we take every reasonable precaution," said the doctor, now using one wrist to dispense a paper towel. "And furthermore—"

"Fine," said Coop, getting irritated. "Just tell me, was she working on the day of the accident?"

"I'm sorry," said the doctor, "but I'm professionally restricted from discussing this matter any further."

"Have you discussed the matter further with her family?"

Presser flinched. "I'm not sure how that's relevant."

"I'm family too," said Coop. He held up a fist, showing Presser the wedding ring. "And I was at the funeral. We were both there, but you came late. Missed the entire service. Like you only showed up to talk with Mrs. Bellante."

He heard his voice rising, felt himself leaning toward Presser. "See, I'm only here for a few days, and I'm just trying to get a sense of what happened. How it could have happened. And if Kay was out knocking on these junkies' doors . . ."

"Junkie. That's a nasty word." The doctor's eyes had a new, hungry gleam. The scavenging look of a seabird.

"Mr. Cooper, I understand you're in a state of grief. And I can't imagine what kinds of things you're seeing overseas. We miss Kay here. It's very sad what happened." The doctor came forward, lowered himself into a seat across from Coop. Studying him. "Maybe I can be helpful in another way," he said. "I have a colleague who specializes in trauma therapy. I'm not sure exactly how the insurance would work with the VA, but if you're interested . . ."

Behind Coop came a flapping. He turned to see that Kay's notes had fallen again to the floor.

"Oh, excuse me," said Presser. He got up to retrieve the sheet. Presser held the paper up to the window light and examined the adhesive, his skeletal silhouette imposed for a moment against the banner of Kay's handwriting. Then he neatly folded the sheet and carried it toward a row of recycling bins at the back of the room. Before Coop was forced to watch the doctor dispose of Kay's notes, he pushed himself up from the table and stalked out.

CHAPTER FIFTEEN

Instead of going back to his hotel, Coop found himself lingering across the street from Next Start. The street was mostly empty. At the end of the block, two men pushed an old Plymouth while a third cranked its engine. A host of pigeons fluttered across the gray sky, flashing their ragtag wings.

"*Please* don't be sitting on my stoop, sir," snapped a small voice, and Coop turned toward a trio of young girls bouncing down the stairs of the building behind him. They all wore enormous backpacks and oversized wool hats. He wasn't sure which one had scolded him.

"Sorry—" began Coop, but one of the girls held up her mittened palm.

"Get yourself to *God,*" she said, in a mockingly deep preacher's voice, and the trio exploded into shrill, piping laughter. They scattered down the street, little neon boots kicking up sprays of slush. Coop faltered in the girls' wake. He felt stupid, purposeless, standing in the cold across from the clinic. *Looking for information,* he told himself. The last traces of Kay. Something he could take with him, some shred of coherence, before he went to the airport and gave himself up.

His instincts told him Eva was his best shot. And there she was, coming onto the street with one arm raised, pulling on a puffy red coat.

Coop followed her for several blocks through the snow

until she turned in to a building fronted in steamy glass. Over the door was a sign that said LAUND-O-MAT below a string of Chinese characters. For a few minutes Coop waited on the sidewalk. His body was bone-weary, and his head hurt from the cold. *What are you doing?* he asked himself. Then he thought: *What else are you going to do?*

Coop was surprised to find the laundromat empty. No sign of Eva or anybody else, but at the back of the laundromat was another door, unmarked, and Coop headed that way, down the narrow alleyway of rumbling machines.

He opened the door on a world of purple darkness, weird geometries of electric color, a static roar of jingles. It was an arcade. Game consoles clumped together in the repurposed storeroom, most of them older titles that Coop recognized— Battle City, Metal Slug, Kung Fu Remix. He found Eva in the corner playing Asteroids, quarters spread out on the dash in front of her.

Coop knew the game from childhood. The asteroids followed a random trajectory, and each time one was destroyed they exploded into smaller, faster-moving rocks. It was impossible to win. In each successive round the asteroids arrived in greater numbers, all of them moving faster until the whole universe was a blur of killing debris.

He watched Eva play until she lost her last life, the ship coming apart with a coarse explosion.

"You want the next game?" she said, and it took Coop a moment to realize Eva was talking to him, addressing his reflection in the countdown screen.

"Look," she said, "I know you're not from the city. But it's a bad look, following people."

To avoid her scolding look, Coop studied Hydro Thunder: dueling rocket boats navigating a tropical canal. He tried to formulate an apology.

"I'm sorry, I'm just sort of wandering . . ."

"It's okay," she said, with a merciful smirk. Coop was impressed with how cool she was, how unfazed.

"So you don't mind if I take a shot?" he asked, pointing to the game.

Eva grinned. "You have the bridge." She fed a few quarters into the machine before slipping off the chair.

Coop seated himself at the console, aware of Eva's warmth at his back.

The little white ship appeared, and big, slow-moving rocks began drifting in from the borders of space. He got the hang of the controls and advanced through the first few stages. While she watched him play, Coop saw Eva take sips from a small glass bottle with a label covered in foreign characters. She saw him noticing and put the bottle in her coat.

"I have a cold," she mumbled. "Watch it," she warned, as Coop narrowly missed a small, fast-moving rock.

"You play this a lot?" he asked.

"Got hooked in med school," said Eva. "My roommate, she was Korean. Said the games make your brain more plastic."

"That's a good thing?"

"I don't know," said Eva. "Some days I think it just helps to blow stuff up."

He smiled, and saw her smile back in the screen's reflection. "Uh-oh," said Eva. "Hear that music? Alien coming for you."

Sure enough, a pixelated UFO came floating out of the abyss, firing lasers in every direction. Coop dodged in a wide arc.

"You know," said Eva, "my grandfather was in the Army. You heard of the Triple Nickel?"

"Of course," said Coop, battering the fire button to take down the UFO. He was genuinely impressed. The 555th Airborne was a legendary outfit among paratroopers. "When was he in?"

"Did almost his full twenty. During World War Two he wanted to go to France but ended up jumping into Montana."

"The forest fires," said Coop, remembering the story. As an experiment in nonconventional warfare, the Japanese had loosed hundreds of incendiary balloons into the eastern jet stream, hoping to set fire to the American coast. The Army's countermove was the first black airborne unit, all recruited from Buffalo, New York. The way Coop had heard it, generals at the time had been reluctant to use African American paratroopers in real combat, so instead they dropped them into the great conflagrations of the Northwestern wilderness, and the Triple Nickel became history's first smoke jumpers.

"Later he was in Korea with the Rangers," said Eva.

Coop whistled. "He must have some stories."

Eva smiled faintly but didn't respond. Then the game ended: rocks came from the darkness to obliterate Coop's little ship.

"I have to dry," said Eva. Coop followed her out of the little arcade. He blinked under the harsh, corrosive fluorescence of the laundromat, watching Eva unload her clothes. He caught sight of a damp tangle of purple underwear and automatically looked away.

"The police," Eva was saying. "Did you talk to them?"

"What?"

Coop had been distracted, but now he looked up and was surprised to see the expression on Eva's face, staring off. Anger. *She's pissed at me,* thought Coop. And then realized, *No. She looks mad at herself.*

"Have you talked to the police yet?" she said again. "About what happened to Katherine?"

"There was a detective at the funeral," said Coop. "But he didn't know shit."

"No," said Eva. "Of course not."

CHAPTER SIXTEEN

All the best soldiers are criminals, Coop had once been told. This piece of wisdom came from a vagrant named Gerard who used to hold court at Tommy's Park back in Portland, Maine, in the fall of 1999. At the time, all the news was focused on Seattle getting overrun by protesters, and the big countdown. Only a month left until Y2K was scheduled to wipe out the universe. Meanwhile, nothing was happening in Portland. Nothing better to do than drift around the Old Port, stand around in the cold. Listen to an old gutter punk tell war stories.

That night Gerard squatted on a boulder in the park, gripping his paper-bagged bottle of malt liquor. Gerard dressed like a beggar, with a mangy goatee and a newsboy cap. He had wrinkles around his eyes and a smoker's voice that sounded like rocks getting crushed in his larynx. Nobody knew much about him, except that he'd been a medic in the Army before getting kicked out, and he still wore a big red cross stitched onto the back of his leather jacket. He couldn't have been older than thirty, but to Coop he seemed ancient.

"You guys know anything about the DMZ?" he asked the scattered audience of teens. "That's in Korea. Where unbeknownst to the general fucking populace, there's still a war going on."

Gerard said sometimes the North Koreans would sneak

over the border, and the next morning his unit would find a sentry with a slashed throat.

"The military always calls it a training accident, because nobody wants a real war. No, you get murdered out on the DMZ and you'll never get a Purple Heart. Never a parade. Just a phone call to your family from some junior officer."

Gerard made his hand into a phone and assumed a tone of mock formality. "Yes, ma'am, I'm sorry for your loss, but please understand that even in the safest training circumstances, accidents can happen."

This led Gerard to the subject of officers. He spat on the brick floor of the park, and with no warning whirled to point a finger at Coop.

"You resemble a smart young man," Gerard said. "Tell me something: Did George Washington ever kill a man?"

Coop faltered.

"Well?" said Gerard, standing up. He seemed emboldened by Coop's confusion. "Did Mr. Founding Father ever put a redcoat between his sights? Did he take saber in hand, did he swipe at another man's bowels?"

Gerard rasped and sputtered, making fencing motions with his beer.

"He did not!" Gerard bellowed. "After all, why would he soil his white fucking gloves? Now what about Lee or Grant? Zero kills between those two. How about Patton, you think he killed any Nazis, I mean personally? Not with his fancy six-shooters, not with his epaulets. But surely—Eisenhower? I mean, *Eisenhower*."

Gerard held up a splayed hand. "Five stars."

He began dropping fingers: "But—not—one—single—kill."

Gerard took a swig of his malt liquor. "You know who wins wars?" he said. "It's the criminals. People who know how to hurt people and break shit. People like me."

Later, if Coop had to pick a single reason why he joined the Army, he'd always think of Gerard. Not his rants but his wrinkles. Because that night, after leaving Gerard alone in the park with his bottle, Coop had gone into the bathroom of Java Joe's coffee shop and looked himself hard in the face. He stretched the skin around his eyes, looking for signs of those premature hard-ass lines. At the time, Coop had liked to think of himself as hard. But in that moment, pulling at the baby skin of his face, Coop had understood that he was fundamentally untested.

Of course, months later when he went to the Army recruitment center on Congress Street, Coop had told himself all the usual lies about travel, college money, and job skills. But the truth was, he never joined the Army to have a future, he did it because he wanted to get a better past.

Now, as he exited the subway at Mosholu Parkway, Coop found himself thinking of Gerard's historical rant. *People like me.*

He walked north under the shadow of the elevated subway track. Overhead the sky was deep and gray, with swatches of blue beneath the heavy clouds.

His coat jingled. Though he'd been forced to leave his demolition kit in Afghanistan, Coop had brought along his sapper's D-ring: a heavyweight black carabiner hung with a jangling assortment of tools—tweezers, hex wrenches, keys, screwdriver bits, odd twists of wire. He also had a tactical flashlight and the Strider knife he'd checked in his duffel bag.

I'm just looking, Coop reminded himself. *Just looking.*

The Mosholu Medical Offices were situated in a narrow three-story building. No lobby, just a locked door with swipe card access. Across the street was a bodega. Coop hunkered down inside, where a jumble of tables and aluminum folding chairs were occupied by hospital employees in white coats and scrubs, slurping coffee and eating sandwiches on big crusty rolls. Coop found a seat where he could watch the building through a few gaps in the Mexican beer ads that were pasted on the windows.

A white van pulled up to the offices, and from the back doors came three guys in coveralls. One swiped an access card while another used a milk crate filled with cleaning bottles to prop open the door while they ferried supplies from the van.

A rumble began down the train line. Coop stood up and left the bodega, cold wind swirling down his neck. Checking up and down the street, he saw a parked police car on the next block, windows darkened in the shade. Coop hunched his shoulders as the noise of the approaching train grew, and he looked back at the open door. Two of the cleaners were carrying a floor buffer through the side doors. The train passed overhead like a giant metal rattle in the sky, and Coop crossed the street. The cleaners didn't seem to notice him; they had finished getting the waxer inside and were back rummaging in the van. On the platform above them the train doors opened and closed repeatedly, and the conductor's amplified voice warned passengers to stay clear of the closing doors. The rumble of the train began again, and Coop followed the cleaners, quickstepping behind the crew as they carried more supplies into the building. He let them get a few paces ahead and opened the first door he passed, then slipped into a stairwell where he paused, listening to the fading clatter of the train.

He crept up the stairs toward Presser's office, which according to Eva was located on the third floor. He heard a movement in the walls, the whirring of gears. A passing elevator. The cleaners would start on the top floor, he reasoned, then work their way down. Coop exited the stairwell on the second floor, into an alcove with a crooked row of vending machines. Beyond, an empty receptionist's desk and a wide hallway. He went down the corridor checking doors, leaving boot prints of dirty water behind him, looking for a place to hide. All the doors were locked.

Coop put his hand on his head and paced in quiet circles, trying to think. Upstairs he heard the slap of mops and the whine of a floor buffer.

He went back to the alcove. The glass-front snack machines looked like they'd been carelessly installed, each turned at a slight angle instead of sitting flush against the wall. Coop looked behind them, checking to see if they were bolted in place. Then he put on his winter gloves and squatted down in front of one of the machines. He worked his fingers underneath the front corner, took a deep breath, braced himself, and lifted, trying to pivot the massive weight. The dispenser trays rattled softly but the machine barely budged. He repositioned himself, panting as quietly as he could, then tried again, his legs and back straining. After a third attempt he finally managed to rotate the machine so it was angled a few more inches from the wall.

Upstairs, Coop heard the buffer winding down. Then a door opened and voices echoed in the stairwell.

He clambered over the top of the snack machine, trying to avoid smearing his muddy boots against the glass, and as the cleaners came down the stairs, Coop swung his legs down into the narrow scalene of space he'd opened between the machine and the wall. He squeezed himself into the gap, one elbow pressed to his side, dusty coils and prongs digging into his body. He waited there, breathing into his sleeve, while the cleaners went to work on the second floor.

.   .   .

"Jesus, where do I begin?" Eva had said, a few hours earlier, after leading Coop from the laundromat to a small Hungarian pastry shop.

"I didn't know it when I started here, but Next Start is kind of a bootleg operation." Eva spoke with her head lowered, fingertips pressed into the space behind her jaw, as if to ease the pain of this unburdening.

"Bootleg?"

"A scam. Let me ask you, does Presser seem like someone who cares about this community? Someone who wants to help people?"

Coop shook his head.

"No," said Eva. "Guys like Presser come to the Bronx talking about the drug epidemic, how they want to do early intervention or introduce new kinds of care. They sell local electeds with this BS and score major grants from the state, then they use the public money as leverage to pitch the private equity firms. Meanwhile they don't know anything about actually treating addiction, so we get these scam clinics that aren't doing a damn thing except making money for people like Presser and his investors."

"People invest in rehab clinics?"

Eva shrugged. "I guess the smart money is on heroin making a comeback. Anyway, there's all kinds of ways to cut corners and make even more cash. Defrauding Medicaid, for one. But honestly, I think Presser might be into worse things."

At this point, Coop had felt compelled to interrupt. "Sorry, help me understand. How is all this connected to Kay?"

"Okay," said Eva, "so I was there when we found out. About Katherine. The police came to the clinic. This was after hours, just me and Dr. Presser, and after they left, I saw Presser carting a box of files to his car. Your wife's case files."

"Why would he do that?"

"This situation is like Presser's worst nightmare. Katherine always made him nervous. He was always asking about her, how she was doing. It's her family—I think he was scared of them."

"Wait, why would he give Kay a job in the first place?"

"I'm not sure he had a choice."

Coop thought about that. "Presser was at the funeral," he said. "Trying to talk with Kay's mother."

"I'm not surprised," said Eva. "He's probably losing his shit right now."

"So what exactly would be in these files?" said Coop.

"It could be a lot of things. But one possibility . . . Jesus, I shouldn't do this to you . . ."

Coop leaned forward and fought the urge to kick her under the table.

"It could be that Kay was hurt by one of the clients," said Eva.

"Hurt?"

"Attacked. Killed, I don't know."

Eva's lips were pressed tight. Her eyes dropped to the table between them.

"We've had incidents before. Staff who've been threatened or grabbed. Mostly nothing serious, but a few months back one of our caseworkers was on a house visit, out of nowhere the client comes at her with hammer, chases the poor woman down the street."

"Goddamn," said Coop.

"Dr. Presser is supposed to report these things to the police. But see, if he did that, the clinic's numbers go down and the government stops paying. I told him we needed to make the reports, that it was only a matter of time until something happened . . ."

"So if Kay was assigned one of these dangerous 'clients,'

that would be recorded in the files you mentioned? The ones Presser took from the clinic?"

Eva nodded.

"Any idea where he might've taken them?"

"I'm not sure, exactly. Why?" asked Eva, looking suddenly suspicious.

"The detective I met," Coop improvised. "I could tell him about the files, maybe get him to look into it."

He wore his most earnest, reassuring face.

Coop waited until the building fell quiet again before extracting himself from behind the vending machine. Afterward he limped upstairs to the third floor row of offices and found 316, the number Eva had given him. As expected, the door was locked. On his D-ring Coop kept a collection of bump keys, each made from a standard house key but with the teeth filed off. He tried inserting these one at a time into Presser's door, found one that offered a reasonable fit, then used the weighted handle of his flashlight to rap on the key head. He flinched with each metallic crack, the sound echoing down the empty hall. After several strikes the pins clicked into place and the door came open.

Darkness inside. Coop turned on his light and swept the room. The lab was made of several workstations, each cluttered with paperwork and medical equipment. Coop saw microscopes, cardboard boxes of slides and test strips, various electronic analyzers, and the open-mouthed pod of a centrifuge. Against the wall were storage lockers and a few miniature refrigerators. There were two other doors, one marked RESTROOM, the other half open, showing the outline of a desk and filing cabinet. Coop paused at this second doorway and aimed his light around the room.

As with the lab, the furniture in Presser's office was simple and impersonal. Scanning the room, Coop's flashlight settled on a crumpled pile under the desk. A pair of corduroy pants. This discovery struck Coop as somehow disturbing. He continued searching the office, uncovering strange new signs of domesticity. There was bedding on the couch, and hanging from the doorknob, Coop found dress shirts hanging in crinkly plastic. Then on the desk he spotted a glass vial, and next to it, three lines of powder. Coop was trying to reconcile these dissonant details—evidence of a drug user living in the office of a rehabilitation doctor—when he heard a sudden eruption of liquid noise. The flushing of a toilet.

All the signs of habitation coalesced into a sick fear, and Coop felt his entire body contract as he turned to see a figure stumbling into the doorway behind him.

Nowhere to hide; Coop instinctively transferred the flashlight to his left hand, aiming it upward at a pinched and suddenly blinking face, and with his free fist slugged the man, pitching him sideways into the doorframe before he fell to the floor. Coop took a step back and shined his light on the man's face.

From the unconscious pile of Dr. Presser came a soft animal whine. He wore a dress shirt, boxer shorts, and one argyle sock, long hair splayed around him, murmuring through his blood-sticky beard.

Coop's fist throbbed in the silence. He reminded himself what Eva had told him, and of the drugs on the desk. Presser wouldn't be calling the police. He let go of the shuddering panic, thoughts coming clear now. The doctor was his enemy, and he was helpless, and with this awareness came a renewed sense of control.

First thing, Coop thought, was to make the situation secure. He knelt beside the doctor and rolled him over, facedown into the carpet.

Presser groaned.

"Sshh," said Coop, and put a knee in his back.

He snatched the pillow from the couch, tore off the pillow-case, and pulled this over the doctor's head. He'd seen a phone on the desk. Coop yanked the cord from the wall and, folding Presser's arms backward, flashlight in his mouth, began to lash the doctor's wrists.

"Fauh," said Presser, beginning to wake up. "Fuck. Hey, no." His voice rising in volume, too loud. Coop shifted his weight, used a boot to push aside one of Presser's legs and drove a gloved fist into the doctor's testicles.

The yelling was instantly cut to a sharp exhale. Then Presser fell into a high-pitched, giggling whine, trying to fold his body like a stabbed caterpillar.

"Sshh," said Coop again.

He finished securing the wrists. Presser continued to wriggle and sob but the volume stayed manageable. Now Coop went back to the filing cabinet. Locked. He took out the Strider and eased the titanium blade into the drawer's lip, manipulating the knife until he found good leverage. He grasped the handle with both hands and leaned into it, extracting a metal squeal of resistance, until something snapped with a violent twang and the drawer came rolling free. Inside he saw endless rows of manila files.

Coop realized he hadn't brought a bag. There was a trash-can next to the desk. Coop dumped the contents on the floor but decided the plastic liner was too flimsy. Over his shoulder, he saw the doctor stirring. Coop looked again around the room, found a garment bag hanging behind the dry cleaning. He threw the suit inside onto the floor.

Now Presser muttered under the hood.

"Hey," said the doctor. "Hey."

Coop didn't respond.

"Please, I wanna . . . Let's have a conversation," Presser said. "We can talk."

Coop kept working. The manila folders slid off one another, slippery between his gloves. Paperwork spilled everywhere within the bag, cascading and intermingled.

"Look, tell them it's fine," Presser continued. "It's not . . . It's fine. Tell them I have it covered. Everything's under control."

Coop stood over him, the open blade of the Strider in his fist. The doctor rolled his head back and forth, still mumbling. Blood had soaked through the pillowcase, a seeping flower of red, and Presser kept talking, his words becoming alien and shrill, unintelligible, pleading with the darkness as Coop left the lab and made his way toward the exit.

CHAPTER SEVENTEEN

Kosta circled a heavy bag, his bare feet squeaking on the gym floor. He ducked and feinted, let off a blaze of right jabs, then dropped low again to rise with a vicious hook to the body. The bag shuddered with every punch, swinging on its chain. Kosta picked up the tempo, huffing and snorting. Cross to the body, hook to the head, another stiff gut shot, and Kosta pivoted away, imagining his opponent doubled and clutching a bruised liver. He chambered one fist for a quick, killing blow to the base of the skull.

The timer buzzed and Kosta took a break from the drill, using both gloved paws to take a deep swig from his water bottle.

He sat on the mat and let his heart rate settle. Nearby he could see Buqa working the kick cactus, a weird piece of equipment sprouting arms at multiple angles. He watched her move through squares of light flashing diagonally from the high slotted windows of the basement space. The fighting gym was almost empty this time of day. Over the last few years since he'd been coming here, more and more of the floor had been converted to padding, a symptom of the American infatuation with grappling. Popular thinking said boxers like himself were outdated, that real fights happened on the ground. There was some wisdom to this, of course. Guys lose control and try to tackle you, then you get all the rolling and humping on the floor, looking for a good submission hold. But real fights weren't staged in an octagon. On the street you could pull someone down for a choke, only to have another guy come up and start stomping on your head. Or you wrap your legs around your opponent's head, but he pulls a razor and gashes open your femoral artery. At his core, Kosta was uncomfortable with the very ideology of ground fighting, the inevitability of entanglement. No, he would keep practicing on his feet. Moving, striking, waiting for opportunities.

Kosta pulled off his gloves and began to unwrap his hands. It felt good to be sweaty from hitting something. He'd been so nervous ever since he decided to make his play. To go behind Luzhim's back.

"Nobody gives you chances," one of his favorite rappers said, "you gotta take 'em." Kosta had repeated this to himself over the last few days while he made his plans, a mantra against the yellow spell of anxiety that seemed to hover around him. Kosta knew that Luzhim would see it as a great betrayal, if ever he found out, but he wasn't sure what the old man would do.

After all, it was Luzhim himself who first gave Kosta the idea to approach the Bellantes. After their phone call Kosta puzzled over the things Luzhim had told him. About the dead girl, and why Sean needed to die, and especially the part about the dead girl's family. The Bellantes. "They're like the Falconaras," Luzhim had said. The Falconaras. It was a name from an older time, when Kosta had been a prisoner.

Kosta was fifteen the first time the Communists had arrested him. They caught him trying to hijack gas cans from a state depot south of Lezhe, and sentenced him to work in a copper mine. He escaped just a month later, only to be recaptured, and for the next several years he was shuffled through a series of juvenile labor camps, a period of bureaucratic chaos he would later understand to be the Communists' death rattle.

When the government fell in 1994, Kosta was transferred to a small detention facility outside Saranda, on the Adriatic Coast.

He preferred the labor camps, where at least they'd slept outdoors. He had grown up hunting in the shadow of snow-capped mountains, through forests of pine and cedar, but in Saranda he'd been locked in a tiny cement chamber with a single slotted window. Prisoners were allowed to bathe twice per week, and they shared a single shower room, which they also used to do laundry. During winter storms the whole prison descended into a bitter, salty chill, and there was nothing to do but slap-box, smoke, and mingle with other criminals. But then a new warden assumed control of the facility, and the prison acquired a television. The warden was a connoisseur of cowboy films, particularly those of Sergio Corbucci. Kosta's favorite was *Il Grande Silenzia*. The snowy mountains of Utah reminded him of home.

There was never news on the television, only cowboy movies, but always there were rumors. Despite talk of a rigged election, President Berisha had claimed a people's mandate to transform the economy. With the support of Western countries and guidance from the IMF, Berisha threw open the gates of the formerly cloistered Albania, and soon there was a frenzy to participate in the free market. Kosta didn't have money or property to invest, but he'd overheard urgent conversations in the prison, men telling their sons to sell the tractor, sell the house, slaughter the animals—anything to free up cash. The warden talked openly and excitedly about the promised return rates, the long lines of people waiting to invest their money, and the cottage he was eyeing, in Calitri, where in a few years he hoped to retire.

One day in January the guards came swarming into the prison, openly brandishing their AKM rifles. They were led by the warden, who yelled and waved a red national flag, and as

Kosta watched in disbelief he began to unlock the cells. The old-timers were skeptical. One man screamed "Don't let them take you" and held fast to the bars. Having been imprisoned under the Communists, he thought it was a ruse, that the guards had come to execute them. But soon Kosta and the others were made to understand the situation: Albania was in revolt. In just a few months the pyramid schemes had crumbled, leaving a sinkhole that swallowed the country's savings, and under advisement from the International Monetary Fund, President Berisha had declared there would be no compensation for the schemes' victims. After all, he said, the blame ultimately fell on those who had made poor investments.

Outside the prison they found Saranda overthrown. Police stations and military barracks had been raided for arms and equipment, and the streets were barricaded with overturned oil barrels. A temporary council of gangsters was formed, and Kosta was selected to lead a team of fellow teenage *rebelimi* on daily patrols. In place of a cell, Kosta took up residence in the empty summer home of a Greek family. The cottage was made of stone, with a small garden and red-tiled roof. When he wasn't on patrol, Kosta sat in the terraced front yard. The rebels had captured a Soviet T-72 battle tank from a nearby armory, and Kosta would sit in his garden as the sun set, smoking cigarettes and drinking bottles of commandeered wine, watching as the tank rolled up and down the beach.

By May the revolution was defeated. Italian troops led a UN mission to stomp the uprising and install an interim government. There were demonstrations and riots, rounds of negotiations that led to a referendum, which was then followed by more rioting. By this time Kosta was on his way north, back to the mountains, following a crew of *rebelimi* who had connections to a gun smuggling operation.

It was around this time that Kosta remembered first hearing about the Falconaras. There were three of them, brothers, and together they had managed one of the largest and most disastrous of the pyramid schemes. During the course of the new government's investigation, evidence began to surface that the Falconaras weren't just a trio of grifters, as had been assumed, but were in fact financial operatives working on behalf of the Italian Mafia. Some even suggested the entire financial crisis had stemmed from this money laundering operation, which had inspired imitator schemes and subsequently triggered a delirium of competition. Though they were never charged, the name Falconara became representative of the whole deceit, the fly trap of capitalism, and for a while it entered the local jargon as a pejorative for greed.

"Don't Falconara all the sausages," a fellow smuggler would say to Kosta over the fire pit as they trucked a shipment of FN SCARS into Montenegro.

And it was this sense that Luzhim must have intended when talking about the dead girl's family, Kosta felt sure. The Bellantes were bankers—"and not just bankers," Luzhim had said—leading Kosta to assume they were somehow connected to the underbelly.

But the name triggered another memory for Kosta. The reason the brothers were never charged. Despite endless interrogations and debriefings and international pressure, despite death threats and raging mobs, the Falconaras never gave evidence against one another. Even though the whole country knew what they had done, each of them refused to indict his brothers. It was a strategy that had led them to prevail under the law, and eventually in the public eye, as this fanatic loyalty suggested a supreme Albanianness. Something Luzhim would never understand. He saw love of kin as a corrupt kind of sentimentality, whereas in Kosta's homeland, family was all.

For instance: Once during the months of the Uprising, Kosta's patrol had captured two Serbians, a husband and wife trying to flee from Durres. The couple had acquired a small cabin boat but been chased back from the maritime border by Greek helicopters. Then they'd run out of gas and become shipwrecked.

When the couple had finished telling their story, Kosta drew one of his Tokarevs and shot the husband in the throat. They shaved the woman's head, hung a heavy Orthodox icon around her neck, and chased her naked down the beach, whipping her body with steel antennas taken from abandoned cars. Finally the woman ran screaming into the surf and Kosta followed. When she fell, he pounced into the waves and held her down in the roiling saltwater. He was twenty-two years old, and it was the first time he had ever been with a woman.

Why did he do this? Because Kosta's grandparents had originally come from Kosova, and his mother had told him stories about their treatment at the hands of the Serbs. And even though Kosta had run away when he was fifteen, had abandoned his mother and their tiny mountain village, he knew that he lived under certain obligations, debts acquired before his birth. He and the Serbs were in blood, because of what their people had done to each other.

This was the thing Luzhim couldn't appreciate, being a Communist fuck first and an Albanian second. He didn't understand the power of ancestral law, the Tree of Blood. What Kosta knew, what had inspired him to go against Luzhim's wishes and approach the Bellantes, was this: True clans will do anything to avenge their family.

So instead of killing Sean, as Luzhim had ordered him to do, Kosta had kept him a prisoner. Then he sent Zameer to the dead girl's funeral, with a letter for her family: *I have the man who killed your daughter, and I will deliver him to you. For a price.* A ransom big enough for Kosta to finally get himself free of his debts to Luzhim. Enough to go out on his own, build up his own crew, chase down his destiny. And yes, Luzhim would be murderous with rage when he found out what Kosta had done, but what could the old man do?

Balkan rave music came from the phone inside Kosta's gym bag. Kosta used his teeth to unstrap a glove so he could pull out the phone: incoming call from Presser. He paused before answering. It was a thing undealt with. The doctor ran a rehab clinic but had a habit himself. In exchange for product, Presser gave Kosta access to cheap methadone and other pharmaceuticals, not to mention a revolving customer base. But it was also the place where the Bellante girl had worked. Presser shouldn't have any way of knowing Kosta had been involved in her death.

But here he was, calling.

Kosta answered and right away he could tell the doctor was just resurfacing after a long nod: his voice dull and distant, stoned, but edged with panic. Something about his lab getting "invaded." Kosta closed the phone and wiped sweat from his forehead. He whistled to Buqa.

CHAPTER EIGHTEEN

Coop tracked the progress of a black squirrel as it dashed across a telephone wire. Everything was gray and quiet outside the hotel, a silent film except for the acrobatics of this weird scrabbling creature. Coop hadn't realized squirrels came in black, and he wondered if they might be bad luck.

A hiss came from the coffee pot. Instead of pouring himself a cup, Coop emptied the urn back into the feed tank, reloaded the filter, and set the pot to run a second time, using the fresh coffee in place of water. Battery acid, Anaya called this concentrated brew. The coffeemaker chugged through its second cycle, occasionally spitting drops of black sludge against the pot.

All night Coop had scoured the files, going without sleep and still only making it halfway through the stack. Each file contained pages and pages of personal histories, medical evaluations, treatment plans, notes from counselors and transcripts from support groups, most of it rendered in a cryptographic salad of medical jargon: acculturation, cross-tolerance, enmeshment, psychopharmacological intervention, ACT and PAWS and CBT. But some words Coop knew: hallucination, relapse, remission, and, of course, heroin.

Heroin, heroin, heroin.

With his coffee, Coop came back to the window. Cold air was breathing through the glass but Coop hardly noticed. In the last few hours his adrenaline had sputtered out, replaced by an intestinal anxiety, something releasing drops of molten worry into the cavities of his body.

He thought about Dr. Presser again, bloody on the floor.

Coop didn't believe himself to be a man who enjoyed hurting people. It was true that he was proud of his earned proficiency with violence, but in his mind there was a vast and crucial distance separating those who were capable of fighting, should the need arise, and the crazy folks always looking for the next throw-down.

The squirrel was still balanced on the frozen wire. In the wobble Coop felt a haunted kind of unease, an itchiness of ghost-fire and hissing snakes, a nauseous tug in the direction of October.

He wouldn't think about that, he decided.

There was something in front of him. Some mystery in the interplay between Presser, Theo, the stranger at the funeral. It reminded him of his time downrange, where through the sandstorm of mission briefings, news reports, and ancient tribal rivalries he would intermittently perceive the barest outline of coherence, a sense there was some structure of meaning hidden just beyond his sight.

Coop went back to the files. He lifted one of the patient records, Nolan Hernandez—gaunt, dark-skinned, his lips drawn back like a wolf—and skimmed the notes. "Client has become agitated and hostile following surgical amputation of left leg; describes violent sexual fantasies, often involving staff." Keeping his eyes on the photo, Coop transferred Nolan to a stack on the nightstand. Next came Diamond, a twenty-eight-year-old mother of three. "Client brags about hitting elderly grandfather with a phonebook." Stack. A growing pile, the violent and possibly guilty. Eva had shared her theory that Kay was killed by one of the addicts she was treating. This made sense to Coop. It explained why Dr. Presser had taken

Kay's paperwork from Next Start and hidden the files in his personal office. He had known that some of the clinic's patients were unstable, but instead of reporting them, Presser had kept sending Kay and the other caseworkers to meet with these violent, deranged junkies. The kind of people who would run a woman down and leave her to die in the snow.

Coop closed his eyes for a moment. He hadn't slept in days and he knew his time in America was running out. What he wanted to do was tear through the folders and find his enemy. But he needed to be deliberate about this. *Slow is smooth,* he heard Anaya say. *And smooth is fast.*

Coop opened the next patient file and studied the photograph inside. A scrub-faced old man with a wide mane of white hair and glassy eyes. No incident reports, just a quick notation from his most recent visit: "Jenning has relapsed following job loss." Coop set the folder down, adding to the other, smaller pile of exonerated junkies.

He closed his eyes again, felt himself circling in the dark, an Ozark wilderness of his own confusion. Trees wheeling around him, a single star at his back. He opened his eyes. Night land navigation, the sapper's course at Fort Leonard Wood, another memory flaring in the sleepless cave of his brain. He had to get back to the files but he was already moving down the path. With your compass you shoot an azimuth, following the directions on your laminated orders. Dead reckoning was a dangerous prospect at night, especially with just a quarter moon under heavy clouds, so you fix on a major terrain feature, and in Fort Leonard Wood, that means a big tree. The woods are dense, six miles of tight growth, crisscrossed with muddy ravines. And all those species of pit vipers they'd been forced to learn: Osage Copperhead, Water Moccasin, Pygmy Rattlesnake, Massasauga Rattlesnake . . . or were those snakes from the postcards? Kay, the queen of adopted snakes . . . but there were definitely pigs out there, muscular wild hogs with razor tusks, you could hear them crashing and snorting in anarchic herds. You sight an azimuth, decide on it, walk. Keeping mental count of your pace. If all goes well, after a certain distance you should arrive at a code-marked tree. But sometimes you complete your pace count and there's nothing around but more woods. This is a crucial moment. The exact spot you are standing in is the result of all previous work. Lose the line and you're lost, with no reference of how you arrived. In these cases you are permitted a single glowstick, which you can drop at your feet . . . a village of huts, each mouth glowing, the blue ghost and her baby with the turquoise pajamas . . . and you walk in a circle around this tiny beacon, widening in a spiral, hoping to blunder across your point. So you circle outward. The panic grows. You have to keep circling, circling in the dark . . .

When he woke again the room was hot. Afternoon had come inside, the sun blazing against the window. Coop surveyed the chaos of papers around him. He poured another cup of burnt sludge from the pot, retched after the first sip, and poured the whole mess down the sink, where it steamed in a black pool. He started picking up the files, flattening them out, re-sorting them. The hours counted down.

Then he came across a new batch of paperwork, one he'd initially discarded. Employee Equipment Sign-Out. A spreadsheet of names and phone numbers, and there was "Katherine Cooper." Next to her name, the word "cellphone" had been printed under the equipment column, along with a number. Next Start had assigned cellphones to all of their caseworkers. Coop tried the number on the hotel line, expecting it to be dead.

But then he was hearing a voice. Her voice.

"Hi, you've reached Kay at Next Start. Please leave a message with your number . . ."

A beep, and Coop listened to Kay's voicemail recording his breath.

He redialed. Listened again.

Kay's phone was still activated.

Coop started to think about where the phone might be, but very quickly he knew. Whatever property hadn't been kept by the police as evidence would have been returned to Kay's next of kin.

CHAPTER NINETEEN

Coop saw glimpses of the Hudson from the window of his taxi, the river flashing at him through a canopy of well-groomed trees. Fresh banks of snow were piled up on either side of the road, and the driver almost missed his turn-off: a green placard delineating the border between Fieldston, "a private community," and the rest of the Bronx. The taxi made its way into the walled neighborhood, a kingdom of country-style estates with white lawns, terraces of intricate stonework, gazebos standing watch over frozen ponds. They came to the address Coop had given the driver, where a shoveled path led upslope toward a stone mansion.

The entrance to the driveway was protected by a heavy arched gate. One of the gateposts featured a subtle aluminum plate with a perforated microphone, keypad, and small video screen.

Coop cleared his throat.

"Hello?" he said, and the screen popped to life, showing the face of a young Asian woman.

"Delivery?" she said.

"Oh," said Coop. "Um, who are you?"

"I'm Sue," said the woman, as if explaining something obvious.

"I'm looking for Mrs. Bellante," said Coop.

"Are you expected?"

Coop shook his head.

"I'm sorry, if you don't have an appointment . . ."

"Listen, I think she'd want to see me." Coop gave the monitor his best attempt at a harmless grin. "I'm her son-in-law."

Sue blinked.

"Just a moment," she said, and the screen went dark.

Coop waited in front of the gate with his hands in his pockets, biting the inside of his cheek. Several minutes passed. Then came a welcoming chime from the intercom, and a mechanical click as the gate lock opened.

Coop walked up the driveway, tugging occasionally at his new clothes. He was still uncomfortable in the wool slacks, button-up shirt, and red cable-knit sweater. The outfit cost him nearly two hundred dollars, but it was an essential part of the act.

Even if Kay's mother was in possession of the phone, Coop suspected she'd have reservations about giving it to him, and he had spent the morning considering the most persuasive approach.

Luckily, the Army had already schooled Coop in a range of dramatic roles. Each a different take on "soldierness," and each associated, in Coop's mind, with one of the four cultural polarities that defined military life. These were Texas, Miami, the Appalachians, and New York City. From Texas you got mass and spectacle, shiny tanks and marching bands, the love of bigness, and a whole system of clean-cut, patriotic mannerisms: calling all women "ma'am," taking your hat off indoors, saluting whenever you heard the national anthem. If Texas was the game-time pageantry, Miami was the dark side of the sun. Here's where you got your obsessive tanners, guys who lay out in the radioactive sun of Afghanistan and spent every free hour at the gym, using improvised weights made from rebar and coils of concertina wire. All the questionable mail-order nutritional supplements, the local hash scored from Pakistani truck drivers, the drunken volleyball tournaments back at Bragg. Miami was the party you went to after football practice. Next were the hill people, folks from states like Tennessee, Kentucky, and West Virginia. This was where the Army got its wolf-dog mentality, the love of ditches and mud and raw meat and chewing tobacco, the homoerotic folk magic called "grabass," and most important, the clannish divide between soldiers and civilians. And finally there was New York City, where you learned everything that wasn't covered in field manuals: how to sham your way out of work details, how to get the best supplies, how to get promoted. "If you're not cheating, you're not trying." An entire world of winks and nods, trades and deals; the cool, clued-in practicality that every lifer learned to assume.

For the current situation, Miami and the Appalachians were out for obvious reasons, and Coop knew he couldn't hope to pit his secondhand New York against a native of the tribe. To give himself a fighting chance against his mother-in-law, Coop knew he'd need his best Texas.

"You'll follow me," said Sue, as she opened the door with a practiced smile. Sue wore a long, intricate braid down her back, and Coop watched the braid sway as he followed her through the massive house. He remembered Kay telling him once that her mother maintained a special and intense partiality toward women with long hair. Once when Kay was a teenager she'd given herself a scissored crop, then dyed the spiky remainder with blue Manic Panic. "I was proud of myself," Kay had told Coop. "It looked good. But my mother? That woman cried like she'd lost a child."

They came into a high-ceilinged foyer of polished wood. Overhead was a massive chandelier, its crystals throwing glittery light across the oriental rug. Sue cast a shaded glance toward Coop's footwear. He realized his combat boots were dripping with mud and melted snow.

"Shit, sorry," he said, and crouched to undo the laces. Sue ducked out and returned with a pair of calfskin slippers. Coop made a show of self-conscious goofiness while he struggled to put them on.

"So, do I tip you, or what?" said Coop. Sue remained expressionless.

They went up a flight of stairs, then down another hallway. Sue indicated a painting with a quick hand-wave, like she was throwing salt.

"This is the family estate, outside Gravina," she said.

The painting showed a white farmhouse on flatlands of umber and sand, the landscape dotted by horned flecks of cattle and twisted trees. As she swished down the hallway Sue gestured at another. Twisted trees growing from a stony plateau.

"The Bellante olive plantation, in the lower Murge."

Next Sue pointed to a chunk of red marble in a glass display case. To Coop it looked like a polished cross-cut of meat.

"From the Bellantes' quarry," Sue was saying, but Coop had stopped paying attention. They had passed several doors, and Coop wondered which of them might lead to Kay's old bedroom. If they had her cellphone, where in this house would they be keeping it?

Emerging from the hallway they came into an unexpected burst of sunlight. Rivulets of water cascaded down a wall of bay windows, through which Coop saw a green cluster of fir trees. It seemed they had come the length of the mansion and were now overlooking the rear lawn, but Coop couldn't see any sign of the river. Instead, as he peered closer, he was bewildered to see another set of windows looking back at him through the snow-draped foliage. Then Coop understood. The forest was actually a courtyard, all contained within the enormity of the mansion.

"Let me clear you a place," said Sue. "Mrs. Bellante will be here shortly."

A pair of armchairs were set against the windows, both of them surrounded by books. Coop had been so distracted by the view, he hadn't noticed the many papers and old volumes spread around the room. Lying on one of the chair cushions was a large tome, its pages opened to a strange illustration: three she-devils, naked and flying in an entanglement of wings. Coop checked the spine. Dante's *Inferno*, as illustrated by Gustave Doré.

"Those are the Dirae," said a voice. Coop slapped the book shut and he turned to find Mrs. Bellante standing behind him. She was draped in a blue shawl, regarding Coop over a delicate pair of gold-rimmed glasses.

"Hello, ma'am," said Coop, rising from the chair. He resisted the urge to come to attention, as he would for an officer. "You surprised me."

"May I?" she said, and took the book from his hand. Her breath smelled of wine, and as she leaned forward the shawl momentarily drooped, briefly revealing the shadowed ridges of her sternum.

Without taking her eyes from the book Mrs. Bellante lowered herself into one of the chairs, licked her thumb, and began flipping through the pages. *Must be pills,* Coop thought, watching the methodical, slow-motion movement of her eyes. Pills and wine. No wonder Sue was trying to keep visitors away.

"You know I studied Classics at Fordham," she said. "Before I met Katherine's father."

"I didn't know that."

Mrs. Bellante nodded to herself, still only absently aware of

Coop's presence. "Switching to law, now that was *his* idea," she murmured, then suddenly brightened, finding the page.

"Here they are," she said. "It's Aeschylus. You know the story?"

Coop shook his head, wearing a polite smile. It wasn't at all what he'd expected, this scholarly disorder. But he could adapt, he decided. Stay patient, wait for an opening to bring up the phone.

"*The Oresteia* was the first written account of a trial by jury," Mrs. Bellante continued, as if reciting. "A murder trial."

She curled herself more deeply into the chair, spreading the shawl across her legs, and Coop saw she wore a girlish pair of silk slippers.

"Who got killed?" said Coop.

Mrs. Bellante smiled, showing wine-red teeth.

"A mother," she said. "By her son."

"Did he do it?" said Coop.

"Oh yes. He'd already confessed. You see, Orestes—that's the son—he was acting on orders from Apollo, one of the gods. Orestes' mother had killed his father, Agamemnon, which itself was an act of revenge, because Agamemnon sacrificed Iphigenia—that's Orestes' sister . . . *Iphigenia,* you know that one? There was a movie with Irene Papas. No?"

Mrs. Bellante let it trail with a wave of her hand. "Anyway, it all started with the invasion of Troy."

Coop nodded with bewilderment. He couldn't tell if she was giving a lecture, mocking him, or genuinely trying to make conversation.

"So the demon ladies," Coop ventured, pointing to the book. "Where do they come into play?"

"Yes, the Dirae," Mrs. Bellante said. "Well, the Dirae are old gods. Spirits of vengeance from the underworld. They want to punish Orestes for murdering his mother, but Apollo, he claims that Orestes was merely delivering justice. Killing his father's killer."

"Who was also his mother?"

"Exactly," said Mrs. Bellante. "Very good. So you see, Mr. Cooper, the real matter of this dispute?"

Now she looked up at him, adjusting her gold-rimmed glasses. The wine-drunk abstraction was gone from her eyes, leaving a gray hardness. In his periphery Coop saw a tremble of movement, heard the light clap of wings as small birds flickered between the boughs of the fir trees.

Slowly he shook his head.

"The question is this," said Mrs. Bellante, gently closing her illustrated *Inferno*. "Which do you think is of greater value: the contract of marriage? Or the bond of blood?"

Coop found himself looking away. He remembered Kay's words. *My mother will destroy you.* Mrs. Bellante placed the Dante atop a stack of nearby books, then folded her hands.

"Now, Mr. Cooper, I'm hoping this is the part where you tell me what you expect to get from this meeting."

Coop looked back at her. He felt the blood rushing up into his face, a wildfire rash of shame.

"And just so you know," she continued, straightening herself, "you and I can speak in generalities, but Theo is best equipped to handle any detailed proceedings. He manages most of the family assets, these days. Including Katherine's affairs."

"Wait, wait," said Coop. He held up a hand. "Are you talking about *money*?"

Mrs. Bellante smiled politely. She cocked her head. "Are you telling me you're not here because you want something?"

"What I want—" Coop stopped himself, hearing the harshness of his voice. He clenched his teeth while Mrs. Bellante watched with an expression of casual, expectant professionalism. Her War Face, he decided. Probably earned over decades of bargaining and litigation, the inscrutable varieties of white-collar combat.

"The thing is, ma'am," he began again, taking deep breaths through his nose, gathering the weapon of humility. "I realize you don't much know me. And I know you never approved of me marrying your daughter—"

Mrs. Bellante opened her mouth, as if to object, but Coop preempted her with both hands, raised in peace.

"Ma'am, it's all right. I understand. You were just looking out for her interests, right?"

Mrs. Bellante frowned.

"Look," said Coop, "I don't expect anything from you folks. And I know you're busy people, so I truly appreciate you making time, especially with me showing up like this. As for the reason I'm here, well . . . I'm going back again soon. To Afghanistan. And then Iraq, probably. And ma'am, you see, the thing is . . ."

Coop rubbed his hands together anxiously, looked at the floor. Summoning up a handful of Texas oh-gosh from the toilet of his heart.

"I just wanted a chance to *know* you folks better. Before I go back."

Coop looked down in his lap. A shaky finish. He worried he'd overdone it.

A moment of stillness followed. Coop glanced up and saw Mrs. Bellante staring at the glassed-in woods.

"You know," she said, her eyes caught in the distance, "Theo was working that day."

Coop nodded sympathetically. He had no idea what she was talking about.

"He was in another building. Saw the planes hit, saw people *jumping*. He was very affected by that, I think."

She used the edge of her shawl to dab at her mouth. Then her eyes popped wide. She stood up and went to the wall of shelves.

"Can I show you something? About our family?"

"I'd be honored, ma'am," said Coop, and he scooted forward with real eagerness. Coop sensed he'd retaken some kind of advantage—*Congratulations,* an inner voice scolded him, *you just bullshitted your grieving mother-in-law*—but he wasn't sure where to pivot from this new position. How to bring up the phone.

She came back to her chair with a sheaf of handwritten letters. "For some context, you must understand that Katherine's grandfather was a fascist."

Coop opened his mouth, not sure how to respond. Mrs. Bellante smiled. "Oh yes, a big family secret. But you know lots of people were, even in Italy, where they say it wasn't about ideology. Anyway, in June of 1943 he writes to a colleague in Berlin. And mind you, the Axis is beginning to crumble—and here's this man, a *believer*—and this is a translation, you understand, but he writes: 'Even in defeat, we will have demonstrated the truth of our vision: it is only force that matters. Our destruction can only arrive at the hands of a greater power, a greater darkness more terrible than ourselves, which we have ushered into the world. And this will also be a victory.'"

She set the letter down. Took off her glasses.

"And this will also be a victory," she repeated. "Isn't that incredible? This man's world is collapsing . . ." she trailed off again, put her fingers to her brow. "I'm sorry, Mr. Cooper."

"For what?"

"You're probably thinking you made a mistake."

"Ma'am?"

Mrs. Bellante smiled, almost shyly. "Wanting to know us better."

"No. I'm enjoying this," said Coop. "And, look," he said, gathering himself up, "there is one thing I wanted to ask you about."

"Of course." One eyebrow crooked up with new attention.

"It's silly, but . . . there's this picture of us." He'd worked out this speech ahead of time. "A picture of me and Kay, taken on her phone."

"Her phone?" Mrs. Bellante looked confused.

"I don't know if that got returned? It's a sentimental thing."

"Um, yes, I think that the police—yes, we should have it."

She stood, eyeing him, and spoke quietly into an intercom on the wall. Coop thought he heard Sue's voice but couldn't make out the words. Mrs. Bellante retook her seat and watched Coop sidelong while they waited.

A few minutes later Sue came into the den with a plastic bag, carrying it in both hands like a kid with a dead bird. Immediately Coop could see that the phone was badly damaged.

"I'm not sure how you'll get anything from it," Sue said with a frown.

"May I?" said Coop, and he tore open the bag. There was a crack through the casing and the screen flopped sideways, hanging half-amputated from its hinge. He held the power button, but the screen stayed flat and black.

"It might still work with a charge," Coop said, as he inspected the mangled device. "All depends on whether the storage chip is damaged. Would it be all right if I brought this back?"

Mrs. Bellante and Sue were looking at each other. "Oh. Well, I'm not sure if that's a good idea," said Mrs. Bellante.

"I'll just need an hour," said Coop.

"Mrs. Bellante, didn't the police say they might come back for these things?" said Sue, and Coop shot her a look of accusation.

"Trust me," he said. "The police aren't doing anything."

Now Mrs. Bellante stood up. The warmth had drained from her and she was the matron of the house once more, icy and elegant. She reached out a hand.

"I'm sorry about the photograph, but I think you should leave that here."

Coop looked away from Mrs. Bellante, out into the glass-enclosed forest.

"Mr. Cooper?"

He tucked the phone in his pocket and walked quickly away, past Sue, through the hall and the rows of paintings, across the oriental rugs, down the stairs where he retrieved his boots, not even bothering to relace them as he left the mansion at a half-jog, keeping his hand on the phone the entire way.

CHAPTER TWENTY

They walked out on the ice, Kosta in front, Buqa behind him, dragging the sack through the fresh snow that capped the lake. The city was all but absent from these massive woods, save for a faint electric glow in the sky. Zameer waited behind them, back on the shore. He had volunteered to be the lookout. *Of course he did,* Kosta thought. Not like Buqa, who followed. Who was loyal.

Kosta loved this park, where the Bronx gave way to old trees and culverts, the rusted outline of the derelict railroad, open fields littered with abandoned cars. The snow was pristine except for the tracks of wild dogs. It reminded him of home, the thundering winters of his childhood. This place, it was almost a shame to contaminate it.

Just another concession to his week of hells.

He had gone to meet Presser, only to find the doctor sprawled on his back, his face a bloody mound of gauze. At first Kosta thought he'd been beaten to death, but then he spied the scorched glass pipe on the carpet, not far from a small pile of glassine bags. Doctor got his ass beat, Kosta reasoned, so he turned to the habit. But his nose was too busted to snort anything, so he tries smoking and ends up overdoing it. Kosta got down close and held his hand over the doctor's open mouth. He wasn't breathing.

So Kosta called Buqa and Zameer. Together they rolled Presser into a sleeping bag and spent some time cleaning his office, all of them working in painter's outfits and hairnets. During the cleaning, Kosta stopped to run a rubber-gloved finger over the warp mark in the filing cabinet. It looked as if someone had violently pried open the drawer.

Now they hauled the sack farther along the lake, passing the ribs of a rotted skiff. Everywhere was death, mused Kosta, decaying corpses of stray dogs, raccoons, and birds, all buried just under the snow. But he and Buqa were very much alive, sweating and huffing out big breaths of steam, struggling under the weight of their load. *It would have been easier with three people,* Kosta thought.

"Swing it around," he said, as they came to the hole.

Here was a gap in the ice, where tall weeds pushed up from the lake. He shoved the bag to the edge, knelt, and unzipped the length of the sleeping bag. The doctor lay inside: pale, cold and bloody-faced.

"Give me the head," said Kosta.

From Presser's office they had taken a heavy bust of an old man with a wavy beard and empty eyes. Now he placed the stone head at the doctor's feet and rezipped the sleeping bag.

"Help me," Kosta said, and they slid the bag to the lip of ice, where it teetered for a second, then flopped into the water, vanishing in a flurry of bubbles. *Just like that and you're gone,* thought Kosta, watching the rippled surface. *It can happen that fast.*

CHAPTER TWENTY-ONE

Kay's phone reminded Coop of a heavy gray beetle, crushed on the polished landscape of his hotel desk. He examined the broken hinge, gently working the lid back and forth. Where would her fingers have fallen around the ovoid shell? There were scuff marks at the corners where the metallic plastic enamel had chipped off, and on the back, a faint spiral of abrasions. Kay was a compulsive spinner. On bad days he remembered her sitting in the kitchen, a butcher's knife laid flat on the speckled counter. With one finger she'd sweep the blade into a slow spin, watch it go round and round like a sharp, fast clock. One day, in the weeks before he had deployed to Afghanistan, the knife point had ended its spin aimed at Coop. "If that were a bottle we'd have to kiss, right?" he had joked. By then it had become difficult to make her smile.

Coop assembled his tools. A Gerber multitool, a miniature screwdriver set, and a soldering kit he had picked up from a Radio Shack. He popped off the battery case and started removing the miniature screws. His mind floated beyond the desk, spinning like the knife on the counter, settling on the dark, pockmarked skin of Sergeant Gayle's arm. The wrist with its red lump, a little metal sandfly under his skin. Gayle was an ammunition technical officer who'd been brought to Kandahar to train Coop and his fellow sappers on the intricacies of IEDs. A few years ago Gayle had been wounded by an IRA car bomb in London. He was just outside the kill zone but got peppered with debris, leaving a constellation of scars across his face, chest, and arms. One morning Gayle had appeared at the engineer's tent. "You mates ready for some true fucking grottiness?" he had asked them, holding up his forearm under the tent's fluorescent light. Just below his hand there was a tiny laceration. "Appeared overnight," he told them, and began to squeeze the wound like a pimple. Coop watched as a curled sliver of half-digested shrapnel was birthed from the fat of his arm. "Got about a hundred of those little cunts left, just waiting to come out. You should see the fun I have at airports," Gayle said with a wink.

Gayle had taught Coop and his colleagues that "mobiles" were the most popular choice for detonators; all the bomber needed was a second phone and a blasting cap wired to the vibration circuit. To properly dispose of such a device you needed to get at the phone's guts.

Coop pulled out the battery and the protective plate of Kay's phone. He pried away a ribbon of wires and there he found an exposed wound of copper filament. He rubbed his temples. The circuitry had to be mended, and even then it was guesswork. The phone might simply be dead.

The iron was ready. Coop touched the tip to the soldering wire, and wisps of smoke rose to the lamp. A metal globule came free, quivering at the tapered point of the wand, and gently Coop smeared a molten line along the cleave of circuitry. Slowly, carefully, he bound the damages of Kay's phone.

The cellphone battery was a lithium-ion firecracker, and if ruptured, it would melt Coop's hand in a flash of superheated chemicals. Behind the faux sandstone wallpaper of his hotel room, flammable gases whispered through buried copper pipes. Every day people held bombs against their faces, commuted inside explosive shells, walked over rivers of possible fire. September 11th should have made it clear: the Explosion was everywhere, just waiting to be summoned.

And if you knew, the Explosion spoke to you. Wasn't that the real problem, Coop thought, that the Explosion was inside him? And that maybe it had been inside him before Afghanistan, perhaps even before the Army . . .

Coop heard a voice.

The phone was a string of pieces, connected by ribbons of wires and fresh metal globs. He had been holding down the buttons on the numeric pad, a small light above the keypad flickering to life, but the screen was still flat and dull, even after rubbing at it with the back of his screwdriver. He pressed the buttons, heard the voice again, crackling. A faint cough from the damaged speaker component.

"Lisshhhenshen . . ."

Coop got down close and shut his eyes. It sounded like a voice message. Coop pressed the End button, then Call, and again came the voice. Hurried, jumbled, an edge of panic to the incoherence.

"Lissen, isshaun . . ."

Coop listened again and again, until he was sure:

"Listen, it's Sean . . ."

CHAPTER TWENTY-TWO

Somebody had left the light on in his cave. Most likely it was Kosta, Sean guessed, but the specifics were lost in a narcotic haze. Under the new polar glow he'd finally been able to examine his prison. It had a sharply angled ceiling, the space too small to be a bedroom but too big to be a closet, and one wall was half-finished with white subway tiles, a jigsaw of teeth, out of which sprouted a rusty plumbing fixture. Probably someone had considered making it into an extra bathroom. One of those lost spaces of geometry inside apartment buildings. You took an old family tenement and subdivided it and there was always some diagonal remainder.

Sean was acclimating to the downers, his mind slowly achieving the coherence he needed to think clearly. To be scared. He'd stolen from the Albanians, and now they had him. What was their endgame? Sean told himself Kosta was just trying to fuck with his head. Maybe release him after a few days of terror, then make him work off the debt. In the year or so he'd been slinging for Kosta, the enforcement angle of the business had rarely came up. So he didn't know the standard procedure, how they dealt with problems like himself. But he'd heard enough gossip to imagine this period of isolation being a prelude to some nasty example-setting.

In the interim, all he had was regrets. He was only twenty, but already Sean worried he'd squandered his easy days. As a freshman at Pratt he had managed to score a great apartment filled with fellow art students, way down on Taaffe, deep in the kingdom of Hasids. It was one of those apartments people said you couldn't find in New York anymore, a five-bedroom with high ceilings and a big central living space that had been sloppily painted in turquoise, an electric tidal wave crashing in spatters. Best of all was the deck, their neighbor's rooftop, which previous tenants had layered with rolls of AstroTurf. Here Sean and his roommates would sit and smoke and drink and watch the costumed black throng of nineteenth-century Jewish toddlers playing in the park across the street. At night everyone would be working on their assignments, the apartment dizzy with spray adhesive and the grassy burn of yerba mate, mirrors dusted with pink and blue lines of Dexedrine. These had been good days, and Sean liked to imagine what alternate life might have developed if he'd stayed the course.

At Pratt, Sean had rapidly come to understand that in the art world, being black put certain obligations on his past. Instructors always wanted to talk to him about where he'd grown up, what his childhood had been like, how he'd become interested in art. As if he must be some kind of refugee, someone *who made it out.* And upon revealing his roots in suburban New Jersey, how his parents were still together and his older sister worked in real estate, Sean always caught the scent of disappointment at the unspecialness of his achievement. Which was a problem because it didn't take excess savvy to realize your relationships with instructors was pretty much the whole deal. Sean had gotten accepted to Pratt with a mixed portfolio of black-and-white photography and charcoal studies. After foundation courses he planned on going down one of the fine art tracks, which basically meant zero money, unless you had the endorsement of a big-shot instructor, someone who could land you assistant gigs and maybe even recommend your work to a gallery. Realizing that these possible mentors were more interested in his past than his future, Sean learned to change up the story. He started saying he was from Camden instead of Cherry Hill, and he learned to assume a wounded quietude, speaking only in suggestive generalities. "Yeah, you know, art, where I'm from? It wasn't exactly *encouraged*." The instructors would nod along. *Of course, of course, no need to say more. Let's talk about your work.*

But Sean knew that prodding folks' assumptions would only take him so far. To make it as a black artist in New York, he'd eventually need that precious credibility of the underworld. And thus in retrospect it was easy to see why he had been drawn to Jasper and Gem, a notorious ex-Pratt couple who had abandoned their studies but still hung in the proximity of Bed-Stuy. They called themselves artists but it was hard to know what exactly they were up to, creatively speaking, since their primary vocation was selling heroin. Together the two of them had cornered the market on Pratt students and teachers who lived scattered around the campus in Bed-Stuy and Clinton Hill. Jasper got his product from the Bronx, where he knew people who could hook him up with a little weight, usually five-gram bundles of dubious purity. Jasper and Gem would dilute the product further, cutting in a mixture of ground-up caffeine pills and powdered milk, then repack it into custom-stamped bags they sold for fifteen a pop.

Sean got in on the operation through the manual labor of cutting, weighing, and repacking. Eventually he worked with Gem to design the stamps for the baggies. The medium made it hard to do anything complex, the ink didn't hold well, but Sean had figured a way to do these geometric sigils, and pretty soon "Hex" became a trusted brand.

And of course, Sean had started using himself. Why not? As Jasper liked to say, try naming a great artist who wasn't a junkie. If you *can* think of one, it probably means they were true users, the habit so bad they had to conceal it. Sean never shot up—thank you *Trainspotting,* thank you *Requiem for a Dream*—but he was sniffing the stuff for a few months, and then, after a particularly fearsome respiratory infection, moved on to plugging, where you put the heroin in a dissolving suppository and cram it up your ass. Probably the least sexy and most effective way to get loaded, short of shooting.

What followed was a predictable decline of his life situation. School became impossible, and Sean joined his roommates in an extended leave of absence.

Looking back, as he waited in captivity, Sean could see this period as the point of rotation, the moment an outsider would have pegged as his opportunity to turn things around. To intervene in his own destiny, to resist the trajectory of his downfall. But they would have been wrong. If he'd read the signs of disaster, maybe he never would have moved to the Bronx. And then he never would have met Kay.

CHAPTER TWENTY-THREE

Coop staggered down the stairs to the hotel lobby, his eyes half-closed against the morning light. He'd been awake all night with Kay's phone and files, but the electric coffeepot in his room had stopped working, so he'd come down to get a refill from the vending machine.

"Specialist Cooper."

Coop snapped his head toward the voice. Detective Melody sat in the waiting area of the lobby reading a newspaper. He wore a bunched-up overcoat with a plaid scarf looped around his big neck. He was still wearing his Mets cap. Other than the two of them, the lobby was empty.

Coop had frozen on the stairs, and his fist going tight around the quarters in his palm. In the swirl of his head he heard Jackie's advice: *Your best bet is to turn yourself in.*

"Let me guess," said Melody. "Right now you're thinking, how'n the hell did this guy know where I was staying?"

Coop fought the urge to run back up the stairs and lock himself in his room. He cleared his throat.

"You surprised me," said Coop. He forced himself down the last few steps and went over to the vending machine. *Get your coffee,* he thought. *Try to be casual.*

"So what can I do for you, Detective?"

"Are you buying coffee from a *machine*?" said Melody. "Nah, c'mon. What say we get a cup of the real stuff? I got my car, it's right outside."

Coop patted his pockets, as though he was worried he might be forgetting something. Melody squinted at him expectantly.

"Unless you have somewhere else to be?"

They drove west to the bridge over Ward's Island. Melody gunned it the whole way, his fat body squeezed into the driver's seat of his old Nissan Altima, doing twenty over the limit to cross the solid HOV line.

"They used to call this Hell Gate," said Melody, pointing out at the narrow, rust-colored waterway below them. "Still about a hundred ships sunk down there, you believe that? Probably more dead sailors in the East River than there is mud."

The traffic pounded in Coop's ears. He stared out the window, thinking of all the files from Presser's office spread across his hotel floor ever since he got Kay's phone working. He thought of two red X's he'd scribbled on his map of the city.

Melody took them up the Bronx River Parkway for a few miles, then pulled off, swerving down a side street where he halted the Altima in front of a small café with a green awning. He came back a few minutes later with two coffees.

"You up for a little walk?" he said, handing one of the coffees to Coop. "Weather's perfect and my leg gets funny, I stand around too long."

They crossed East Fordham Road on foot, Melody quick despite his limp, dragging one wingtip behind him. The sun sat low in the polluted canopy, a shadowless morning haze over the morning traffic. After a few blocks they came to a large public park, where the sprawl of the city collided against a wall of trees. Melody led them off the sidewalk and down a winding stone staircase to an isolated circle of stone benches.

Melody used his gloves to swipe snow from a bench before lowering himself onto the seat. Coop stayed standing. He sipped his coffee but didn't taste it, wondering how long this would take. Whatever this was.

"You see over there?" said Melody. He pointed up over the park toward an orange glint of sun. No, not the sun. Looking through the branches Coop realized he was looking at a massive bronze dome rising above the trees.

"Botanical Gardens," said Melody. "Nice, huh?"

They sat in silence for a while, watching the orange light reflecting off the dome and out across the frosted park. Coop was impatient; he wanted to go back to the hotel. Even though he knew he should be focused on the present situation, figure out what Melody was after, his mind kept going back to the files in his room. One in particular: Sean Hudson, age twenty.

"You know," said Melody, "when I was a kid, me and the guys would come out here with slingshots, try shooting for the glass. Later on, we're older, sometimes if we were hard up for cash we'd come down here looking for tourists to roll."

"Roll?"

"You know, mug, hijack. Robbing people, whatever."

Coop raised his eyebrows in obligatory surprise.

"This old tour book, I guess they had this spot marked as a good view of the Gardens," Melody continued. "So we'd just come up and say: 'Good afternoon, where you folks coming from? Oh yeah, Milwaukee? Welcome to the neighborhood. Now give me your wallets, you dumb fucks.' "

Melody chuckled to himself, making jabbing motions with an imaginary weapon. "Different neighborhood back then. Total fucking bedlam, you wouldn't believe how bad."

"Huh," said Coop, absently.

Melody sipped his coffee. "Not like Maine, I guess."

Coop turned toward the detective. "You might be surprised," he said.

"That right?" said Melody. "What, you get in trouble for

fishing lobster out of season?" He laughed to himself. "Maybe some nautical infraction? The incorrect placement of buoys?"

"Larceny and aggravated assault," said Coop, sipping his coffee.

"Well hey, all right. That's some respectable delinquency."

But you already knew about my record, didn't you, Coop wanted to say. His instinct told him Melody had already pulled his juvenile rap sheet, and now he was using the information to build trust between them. Regaling Coop with his own stories of lawless youth.

"One thing I thought was interesting," Coop said, "when you get arrested, during booking, how they rate your vocabulary."

Melody nodded. "Yeah, they do that in some places. What score you get?"

"Articulate," said Coop. "I think it was the highest one."

"Yeah, it is."

"Another thing I thought was strange," Coop continued, "was how, when they brought me in for the interview, the cop just sat there for a while, looking me right in the eye. Not saying anything. Finally he asks a few questions, then takes a while, looking through his paperwork. It kept going like that. He'd ask a few questions, always followed by these long periods of silence."

"Wasn't what you expected, huh?" said Melody.

"Nope. I thought it would be like in the movies, you know? Two cops, both of them throwing questions at me. Instead I was wondering, is there something wrong with this guy? Like maybe he had autism or something."

"Lotta guys think that," said Melody, chuckling. "They wait for the bright light in their face, the bad cop act."

"Right," said Coop. "Then, two years ago, while I was at sapper school, I met a guy who used to be a cop. I don't remember how it came up, but I was telling him this story, how I got arrested and interviewed by this weird, quiet detective. And my friend is laughing at me. He told me the silence, it's a technique they teach you guys."

"Sure," said Melody, shrugging it off. "We got all kinds of tricks."

"My friend said what probably happened was this: they tagged me as 'articulate' during in-processing, so this cop's training tells him to let me sit there, waiting. The theory being I'd overthink the situation, being a smart guy, and start asking questions. Incriminate myself by showing him what I did or didn't know."

"Huh," said Melody. Coop thought he sensed a subtle tightening of the detective's posture.

"So here we are," Coop continued. "You invite me for coffee, no explanation on why, or what we're gonna talk about—and hey, it's good coffee—but here we are, sitting. In silence. And I keep thinking, well this feels familiar."

Coop turned to face Melody and he saw the cop's eyes searching over him, like Coop had just changed shape and Melody was looking for a trace of the familiar. The detective took a moment to recompose himself before replying, and when he did, it was with a resigned sigh.

"To be honest, Specialist Cooper, you know what I've been doing?"

Coop shook his head. "Tell me."

"Deliberating."

"Deliberating," Coop repeated. He studied Melody, wondering what new line of bullshit this could be. "About what?"

"Yeah, see—this is tricky. There's been a development. And we see a possible linkage between this development and the investigation regarding your wife's death."

"What development?" said Coop. He hadn't expected this.

"Well, it's only a possibility, see? If it turns out to be a separate, unrelated crime, I can't be sharing information with you—"

"What development?" Coop repeated. He suddenly needed to know what Melody knew, and at the same time he couldn't help thinking, *I could share some information with you, Detective. Some shit you don't know.*

Melody's frown suggested he was being patient with someone who had disappointed him. "The manager of the clinic, Dr. Richard Presser? He's gone missing."

The temperature seemed to drop, and in the distance Coop heard a sharp cracking noise. A tree branch splitting under the weight of ice. In his mind it was Presser's head slammed sideways into the doorframe.

"Like I said, we're not sure if there's a connection," Melody was saying. "But the timing of this, it makes me think we need to expand the zone of inquiry."

"Zone of inquiry—what does that mean?"

Melody scrunched up his face and leaned a little closer. "I know I brought this up at the funeral. And I understand why you wouldn't want to go into it. But given this new information, which I'm sharing with you, I'm wondering if you can walk me through a few details."

"What details?"

"How things were between you and Katherine."

Coop blinked. *How the fuck are those related?* he wanted to yell, but before he could say anything they were both interrupted by a sudden electric ringing.

"Ah, hang on," said Melody, and he fumbled around his coat, producing a phone.

"Shit, I gotta take this," he said, checking the number, and got up to limp a few steps away.

"Yeah?" he said, and Coop was close enough to hear a

man's urgent voice on the other line, but he couldn't make out the words. Melody looked over his shoulder and took a few more steps away, mumbling into the receiver.

Coop bunched up his fists and hid them inside his jacket. Behind his eyes he saw a red blooming. A lake of blood seeping across the floor of Presser's office.

"Listen, it's Sean . . ."

Inside Sean's file Coop had found a page listing his contact information, including last known address. He consulted his foldout map and found the street, Briggs. He drew an X at the approximate cross streets. Then recognized a nearby intersection. Coop drew another X, barely two inches from the first mark he'd made. Stepped back from the map. What were the chances of that?

Kay was killed three blocks from Sean's apartment.

Seeing those adjacent marks, Coop had felt a new heat come to life in his chest. He folded his hands on top of his head and paced around the room, keeping his eyes on the map. The longer he looked at the pair of red X's, the more he felt the certainty of rage. He tore through Sean's file until he found a phone number, and without waiting punched the numbers into the hotel phone. No ring but here was the voice again, unmistakable ("You got Sean, leave a message at the beep."). Not knowing what else to do, Coop had left a message.

Watching Melody hunched over his cellphone, Coop briefly considered sharing all this. But then the detective came back over with a sly, apologetic grin, holding the open phone against his chest like he was saying the Pledge of Allegiance.

"Fuck, I'm sorry about this," said Melody. "Duty calls."

Coop narrowed his eyes and pointed at the phone. "This have anything to do with—"

"No, no," Melody said. "It's another thing." With his other hand Melody dug in his back pocket for his wallet.

"Listen, I give you twenty bucks, you can take a cab back?"

"No, keep your money," said Coop. He felt conflicted; it was a relief to escape Melody's scrutiny, but insulting to be so suddenly dismissed.

"Hang on," said Melody, covering the phone with a hand. He looked at Coop. "What's up?"

"You never told me how you knew where I was staying."

Melody grinned. "This is my jungle, I know all the little animals." Using one gloved hand he made scurrying motions in the air. "Not a branch gets disturbed without me hearing."

CHAPTER TWENTY-FOUR

Coop returned to the Crotona in a trance, his mind crowded by new uncertainties. The hotel was quiet in the late winter morning, only a few cars in the parking lot. Upstairs he fumbled with his keys. When he got the door open he tried the light, but the room stayed dark. Coop stood for a few moments in the entryway, flipping the switch back and forth. Nothing. Peering into the shade Coop could see there was something wrong about his hotel room. His mattress was capsized, all of his gear had been dumped on the floor, and the whole mess was layered in a snowstorm of Kay's files.

Fucking cops, he thought. This must have been Melody's ploy all along. Get him out of the room, keep him away just long enough to search the place. But what would they be looking for?

Then a monster-faced man rose up from behind the bed, snarling from the shadows, and Coop understood, too late, that this situation was something else entirely.

The man was dressed all in black, and he wore a savage expression, bearded and inhuman. Coop jumped back, putting distance between himself and the creature, only to have a paw land on his shoulder. He drove an elbow backward and tried to backpedal but found himself facing two more snarling faces. They had him blocked in. A leg flashed out and the wall hit Coop in the back. He coughed and fell forward with a *whoof* of stolen air. There was a hiss—like spray paint, a bright venomous snake—and his eyes exploded in orange fire. Coop fought against the bulk behind him. Someone punched his ear. Someone kicked him in the stomach. Coop doubled over, coughing in the cloud of what he realized was pepper spray, and smothering blows fell down all around him. He tried to call out for help but only managed to suck in more of the hot, bleeding air.

I'm dying, he thought, *they're killing me,* and as he fell sideways he thought for some reason of the chaplain.

He yelled for them to stop. Begged them, but the monsters kept chipping pieces away from his body. Coop rolled into a ball and through bleeding lips found the words to a new and shameful prayer: *Just let it stop.* In answer, Coop felt his head tugged upward, and then it was over with three quick jabs.

CHAPTER TWENTY-FIVE

Among the shadows there were spots of light. Coop felt that the world was somehow out of reach, that he had been cast into a dark place where only the faintest remnants of sensation could reach him. His head was covered by some kind of shroud, he could feel the fabric sticking to his nose and mouth. The pain was everywhere, so widespread that Coop found it difficult to pinpoint the individual sources of his injury. There was a squelching in his ribs whenever he twisted in his bonds; he was tied to a chair, he realized. One of his eyes felt gooey, and with the tip of his tongue Coop located the jagged corner of a freshly broken tooth.

He remembered hushed voices, people speaking in a language that sounded like Russian. Then police sirens, clattering doors . . . or was he hearing that *now*? Somewhere under the blanket of pain he'd lost the sense of time, everything converging into sound-fuzz. Then came a brushing across his face and the darkness was torn away, replaced by three trollish heads. *Cavemen,* Coop thought, *they look like cavemen.*

"You gave him too much," said Kosta, speaking in Albanian.

He put two fingers under the stranger's chin and lifted his head toward the light. The oozing face made contortions, one eye dilated and filled with blood.

"It's only the first shot," said Zameer. "We did exactly what Luz—"

"No names!" snapped Kosta.

"We did exactly as we were told. *She* probably kicked him too hard," Zameer said, pointing at Buqa. "But it's fine, I have an idea."

Zameer went upstairs. For her part, Buqa was silent. She stood with arms folded, head bent slightly in the direction of the soldier, willows of fake hair trailing down from her rubber monster mask.

Irritated, Kosta dug his fingernails under the seal of his own mask, sweating in the heat of the basement. It was another fuck-up of Zameer's, and looking back, Kosta realized of course he should have specified: Fetch something simple, Zameer. Maybe ski masks from a hardware store. Whatever you do, don't spend $60 on three elaborate silicon disguises, not like the "Bigfoot Costume" heads he had proudly presented. But this was a surface problem, Kosta reminded himself. Especially compared to the dilemma of what to do with their new prisoner.

The contents of the man's wallet were spread out on a folding metal tray table. Kosta picked up the U.S. Army ID card and studied it against the man's face. He'd been hoping for some kind of dissimilarity, but the wide-eyed, uniformed teenager in the photograph was the same as the beat-up stranger. A soldier. Kosta shook his head. They had kidnapped a fucking soldier.

Killing him was out of the question, of course. You never killed soldiers, not if you could avoid it, a lesson ground into Kosta's head during the days following the Uprising, when their country was swarming with NATO troops. "Armies are just another clan without *besa*," Luzhim had told him, "like the police, or the mixed gangs. When people join for the advantages, there's only one way to build loyalty: You have to protect your troops while they're alive and avenge them if they die. So if you kill a soldier? There's never bargaining. They'll have to hunt you down, or their own men will lose faith."

So Kosta had decided to inject the soldier with the formula. He figured the drugs would get him to talk, they could determine how he was connected to Sean. Then abandon him somewhere. After all, soldiers were just like drug addicts, they went crazy all the time.

But now they had a new problem. The first shot of the formula was working too quickly. Or maybe Zameer was right, the beating they'd given him had been too severe. Because the soldier was just sitting there, staring deeply into the walls, not answering any questions. Occasionally his eyes would go wide, like he was seeing something terrible. Or mutter through his bleeding lips and go back to staring.

Zameer came back downstairs from the kitchen with a half-empty jug of vodka, sloshing it in the light.

"This is your idea," said Kosta. "To get drunk."

"No, no," said Zameer. "You ever been tripping?"

Kosta shook his head.

"When you take LSD, they tell you never to mix with alcohol," said Zameer, unscrewing the cap. "It kills your high."

As Coop's eyes adjusted to the light, other details began to come clear. Puddles on the concrete floor. A light, to which his eyes kept returning. At first this bulb had seemed like a warm, glowing omen, a welcome alternative to the cavemen. But now the light had begun to mutate, and Coop shrank from the poisonous glow. The bulb oozed and became a squirming neon spider. The spider flexed its neon legs and released a droplet of light onto Coop's bare forearm. The light hissed as it burned a pit into his skin. Coop tried to move but his hands and legs were still tied. The drops fell faster on his face and chest, each one landing with a white-hot brightness of pain.

. . .

"**Wake up,**" said a voice, and Coop blinked, shivering. He wasn't burning, but cold fire still licked at his face. Now here was one of the cavemen.

"You awake?" it said.

Coop groaned from deep in his seared throat. He opened his mouth to speak and just ended up sputtering and drooling down the front of his shirt. Another caveman came forward, clucking its tongue, and lifted up Coop's shirt, using it to wipe the puke and alcohol and blood off his face.

A small device was placed in his field of vision, a rectangle of pale blue light. Coop heard beeping noises, and then, weirdly, the sound of his own voice.

"Sean," said the voice. "Listen to me very carefully, I know what happened, and you better call me back in the next twenty-four hours or I will tell the police. I will tell everyone, do you fucking hear me, I will make your life hell, you fucking junkie, I will end you finally and forever. Call this number, Sean. Call this fucking number."

Then came the phone number at Coop's hotel. It was the message he'd left on Sean's phone the previous night.

"Now we're going to have some conversations," said the caveman. "Do you hear me?"

Coop blinked sleepily. His face rang like a bell, someone had slapped him. He heard the sound, but the pain was distant. Then he began throwing up again.

This was going nowhere, Kosta decided. If anything, Zameer and his vodka had made things worse. In the process of trying to administer the liquor, Zameer had upended the bottle all over the soldier, making him scream and thrash like a man being burned alive. Finally he calmed down, but the vodka had only made him less intelligible. Perhaps the damage of the formula had already been done. If so, Kosta had to admit Luzhim was right about the formula's potency. He wondered how much worse it would get when they administered the second and third doses.

Kosta flinched as a sudden electric buzzing sound cut through the basement air. Moving catlike, Buqa jumped up on the radiator, her shaggy Bigfoot mask pressed up to the slit window.

"Someone at the door," she said in Albanian.

"Ssshhh," said Kosta, holding his fingers to the lips of his mask. "Who is it?"

Buqa shook her head. Kosta considered the situation for a second. He pointed to the soldier. "Keep him quiet."

The buzzer rang again as he traveled up the stairwell. Someone impatient. *Probably the neighbors,* Kosta thought. Was it possible they had heard the commotion? Then, in the hallway, he heard a noise and froze: the unmistakable hiss of a walkie-talkie. Now he knew exactly who was waiting behind the door.

Kosta closed the basement door behind him, making sure he heard the lock click shut. Then he pried off his sneakers and slid carefully down the carpeted hallway. Still eyeing the front door, he reached into a broom closet and with his fingers located the small shelf over the doorframe, where he kept his favorite gun: a snub-nosed Colt Sheriff with a cow skull engraved in the grips.

The door buzzed again. Kosta slipped the revolver into the back of his jeans. It was a hollow precaution. After all, he had two men imprisoned within his duplex; if the police had a warrant, firearm possession would be the least of his worries. Kosta tightened his belt and continued down the hallway for the door.

. . .

Something shifted in the darkness, a hidden immensity, greater even than the pain. Coop had noted a stifling to the proceedings, a sudden hush, before all lucidity fled again, his awareness now zeroed in on this new *thing,* the great presence breathing in the dark. Something clopping toward him from beyond the lamp's glow. He could feel the heat of its eyes, studying him. Judging him. "Please," Coop whimpered. "I'm sorry I'm sorry I'm sorry."

Someone kicked his chair. The basement wobbled for a moment, then Coop crashed backward onto the floor. Now one of the cavemen was straddling him, pressing its hands over his face, suffocating him. Coop remembered with sudden clarity that he had been abducted, beaten up, possibly poisoned. It was a *person* on him, a person pressing a rag into his mouth. From this revelation came an outfanning of solutions. Coop twisted his neck, got several of the fingers in his mouth, and bit down as hard as he could.

Zameer had intended to quiet the soldier with an old hand towel, but now it was his own scream he had to muffle as he pried away his mangled fingers. He scuttled backward and held his bleeding hand against his chest, humming hysterically. He had seen deep, toothy punctures, knew it was bad, and he cursed *fuck fuck fuck* while overhead the door buzzed again. Where was Kosta? Buqa came over to help, but in his fury Zameer pushed her aside. He staggered toward the basement wall, where laid out on a counter were the remaining glass syringes.

Upstairs Kosta was combat-crouched against the door, one hand angled at his back. Slowly he raised himself to peer through the keyhole. Then he saw the figures on the porch and laughed with relief. He untucked his shirt to hide the pistol before whipping open the door, where two teenage girls were standing on his stoop. Daughters of the Homeland, both of them carrying clipboards, walkie-talkies, and messenger bags. Across the street Kosta saw another pair of them, the girls sticking together for safety while they canvassed the block. Volunteers for Luzhim's charitable organization, which organized monthly fundraising crusades through the neighborhood, drumming up funds for Kosovar independence.

Kosta folded his arms and grinned at them, waiting for the pitch—he was momentarily unhinged with a frenzy of manic relief—but instead they jerked back with surprise from the door.

"Um, trick or treat?" said one of the girls, finally. They exchanged between them a disbelieving look.

"What's the joke?" said Kosta, still a little nervous. Only then did he realize that in the delirium of his anxiety he'd completely forgotten to take off the stupid Bigfoot mask. Which he now peeled away with a grin.

"Oh, too bad," he said, scratching at the suction marks on his neck. "I was trying to scare you."

Distant sensations: the cutting pain in his wrists, the greasy taste of blood in his mouth. Nearer was the world of his chair. Coop was still on his back, wrists bound to legs that were fused with the hard seat. The chair was part of him, the architecture of his suffering. And deep within, like the guilt in his bones, he felt the chair's creaking flaws. Somewhere in the room there was an argument taking place, a muted fury of Russianish. Coop grabbed the chair's midrail and strained, spit bubbling up from between his lips. He gasped as one foot twisted free.

Just then the thin man fell upon him. It was the one whose hand Coop had chewed, looking like a batshit Napoleon with one arm crammed under his jacket, the other gripping a fistful of needles.

Coop cocked his leg, now free, and booted the man directly in his neck. Jaw-clack. The man looked up the ceiling, tracking, Coop imagined, the uptrail of his own mouth-blood. Coop gripped the chair and kicked again, the man falling away into the darkness. There was a scuffle. And then someone started screaming.

Zameer backed away from Buqa, his nerves electrified by her howls.

He tore off his mask and spat blood on the floor. The soldier had kicked him in the face, he'd fallen backward. Buqa had tried to catch him.

And now she was on the ground, clawing at her neck, making that horrible *wailing,* the noise shooting electric through Zameer's skull. In a panic he hissed "Sssshhhh" through his bleeding mouth.

Then he saw the broken ampules around her, the slivers of glass. He'd been holding the second two syringes when he'd fallen, when he and Buqa collided in the darkness. She'd tried to catch him. And now the needles protruded from the muscles of her neck, twitching with each spasm like a cricket's antennae.

With his freed leg Coop kicked at the chair until he was disentangled, then peeled away his hands and rose upward in a stagger through the warping blackness. He moved liquid past the two figures screaming and groping each other, one kneeling over the other, and as he approached the shape of a doorway he heard a pounding of footsteps. Coop sidestepped behind the door as it opened. He curled himself into the open doorway and pattered up the stairs.

Zameer was trying to help, but he wasn't sure—should he pull out the needles? Buqa was moving too much, her face red and so full of fear. Then the lights came on. Here was Kosta standing in the doorway with a gun, and Zameer thought: *Oh fuck.* Then he saw the soldier sneak out from behind Kosta, slipping through the open door to the stairwell. Zameer stumbled to his feet and chased after him.

Coop fast-crawled up the stairs with helpless momentum. Again he felt the snarl of *something* at his back, fast wasn't fast enough, but as the hallway light rushed toward him Coop stopped and spun, ready to face his pursuer.

Kosta made it back to the ground floor just in time to see Zameer collide with the soldier, the two figures spinning in a graceless orbit of elbows and grunts. And before he could get to them, they crashed through the storm window, toppling out into cold air. Kosta came to the broken window, panting, and saw Zameer splayed below on the snow-covered awning in a halo of shattered glass. And there was the soldier, on his feet now, gaining distance down Arthur Avenue.

CHAPTER TWENTY-SIX

Coop sprinted down the sidewalk with the exhilaration and terror of a fugitive, his bare arms pumping. He vaulted a snowbank, skidded, found himself lying in the snow and hopped immediately back to his feet. He ran down an empty corridor of cafés, delis, and seafood markets, his nerves embroidered with bright poison, and Coop knew he was fast, *uncatchable,* that all the city's instruments—the ambient thumping of a radio, the crashing of dump trucks, the shrill chorus of sirens—each was orchestrated to the rapture of his stricken mind.

The glow of the city seemed to warp, streetlights narrowing into tracer fire. All around him flew streaks of killing light. Coop understood that he was outdistancing the city itself, crossing into a new, private world; a territory governed by the derangement of his senses.

Instead of running through the Bronx, he imagined he was sneaking from his father's house. Out onto the sloping yard, past the drum barrel grill, its rusty belly layered with fish bones, then down to the iced-over marsh and its brittle maze of cattails, where pockets of mud ballooned under each crackling step. Then Coop was back on the streets of the Bronx and his nose was filled with smoke. The city was burning. No, not just the city, a whole nation on fire. And his own body glowing stove-hot, cracking with a dry fever, flakes of skin peeling off him as he ran, blowing around in a flurry like white ash from the bonfires they used to build in Maine. He and the other kids would start fires in the forts, these old concrete bunkers that had been abandoned since World War II. Originally constructed to spot submarines, now occupied by gangs of teenagers practicing the old religion of fire worship, heaping up stacks of driftwood, construction supplies, dried-out Christmas trees, whatever they could find that would burn. But the tragic thing about a bonfire was you couldn't ever brag about it afterward, no matter how enormous you got it going. Fire left no trophies, just branch bones and craters of wet ash.

Now his hands were empty and frost-burned, trembling with blue heat. *A bad sign,* said his distant brain. Chilblains. Hypothermia. Prevention of cold injuries is an individual responsibility. You had to be mindful of evaporation, respiration, convection, conviction. *It's cold out and you're bleeding,* insisted a small voice. Probably killing yourself. How had he ended up here? *I was taken,* Coop remembered, they came for me, ambushed me in my hotel room. *Ambush.* The word had dangerous echoes . . . and there, summoned by his wayward thoughts, there was the burning boy of Afghanistan, his reflection in the dark glass of a storefront. The boy's feet were bare, floating just inches above the street, lifted by the slightest murmur of wind, his eyes exploded . . .

Coop ran harder through the snow. *You're tripping,* he told himself, *you're just tripping. People do this for fun.* But the boy kept following him, his passage leaving a molten trail in the pavement.

Then, in the distance, Coop saw a bright red column of neon: ST. BARBARA'S HOSPITAL.

He ran toward the sign, escaping into a changing geography, where thin minarets grew like droplets of stone falling up toward the sky. Everything was melting together. He was running to the tower and he was stumbling toward the hospital through the vast dark Bronx and he was freezing to death.

He came through sliding doors into the flickering light of a weird-angled chamber, with three windows overlooking three different skies, each containing a vast constellation of stars.

And there she was, her naked skin lambent in the starlight. Saint Barbara, Mother of the Bomb. From her head fell a mane of coppery fleece, pinned by a crown of orange peacock feathers. The dips between her ribs were like the salt-polished curves of a seashell, and cradled in her lap was a long curved lamp, illuminated with Arabic script. She held the handle like a teacup, and with her other hand she stroked the lamp's nose.

"That's mine," said Coop.

"My father bound me to a stake," she replied. There was an opening in her neck, and when she spoke it gurgled blood.

"He burned me with sheaves of straw. I was put inside a barrel, studded with nails, and rolled down a hill. Then my father took my hair in his fist, dragged me up the rocky face of a mountain, and only then did he put the knife to my throat."

"Why?" said Coop.

"He hated me for my miracles. I divined the nature of the cosmos by looking out these three windows. I reattached a knight's head to his body so that his soul could pass into Heaven."

"Here." She handed Coop the lamp. "This is your Jinn."

"I get a wish?"

She laughed: white teeth bared like lightning.

Coop opened the lid and saw red-painted rocks, coals burning in the copper recesses. And there was the boy again, fire dancing around his feet.

The best soldiers forget. They told you this on day one. Right off the bus, when Coop stood in a room with twenty other raw-headed recruits, their pitiful civilian things dumped on the linoleum floor of the intake center, the drill sergeant screaming: *You think y'all are men, but you're not even boys. You know what I see? Infants, a whole maternity ward of little pink babies. And not even strong babies. Y'all are like preemies with those undeveloped lungs, and I'm not thinking y'all are going to survive. See, you don't know how to talk, you don't know how to walk, and you sure as shit don't know how to fight*, said the drill sergeant. *You think you brought skills, experiences, God forbid, ideas. You're a hundred percent wrong, troops. One hundred. Percent. Wrong. And the faster you understand how wrong you are, the faster you forget the shit you learned back on the block, the faster you'll be a soldier and a man. So you best start forgetting, privates. You know what we do here on Sand Hill? They been saying it since Vietnam. We kill babies, and I will kill you right back to your hometown, where you can roll around and drool and get your diaper changed by Mommy.*

And here Coop remembered the drill sergeant pausing at the door of the barracks, turning his head toward Coop and the other recruits, his round-top hat tilted like that of a villain in a cowboy film, and he said: *Us men have work to do in this world.* And already Coop was thinking, *Yes, let me forget*, because he sort of loved this man.

Replacing his memories of home were weapon velocities, the correct application of field dressings, camouflage patterns, and how to correctly ease an enemy into unconsciousness via rear blood-choke. He learned to iron his uniform and spit-polish his boots and march with his shoulder blades pushed straight back. He learned that *hooah* is a question and *hooah* is the only answer.

Some recruits tried holding on to something. Like faith. Coop recalled one poor kid—from Montana, maybe, one of those M states—who didn't make it because one Sunday during barracks cleaning Drill found him curled up near his cot, nose-deep in the Psalms. Drill said: *I know that's not a book, Private. I know that's not a book you're reading while your battle buddies are waxing the floor and fixing their hospital corners.* And the kid actually tried to reason with him. He said, no, Drill Sergeant. This is the good book. And this is the good day.

Not for you, said Drill.

Some people forgot their hometowns and their faith but couldn't forget their bodies. If you were fat you had to get hard fat, skinny guys forgot their leanness and got real necks. You did push-ups like there was a plank on your back, sit-ups like your waist was a lever and your knees the fulcrum. There was no proper form for running, you just forgot you were ever slow. And when others didn't make it, you forgot them, too. The dead babies ghost away and you graduate, you go to Combat Engineer training and Airborne School, and then the first day at your new unit in Fort Bragg, the 303rd Engineers, the first thing they tell you is: *Listen, Private Cooper, you seem squared away, but you better forget that shit you learned in training. That shit will get you killed, and it sure as hell won't get your ass promoted.*

Then you finally go to war and nobody knows anything at all.

Which is all the more reason to remember the one thing you're supposed to remember: the best soldiers forget.

And now Coop remembered.

CHAPTER TWENTY-SEVEN

Coop lifted his head off the dashboard. The windshield was darkened with sand, and a blunt crack echoed through his skull. He heard a sputter of radio life, beeps and static.

RPG, RPG, RPG.

Everything outside his vehicle was fallout and smog. In front of him there was a fire—a burning humvee. Coop flinched as a hailstorm fell upon his truck, accompanied by the clatter of return gunfire.

Fire on the right, yelled the radio, and something punched into his windshield with great force, leaving a star-shaped fracture in the glass. Coop opened his door to peer out, but couldn't see anything through the smoke. By the time he dropped into a crouch against the open door, the shooting was over.

The convoy had been following the road back to FOB Castello when the ambush started. Nobody was killed but one grunt had taken shrapnel to the cheek. Coop listened to him scream while the doc applied QuickClot, but the doc still couldn't get the bleeding stopped and they had a long drive ahead. First Sergeant Walker opted to call in a nine-line medevac and the convoy waited on the road, everyone's weapons aimed up at the canyon walls, until a wavering speck of black appeared in the afternoon sky. Cold grainy wind became rotor wash as the bird touched down. Meanwhile, it was up to Coop, the only engineer attached to the convoy, to strip comms from the destroyed humvee that lay in front of him. He used a pickax to pry the demolished radio from its console, choking on black gouts of diesel, then hucked a thermite grenade into the cab. Coop watched the skeleton of the vehicle vanish in fireworks and white smoke before returning to his own truck. By that time they'd dusted off the grunt with the face injury. Everyone was ready to get back to Castello.

The convoy returned through orange dusk, gunners whirling in their turrets, engines revving as the drivers muscled over every hill. Coop's uniform smelled like truck smoke and cordite and there was a crust of red soot on the skin of his face and arms.

Corporal Paulikas from the infantry took over the driving. He was a freckled and forward-toothed National Guardsman, a stranger, and they both stayed quiet in the aftermath of the firefight. Coop sensed a mutual need to demonstrate their professionalism. Neither wanted to be the wide-eyed cherry, asking, "Can you believe what just fucking happened?" He appreciated the silence, it gave him time to make sense of the event. We were *ambushed,* he thought.

He was looking out the window when he saw a distant figure, unmistakably human, crouched among the clay teeth of a ruined temple. The convoy was crossing an older trail which sloped downhill, past the ancient rubble, and the last daylight brightened a patch of desert at just such an angle that Coop spotted the shadow, his shape framed by a half-collapsed archway.

"I see a guy," Coop said.

"A guy," Paulikas repeated, his eyes on the road.

"Stop, stop, stop," Coop said. The truck slowed and Coop twisted in the cooling air to look back at the ruins. No figure could be seen in the red light.

First Sergeant Walker came loudly over the radio. "What the fuck, over?"

Paulikas clicked his mic. "Sapper said he saw someone."

"Say again? We're stopped because we saw *someone*?"

Coop had a Leupold in his kit bag. He blew sand off the lens and scoped the sun-drenched lower road. There was the man again, his shape gathering itself up into the light. Something in the man's hand. A canister.

The radio crackled again. "Nobody out here sees shit," First Sergeant Walker was saying.

"Possible mortar," said Coop, and he dropped out of the humvee, lifted his M4, and through the sights hunted for a wavering silhouette.

In the days following Coop would reflect on this moment and wonder about his state of mind. Certainly he remembered the rage. He'd just been ambushed, and now here was someone aiming a fucking mortar in the direction of the convoy. It felt personal. And of course he'd been scared, trying to gauge the distance between himself and the enemy while a panicked part of his brain wondered about a mortar's effective range. There was also the pressure of his colleagues, the electric silence of the convoy behind him. If he was wrong it was more than a fuck-up, it was dangerous. By halting the mission he'd put them all at risk. But if he was right, Coop had chanced his way into an opportunity of transcendent value. It was like those game shows where they stop a random pedestrian and give them trivia questions: one minute you're walking down the road, the next you're on television with a chance to win a million dollars. Except for Coop the reward was infinitely more valuable than money. With the release of a single bullet, his whole existence could be folded into a story of competence, heroism, performance under pressure. Everything before this would become prelude, a slow gathering of aptitudes leading up to the day he saved everyone's life. If he could make the shot.

So in his head Coop was tamping down the greedy exhilaration of discovery, trying to put himself into range mentality. He snuggled the weapon into his shoulder, tried to stop his breathing, find that dead space; the void that would align the sunset phantasm with the barrel of his rifle. And then a moment of pure grace and geometry: the enemy giving up his center mass. Coop heard Paulikas begin to hiss. And ever so gently he squeezed the trigger.

The first sergeant ordered Coop, Paulikas, and three grunts from Second Squad to go down and identify the body. If there was one. Darkness was coming fast across the valley and they hustled in file down a gravel slope, toward the smashed temple. Now Coop could see the ruins more clearly. Clumps of rubble lay buried in a lake of purple shadows, a half-collapsed chimney protruding from the center. Coop wondered if it was Buddhist, Persian, maybe even Babylonian. On arrival in-country the sappers had received an abbreviated archeological survey from a public relations officer, the takeaway being: If it looks old and interesting, try not to blow it up.

"Gotta be over two hundred meters, that's a choice shot," said Paulikas, as they descended.

"Dumb luck, if I got him," Coop muttered back. He recognized the strain in Paulikas's tone. The grunts were clearly jazzed by the possibility of revenge, while also feeling a little sour that an engineer, a fucking combat support element, would be responsible for the kill.

Now the infantrymen were taking a knee and Coop joined them, crouching in the sand. They had come to the perimeter of the ruins and could see the temple up close, its stone flank pocked with old bullet wounds.

Corporal Paulikas called Coop over with a wave of his hand. He was studying the temple through night vision goggles.

"Gotta admit," he said, "figured you were full of shit for sure."

Paulikas offered the goggles and made a single chopping motion toward the open doorway. Coop peered through the field of green, scanning the battered shape of the structure, suddenly depthless. Aiming the NVGs along the path indicated by the corporal, Coop sighted an outturned branch of pixels. The splayed leg of a human corpse.

"Situation is, I don't see how we get there to confirm the kill," Paulikas continued, and he made more chopping motions. Coop saw the problem instantly: around the temple was a scattering of red-painted rocks.

Coop needed to see the body. He *would* see it. It was a question of respectful completion; there was something perverse, even cowardly in the idea of killing someone without laying eyes on the damage. He conferred with Paulikas and put together a quick plan, and for many weeks after, he'd wonder about how things might have gone if he'd just said "Fuck it" and headed up the slope toward a future of enviable unknowing.

Pushing up from the sand around the temple were larger chunks of rubble, columns and wall sections, half buried. A pathway through the minefield. Coop detached himself from the infantry squad and hopped onto the nearest island of stone. In the energy of the moment he was reminded of rock jumping back home, the stumbling dashes from big rock to big rock along the shore. The idea was that pebbles were rivers of lava, so you had to stay on the rocks foot-sized or larger, but only for a moment before they sank into the molten bubbles.

And eerily, as he came through the arched doorway, Coop imagined he could actually hear the fizzle of melting rocks. No, it was something else; a hissing, venomous noise, a weird snake-prayer filling the ancient darkness. Coop flashed his light on the scene. And he stood there blinking, his brain forced to process a host of new details.

First off there was all the blood. Flung out in sharp jets and drizzles, splashing the stone around the fighter's corpse, which was bent backward over a rocky protrusion on the temple floor, with his head turned sideways. *Too much red*, Coop thought, too much to be the blood from such a small body, smaller than Coop had been expecting. No, the red was vapor from a bullet-scored metal cylinder, one of a half dozen pitched around the temple floor. And combined with the smell of aerosol and the Arabic labels, Coop put together that these were cans of spray paint, which, sighted from a distance, distorted by light, and in perspective against a smaller body, had resembled to Coop's trained eye the shape of a mortar round.

The red rocks had been spray-painted. Coop had a flash of respect for the primitive ingenuity, inventing a whole minefield to keep soldiers off your turf. And he'd begun to process that the man he'd shot was a kid. Barely a teenager. He knew it from the small body and the tiny sneakers, from the hesitant shadow of hair on his upper lip. And as Coop studied the broken face he saw a subtle motion in the kid's chest. And heard it, as the hiss of the wounded spray can died. A quiet gulping of air. This last piece of information took the longest to fully register. Coop watched blood spilling steadily from the rupture that only minutes ago had been the kid's mouth, his flashlight traveling over bare wriggling fingers, as if the kid were slowly but insistently trying to find purchase in the reddening sand, and his feet and legs were moving, now, too, heels scraping the ground, as if trying to swim away from Coop's flashlight, or perhaps aimed to fix the imprint of his body into the temple floor, a bloody snow angel. The kid was still alive.

"Cooper, where we at?" said the radio. It was Paulikas.

Coop would never forgive himself for how quickly he came

to a decision. He called back to Paulikas and informed him that the corpse indeed appeared to be a Taliban fighter, but the body had been booby-trapped. Then Coop had begun laying down packets from his demo bag, crowning the scene with crisp white blocks of C4, keeping his eyes aimed down at the ground as he paid out detonation cord from his spool, making his way back across the jigsaw path of rubble, back to where the other grunts were waiting.

"Bug out," said Coop. "I've got it." No one argued with him. He heard the scramble of boots as the fire team moved away from the temple. Coop huddled behind the nearest berm of rubble and sat with the detonator in his hand. Up on the road, the convoy had shrunk to a line of dim orange lights beneath the greater darkness of the mountain. The stars were coming out. He pressed the switch and the blast whooshed up through the old temple like fire traveling up a chimney, sweeping over the berm and through Coop's body, sprawling him backward under the white light of a momentary sun.

And now, lost and freezing to death in the Bronx, sitting against a wall and staring upward at the black unforgiving sky, Coop swore through the brain-scrambling apocalypse of the explosion that he had actually seen the kid's body lifted in flight: arms and legs spread out, disintegrating, a comet flying away from the earth.

CHAPTER TWENTY-EIGHT

Eva came out of the elevator into Three East, an ancient subdivision of St. Barbara's Hospital. It was a dismal unit. Soot-encrusted windows ran along the exterior wall, casting the hallway in a polluted light, and the linoleum floor had been skinned down to the glue. Nearby, a coil of wires hung from an open panel in the ceiling, where it looked as if an electrical repair had been called off midproject. Eva shook her head, frowning at the hospital's exposed innards. It was the kind of hazardous neglect that would have driven her grandfather into a fury. He'd worked construction after retiring from the Army, and in this second career had earned a reputation as a fierce advocate for onsite safety. Two years after his death, Eva still got holiday cards from his union brothers and sisters at Local 100.

Down the hall, Eva recognized a young Filipino man sitting alone behind a cubby of reinforced glass.

"Hey Geo," she said.

Geo smiled and held up a finger to indicate he was on the phone.

"Yes, Doctor, I understand," he was saying. "But I'm not seeing any of that in the EMR."

Geo's voice echoed spookily in the ward, and Eva found herself walking faster to his booth. According to hospital policy there was supposed to be a security guard on every level, but Eva knew they were often pulled from the floors to help with conflicts in the emergency room.

"Sure, sure," Geo was saying into the phone, clearly mustering his patience. He looked at Eva and rolled his eyes.

There were no other chairs so Eva leaned against the wall, blinking to fend off exhaustion. For the last few days she'd been on Q2, pulling overnight shifts every other day, and meanwhile still trying to keep her hours at Next Start, which had descended into bureaucratic chaos ever since Presser went missing. Now it was almost 6 a.m., the end of her shift, but just as Eva had been finishing her sign-outs she'd gotten a page telling her she was needed here, on the third floor, for an urgent consult.

"Yes, Doctor," Geo was saying. "I'll make a call down to Records, but if it was never entered, I can't . . . Okay, sure thing."

Geo hung up and cocked his head at Eva.

"Lemme ask you something," he said. "In medical school, why they don't teach doctors how to use computers? I mean *seriously.*"

Eva managed a weak laugh. "If we could use computers, you wouldn't have a job."

"True," said Geo. "Too true. So what's up?"

"I got paged."

"Yeah, lemme see," said Geo, flipping through a stack of hand-written messages. "Here it is. They want you in Room 316."

"Damn," Eva muttered, and dropped her head. "The Tomb? You're sure?"

"Hope you didn't have breakfast plans," said Geo, frowning sympathetically.

Eva let out a harsh sigh. She lifted herself from the wall and marched away, farther into the recesses of the derelict wing.

Among medical staff, Room 316 was popularly known as "the Tomb of the Unknown Patient," a special ward for the unidentified and insane. The patients admitted here were people without papers, without families, without any discernible history. The city's truest orphans. It seemed to Eva that such people were birthed by the city itself, miraculously conceived in dark places, a by-product of urban life. But of course there was always an explanation, usually a combination of mental disorders, poverty, and social isolation. No one counted on these folks anymore, no one expected them home. And in most cases, nobody would ever claim them. The hospital was required by law to provide them a measure of care, but management didn't want them taking up beds that could be made available for patients with insurance. So they threw them in the Tomb with some poor resident stuck on the case, a junior physician who would inevitably spend hours bogged down in paperwork, trying to get them identified or at least transferred to another agency.

And this morning it's me, thought Eva, as she came to Room 316. It was empty. There were two beds inside the room, both outfitted with restraints. The patient must still be in transport, she guessed. Eva took the interim to sit down on one of the beds. She eased off her orthopedic clogs and rubbed her ankles. A moment's respite from the battle.

"This is a war, doctors . . ."

Something a city official had said during yesterday's morning conference. The whole Psych department had been subjected to an exhaustive presentation detailing the post-9/11 mental health epidemic in New York City. A PowerPoint of grim statistics. Experts were projecting a half million new cases of PTSD among the citizens of the five boroughs, which constituted a 200 percent increase since before the attacks. Thousands upon thousands suffering from alienation, insomnia, and despair, all the modern disorders of urban life, but now jacked up by an animal fear of death. Meanwhile there had been some predictable trends in various indicators of poor mental hygiene, starting with record sales of alcohol, firearms, and sex toys.

Perhaps sensing the bone-dry morale of his audience, the city official had ended on the note of duty. "This is a war, doctors," he told them. "And all of you are fighting on the front lines."

And Eva had thought: *No shit.* Because for her there had always been a war. As a child it was Korea, her grandfather's conflict, which had raged on for decades in the Okori household, a fact of life around which their days had been organized. And now with her grandfather gone, Eva had found her own battle against the Bronx itself, with its shootings and overdoses and infants thrown down three flights of stairs. People burned with chemicals, sick from toxic mold that spread in dark-spotted canopies over the leaking houses, choking on fumes from the Van Wyck Expressway, that gentle poisoning mist. And if that weren't enough it was war with insurance companies, war with the hospital management. You fought your own body, its need for sleep, nutrition, and exercise, its soft susceptibility to MRSA and other bacteria. And finally, you were at war against your own mind. That official had it wrong. Madness wasn't the enemy, it was the field of battle. *And here comes another casualty,* thought Eva, standing up from the cot as she heard the sound of a gurney being rattled down the hallway.

Into the room came one of the transporters, maneuvering a litter, and on it a young man, apparently unconscious. Escorted by Dr. Adjaye, a resident from the Emergency Medicine department.

"Here's a fun one for you," said Dr. Adjaye, speaking in his slightly British accent. He handed Eva a sheaf of paperwork. Adjaye was a foreign medical graduate who had trained in

Ghana, his skin so dark it made Eva feel pale in comparison. He was unshaven this morning, with white bristles on his chin that matched his starch-white coat. "Admitted a few hours ago without identification, wouldn't give his name."

"What's his status?" said Eva, absently flipping through the file.

"But he did know *your* name," said Adjaye.

Eva looked up at her colleague with an expression of total bafflement, then down at the patient. Coop's face was covered in bandages, tape, and bloody gauze, but she recognized him immediately. His chest was bruised and smeared with Beta-dine, and both arms were getting fluid through wide-gauge IVs.

"Doctor?" said Adjaye.

Eva forced her eyes back to the treatment record.

"I'm not sure I recognize him," she said. "But it's hard to tell with all these contusions."

She stared a little longer, distantly sensing Adjaye's impatient gaze. *Probably eager to hand this off,* she thought.

"What happened to him?"

"Security found him near the hospital. He was severely underdressed for the elements, as you can see from the frostbite. Based on pupil dilation, facial tremors, and patient behavior, the ER noted possible drug-induced psychosis, but urine screen came back inconclusive. According to the notes, patient stated that he'd been injected with an unknown substance against his will."

"Jesus," said Eva, under her breath.

She looked at Coop's bare skinny legs and big feet. He was just a kid, Eva reminded herself. Him and Katherine both.

"Any other injuries?" said Eva.

"Hypothermia, obviously," said Adjaye. "A handful of minor contusions. And some hyphema here, perhaps," said Dr.

Adjaye, raising one of Coop's eyelids. "His RBCs are normal, vitals okay. No word yet from Neurology."

Eva stared, thinking about what would happen next. If no one else could identify him, the hospital would be forced to bring in someone from the local police precinct to take finger-prints. Eventually they'd find out he was military and someone would contact his unit. "Military justice," she heard her grand-father say. "That's what you'd call an oxymoron."

"So?" said Adjaye. "You don't know him?"

I am not going to help him, Eva told herself. *Whatever it is, it's too much.* She stared longer into Coop's unconscious face. Found herself nodding.

"You know what," she said. "Yes, I think I do."

CHAPTER TWENTY-NINE

An hour later Eva brought a wheelchair and a plastic bag of clothes to Room 316. Coop was awake now, but barely. They had him on a heavy dose of lorazepam to combat his hallucinations. As she came into the room he gave her a crooked smile of recognition.

"Put these on," said Eva.

She had picked through the donation bin at the hospital and retrieved a pair of black sweatpants, a clean white T-shirt, and an oversized Christmas sweater decorated with white reindeer. She'd also managed to get him a temporary eye patch.

She watched him while he put on the clothes.

"You wouldn't give them a name," she said.

"What?"

"The first doctors who saw you. Why not tell them who you are?"

Coop shook his head.

"What happens when they find out? When the hospital calls the police, and the police call your unit?"

"Trouble," said Coop.

Eva helped Coop off the bed and into the wheelchair, then rolled him down the hallway of Three East. She waved to Geo and pushed Coop into the elevator. As they descended, he studied his reflection in the aluminum interior.

"I look like a homeless pirate," he pronounced, after a few moments.

"You're welcome," Eva replied.

In the lobby a stained-glass portrait of Saint Barbara was set into one of the walls, between two artificial trees. The glass around her was deep midnight blue, with backlit stars in the three windows of her tower.

"Wait," whispered Coop, "they're just letting me leave?"

"I told them you were a patient at Next Start," said Eva, "and that you didn't have any insurance. Trust me, they couldn't wait to get you discharged."

"So that's it?"

Eva smiled wearily, the hallway lights rising and falling as she maneuvered him toward the exit. "That's it."

They rolled through the glass doors, waving to the lone security guard at the entrance, and into the cold glare of morning.

"But the hospital will call someone, won't they?" said Coop, speaking louder now that they were in the parking lot. "My unit will find out."

Eva shook her head. "Nobody's going to call anyone. As far as the records are concerned, you're just another John Doe with a drug problem. Probably not the last one we'll see this week."

Eva left Coop on the sidewalk in front of the hospital. He sat in his wheelchair, blinking against the freezing wind, and watched as Eva trudged out into the street and stood there with an arm outstretched, finally managing to wave down an unmarked Crown Victoria, the gypsy cab flashing its brake lights too late and coasting a half block past them in the slush.

Eva gestured for the driver to hold up while she hustled back to the sidewalk.

"C'mon," she said, leaning over Coop to help him. Her braids were everywhere, her breath hot on his face. "The driver won't wait."

"You'll get in trouble," said Coop, staring at her.

"Maybe," Eva said. She held out her hand. "Now, you good to walk, or do I have to roll you through a snowdrift?"

Coop was shaking by the time they got back to Eva's apartment. As she laid him on the couch he let out a convulsive shudder, his whole body firing with each rattle of his lungs.

Eva stepped back and tried to make a clinical assessment of her new patient. Pneumonia was the most immediate concern. Coop had been discharged with a prescription for oral Levaquin, but antibiotics were always a guessing game, and there was no guarantee that it would be the right course of treatment. It was obvious he was having difficulty breathing, and the damaged ribs would complicate any DIY respiratory therapy.

There were too many things to do. *First things first,* she thought.

From the bathroom Eva fetched the little glass bottle of cough syrup, decorated in Chinese characters, and allowed herself a crystal green spoonful. With great discipline she recapped the bottle and put it back in her medicine cabinet. She sat on the toilet lid and closed her eyes. The bathroom slowed and began to soften. Deep breaths.

She stood up and got to work. First step was to keep him warm. She went to the closet for the spare duvet and found herself standing there, wanting to fold herself up in the darkness of the crawlspace. Pushed herself away from the door and laid the duvet over Coop's trembling body.

She turned up the thermostat as high as it would go, then rescued a few coffee cans from the recycling bin, which she filled with water and set on the radiators. She went to the bathroom and turned on the shower, let it run hot with the door open. *At least the landlord pays for water,* she thought, with a sense of calm that had been impossible only minutes before. She put pillows under Coop's head and propped up his knees with rolled towels, wrinkling her nose at the sweaty male funk of his damaged body.

She stood up and looked around, processing how messy her apartment was. How totally inappropriate for patient care. *Look at you,* Eva thought, *discharging a sick and possibly psychotic young man to your own home.* Good career move for a hungry young doctor trying to make it in the world. *What if he dies here,* she asked herself, *or wakes up and rapes you?* Everybody in New York had heard stories like this: women trapped inside their apartment for days, chained to their own radiator and tortured while the rest of the building went obliviously about its business.

But there wasn't time for regret. Eva had only a few hours before her shift at Next Start began.

She changed Coop's fluid bag and injected a small dose of codeine into the IV port. The bandages on his face were crusty, but they'd be fine until evening. She checked the clock on her microwave and saw she had only a few minutes to change into new clothes after quickly cleaning herself with baby wipes—no time for a proper shower—and soon she was headed back into the cold, leaving Coop unconscious on her couch.

CHAPTER THIRTY

Coop came awake with the terror of drowning in a hot ocean. He tried to breathe, but each attempt caused him to bark in pain. Then something in his lungs wormed itself free, a burning clot that traveled up his throat and lodged in his sinuses. Coop turned to gag. For several minutes he lay with his torso half off the couch, staring at the blood-rimmed loogie he'd left on Eva's floor.

He knew he had survived something immense and brutal, though he struggled to give it a name. It was more a force of nature that had found him, and with the astonishment of a slapped child he couldn't believe how badly he'd been hurt.

Slowly Coop untwisted himself. He lay sweating in the fever of the apartment, which smelled like scorched metal. In his periphery Coop saw the steaming cans on the radiator, under the window, and he watched rivulets of water drip down the glass.

Over the next hour he tried to take inventory of his broken body. There was a new IV in his arm and a tube running into his dick. Connected to the dick tube was an amber bag of urine that lay sweating against his thigh. All over himself he found bandages and gauze, on his hands, his ribs, his face, even an X-shaped dressing pasted to the back of his skull.

For the rest of the day Coop lay in the puddle of his helplessness; too exhausted to move, too much in pain to sleep, feeling the seconds tick away one at a time.

When he next came awake there was light in his eyes.

"Hey," said Eva. She was bent over him with a small flash-light. "Can you follow this?"

Her face was close. Coop wanted to smile but was afraid to flash his broken teeth. Now she clicked off the light and went deeper into the apartment.

"Are you feeling hungry yet?" she called out. "I'm thinking Saltines and chicken broth."

Coop gave a weak thumbs-up, hooking his neck to keep sight of her. The kitchen was narrow with cabinetry, and he watched her point her toes against the floor, leaning her pelvis into the counter as she picked through the cupboard.

Together they sat in the living room. Eva ate with a glassed-over intensity, reminiscent to Coop of his fellow recruits in Basic Training, that sleepless, mechanical recourse to primitive tasks. Hunger as a function. Coop was thankful for the mutual burnout. He'd been expecting a tense silence, Eva waiting for him to explain how he had ended up at the hospital.

"I want to say thank you—" Coop began, and Eva flicked her hand dismissively. From her purse she produced an orange prescription bottle, unlabeled.

"Take two of these now you've eaten," she said. "For the pain."

"What are they?"

"Percocet. Should help you sleep, too."

Ordinarily Coop was resistant to taking any kind of drug, especially after the last few days. But under Eva's care he felt cowed by his debt to her and so uncapped the bottle and up-ended two of the big white pills into his hand. He fed himself the pills and swallowed dry, feeling them go raw down his throat.

Eva kept eating. With chopsticks she moved noodles to her mouth. But she watched him. Waiting for something. Coop had another Saltine. Looked around the room. Cleared his throat and wiped crumbs from his scabby lips.

"So," he said. "There's a thing I should tell you."

Coop heard himself as if at a great distance. He was surprised to be telling Eva so much. Once he started talking he'd gotten the idea he could start in Afghanistan, and this might give coherence to the series of events culminating in the theft of the files from Presser's office. He talked about the way he got the news about Kay's death, about coming home and the funeral and the Bellantes. The cascade of truth being a side effect of the pills, he figured, or maybe just a failure of his body to keep anything else contained.

Eva listened, frowning at the appropriate times. She didn't seem surprised. He wanted to keep watching her, to judge the impact, but found himself losing track as the painkillers did their work. Things began to slow. His head felt heavy with ballast. Coop slumped back into the couch and squinted at the ceiling as he spoke, straining with the effort of reconstruction. He mumbled his way through the next part, trying to get the words correct. Telling her about why he didn't tell the police, how instead he used the information she'd given him and went alone to the lab and found himself face-to-face with Dr. Presser—glancing over he saw Eva's jaw working, but he couldn't stop the mudslide of confession—and he continued through his story to the files and Mrs. Bellante and the broken cellphone, to Sean, then finally to the abduction, where the stream of his memory seemed to accelerate, gaining turbulence before spilling over a cliff in the landscape of his mind.

"I'm glad you told me," said Eva, once he'd finished.

Was she angry? Coop couldn't tell. Everything was glassy under a cloud of relief. Then through the haze he felt hands on his leg. Eva's hands, he realized. Moving on his body.

Coop came up from sedation, jump-started by the thrill of

contact. Was she grabbing him? She had the duvet cover lifted up, his boxers were yanked down from his hips. Now she was touching him with gloved hands. Coop felt moved by unspeakable gratitude, and in the moment of thrilling, guiltless instinct he decided he wanted this, he wanted Eva. Craning his neck against the thudding imminence of sleep he looked up—just in time to see tubing from the Foley bunched in Eva's gloved hand, her other hand braced against his hipbone for leverage. With a yank she removed the catheter.

Cutting through the haze, a perfect clarity of pain.

Coop yowled through clenched teeth and put his hands to his groin, gasping and confused, unable to mend, with pressure, the nauseating urethral pain.

Eva neatly discarded the catheter into a plastic bag.

"I'm glad you told me," she said again, and without another word she went into her bedroom and closed the door, carrying the plastic bag like a small, slaughtered animal.

CHAPTER THIRTY-ONE

Panic arrived only after she'd shut herself in the bedroom and slid home the feeble lock. Eva was awash in adrenaline and embarrassment. At her feet was the crumpled plastic bag, filled with the snaking tube, darkly spotted in blood. Ripping out the Foley had been a cruel impulse. She was furious at Coop, furious at her own stupid investment of trust. Eva leaned her shoulder against the door and wondered how well it would hold. At the hospital she'd seen all manner of brutality in response to sudden pain, and now that she knew what Coop was capable of—he'd broken into the lab, attacked Dr. Presser—it had been even more foolish for her to take chances.

For several minutes she listened to her own breathing in the silence, keeping her weight against the door.

Nothing. No stomping or grunts of frustration, no footsteps padding closer.

Cautiously she stepped away from the door. Then came the onslaught of nerves, panicked breathing. And to her alarm, a kind of perverse excitement, her body suffused with heat and expectation at the proximity to a dangerous stranger. Eva went to her dresser, pulled open the drawer where she kept the cough syrup. Then thought better of it, turning instead toward the small coat closet beside her bed. She wished it were big enough to crawl inside. Really it was a wish for her grandfather to be alive. She wanted to feel the largeness and warmth of his hand on her back, guiding her toward that cubbyhole in her old bedroom. As a child she'd thought it was a game they played, something exciting.

Her grandfather would walk her to the closet and gently usher her inside, always with the same secret orders, the same expression of tender vigilance.

"Stay hushed."

In the closet she would reach up and pull down the sweaters and jackets from over her head, making a nest for herself, snuggling into the mysterious darkness. She'd listen to the floor creak as her grandfather padded through the apartment, hunting for hidden enemies, and Eva would feel a delicious sense of privacy. It was a feeling she had held on to, a kind of gift, even after she'd come to understand the closet games as dissociative episodes, a symptom of her grandfather's "bad time" in Korea. And now, locked inside her room, Eva could see with a certain weariness how this fondness had obliquely drawn her to Coop. Something in him was reminiscent of her grandfather, perhaps the same mix of sadness and good manners, undertoned with a latent violence. Another soldier in a war that was sure to be forgotten.

And now she had a dilemma. Her first instinct was: Get this motherfucker off my couch. Tell him he needs to discharge himself from the premises. Or maybe just call the police, let them sort it out. Except the police would have questions for her, too. After all, she'd been the one who told Coop about Dr. Presser and his shadiness, and then she'd freed him from the hospital. And even if she didn't call the police herself, kicking him out would have the same effect. Inevitably he'd get himself in trouble and implicate her, and the rest would go like dominoes. Bye-bye residency, hello six-figure student loan debt. Sitting on the floor of her bedroom, Eva told herself to accept the true shittiness of her predicament: kicking Coop out could be the end of both of them.

When Eva came back into the living room Coop pretended to be asleep. He wasn't sure what would come next, and under the disorienting effects of the pain pills, Coop had the idea that Eva might come over to the couch and start hitting him. She could hold a pillow over his face. Instead she sat down across from him, wearing a stern mask.

"You'll need time to recover," she said.

Coop fake-blinked awake. Then nodded in dull comprehension. "I need to go back soon."

"Back where? The hospital?"

"Afghanistan."

Eva nodded to herself. "You'll stay here until then. Understand?"

Less an offer than an order.

CHAPTER THIRTY-TWO

Buqa's eyes were horse-wild, and in the darkness of the room Kosta swore he could hear the galloping of her mind. The landscape of her inner world must be horrible, he thought, given the way she was shivering. The guest bed was too small, and every so often Buqa struggled against the quilt, keening in frustration as she tried to cover herself.

Kosta watched from a chair that he'd pulled away from the bed, safely out of reach. He'd managed to extract the needles from Buqa's neck, but all subsequent attempts to care for her had produced a violent thrashing—like a toddler, Kosta thought, but far more dangerous. He had already caught a stray fist while trying to dress her wounds. The punch had doubled him against the wall, and Kosta had sat down, heaving, the pain amplified by bitter admiration. Why did it have to be Buqa who had been poisoned?

Kosta watched her writhe and mutter, her neck a collar of dried blood. From elsewhere in the duplex came a subtle, insistent scraping.

Kosta stood up and listened more carefully. Recognizing the noise, he crept from the room and went downstairs. Kosta found Zameer sitting shirtless at the kitchen table, sharpening his linoleum knife. Zameer clutched a whetstone in his gauze-wrapped paw, the good hand making slow, deliberate swipes with the blade. Stickered across his shoulders and arms were dozens of small bandages.

"She get better?" Zameer said.

"Of course not," said Kosta. "You need to do that right now?"

Zameer inspected the angle of the blade. "The sharper the knife, the less the pain."

Kosta stared at him for a long time. "Try to be quiet."

He put a kettle on the stove and took a box of herbal tea from a drawer. Then Kosta retrieved the box of Olanzapine wafers he'd been feeding to Sean. He surveyed the tools with regret.

Things had gone out of control. All morning Kosta had surreptitiously canvassed the neighborhood. Had anyone perhaps seen a madman running through the snow? The old grandmother who ran the Italian ice cart had spat at Kosta's feet.

"Criminal," she had said. "Shame on you."

Kosta moved on. Ditmir from the electronics store confided that he had indeed seen a figure wandering through the streets.

"His eyes were clouded, and he was followed by crackling light. Like *Rmoria,*" said Ditmir, followed by a hoarse coughing fit. "Hey, you know what my father would do, when he saw a storm coming?" Ditmir had continued. He pantomimed a rifle, aimed at the sky. "He'd shoot at the clouds to chase off the weather."

Kosta thanked him but privately deemed the intelligence unhelpful, as Ditmir was known to blend his pipe tobacco with hashish.

After hours of questioning his neighbors, Kosta found a Daughter of the Homeland who thought perhaps she'd seen a man sitting on the roof of the gazebo in Ciccarone Playground, staring up at the stars. Which meant the soldier had drifted toward the hospital, Kosta thought. Increasing the likelihood he had been scooped up by the police. On the other hand he might be dead somewhere, frozen in a culvert. Had they given him enough formula to take hold? If Buqa's state was any indication, it was certainly possible.

A shirtless man, disappearing into winter. It was an appropriate image, Kosta felt, as the whole situation ran wild, beyond his grip.

Kosta came back into Buqa's room and knelt at her side, carrying a steaming mug of tea. He put a hand to her forehead but she started at his touch.

"Hey," said Kosta. Buqa looked over at him shyly, licked her lips, and burped. Out came a string of apologies in Croatian.

"Here," said Kosta. "Drink this."

Buqa protested at first, but Kosta put gentle pressure on her forehead and tipped the mug toward her mouth. She coughed and sputtered and sat up, trying to wipe it away. Kosta helped her lie back on the bed. Soon her eyelids began to flutter, the Olanzapine already doing its work. Kosta cooed to her as Buqa fell asleep. Soon the room grew quiet.

Behind him Kosta felt a displacement of air and turned to see Zameer ghosting into the room. Kosta held up a hand, indicating that he should wait, and Zameer posted himself at the foot of the bed, shifting back and forth on his feet.

Moving ever so slowly, Kosta leaned over Buqa and began pulling up the quilt around her torso, as if he were tucking her in.

In Kosta's view, there were right ways and wrong ways to kill a friend. For instance, some amateurs put their faith entirely in drugs, and while chemicals could help soften the process, there was no such thing as an ecstatic overdose. In Kosta's experience, death by narcotic was a drawn-out torment of choking and seizures. A gunshot to the skull was instantaneous and pain-free, but for this method you needed a quiet and disposable firearm. Lacking such resources, the gentlest way was the knife.

Gripping a fistful of quilt in each hand, Kosta stretched the folded bedding across Buqa's chest. Slowly he leaned forward with all his weight, pinning her.

"Ssshhh," he said, and felt her lungs empty under the pressure.

He turned back to Zameer, ushering him forward with a nod, but suddenly Kosta felt a deep, convulsive shiver pass through the muscular body beneath him. And then he heard the keening, a horrible moan. Looking down, Kosta was dismayed to see Buqa's eyes flapped wide, awake with naked fear. Looking down at the foot at the bed, and then up at him, her face pleading and terrified.

Zameer was already coming with the knife. Buqa began kicking, so Kosta leaned with all his weight to keep her down while Zameer fumbled one of her arms from under the sheets, and drew a lazy, jagged cut from elbow to wrist. Blood lanced onto his tracksuit and sprayed the bed while Buqa fought, opening her mouth to yell. Kosta yanked a pillow from behind her head to cover her face. Now Zameer was jabbing the knife into her side, huffing rapidly, spittle bubbling from his lips. Kosta watched the blade vanish and reappear, a magic trick. He had seen many stabbings, but had never been so fixated with horror. It seemed wrong that a knife could obtain such casual passage into the body.

The bed turned dark and wet and soon it was over. Kosta stared with amazement, seeing Buqa's face again, her expression at the moment she had woken up and seen him holding her down. The face of a child about to cry, accusing and so horribly *disappointed*. All the world's disappointment in those eyes, he thought.

Kosta eased himself away from the corpse. He turned his

gaze on Zameer, who stood panting on the other side of the bed, his knife still sticking from Buqa's side.

"Why would you do that?" said Kosta.

Zameer blinked. "What?"

"You wanted her to see it," said Kosta, speaking in Albanian now. "Why would you show her the knife?"

Zameer opened his mouth to offer a defense, but the hard rage in Kosta's stare made him reconsider. Slowly Zameer took a step backward, his eyes flashing toward the door.

Kosta stepped around the bed, blocking his escape. Instead of running, Zameer lunged for the knife. But this time he couldn't free it. It was as if Buqa fought back, clutching the knife within her ribs. Zameer let out a weird, frantic giggle as he strained to wrench the blade free. Kosta lunged forward and grabbed Zameer by the throat. "You showed her," said Kosta, his voice a harsh growl, his grip tightening with each word. "You showed her."

CHAPTER THIRTY-THREE

The next day, when Eva had gone to work, Coop decided to attempt the slow, excruciating process of lifting himself off the couch. The ligaments in his back felt as if they had petrified, and it took almost a half hour for him to sit up and hobble across the living room, cradling his bladder.

Standing in front of the mirror in Eva's small bathroom, Coop examined the purple blossom across his chest. He took another Percocet, swished out his mouth, and spat up glassful after glassful of pink water. Next Coop tried walking around the apartment, hands out like a blind person, paddling to grab at counters and doorframes. He hunted for some kind of entertainment, defense against the dull, useless hours of healing. There was no television, and Eva's bookshelf was filled with intimidating titles like *The Pathological Basis of Disease* and *Dialectical Behavior Therapy*. Coop scoured the rest of the apartment, hoping his sapper's instincts might help uncover a cache of legal thrillers, spy novels, comic books, anything he could just enjoy as entertainment while he healed, but the only treasure he managed to locate was a collection of erotica paperbacks and a bullet-shaped metallic purple vibrator, all hidden in a handbag under Eva's bed.

Defeated, Coop returned to the bookshelf. This time he noticed a stack of older-looking books and papers on the top shelf, set apart from the other volumes. Coop pulled down a pocket-sized book from the top of the stack called *Freedom or Damnation*. It was a collection of religious quotations, each presented in large text and accompanied by photographs of black clergy. Coop went back to the couch and flipped through the book until one of the quotes stopped him:

> God is not dead—nor is He an indifferent onlooker at what is going on in this world. One day He will make restitution for blood; He will call the oppressors to account. Justice may sleep, but it never dies.
>
> —FRANCIS J. GRIMKÉ

He liked that: *restitution for blood*. The words captured a swarm of feelings and doubts that had grown inside him ever since he'd landed in New York—feelings about the war, about Kay and her vanishing, about his own crimes and what he might do to make amends. It seemed to Coop that his investigations had brought him to the verge of this idea, restitution, and he had been punished for it.

What he wanted to do was return to the mission. Find Sean, make sense of his connection to the men in masks. But reconstructing his abduction was like scooping up handfuls of dry sand, the memories kept leaking through his fingers. Through the steamed-over windows he heard the sounds of the city, all the commotion rushing through his brain, and spinning in the red-lit darkness behind his eyelids Coop saw the rubber caveman faces snarling at him. He dreamed he was running again through the courtyard of the church on Castle Hill in pursuit of the man in the black suit and sneakers. His footprints were laced with sparks, and suddenly Coop wasn't sure whether he was chasing someone or running away.

When he woke, the sun hung low and orange below the window. But the fact that he had slept through the day was secondary to a new and urgent thrill, something that had come up from the cauldron of his brain while he was sleeping: Coop remembered that his enemy hadn't always been disguised.

CHAPTER THIRTY-FOUR

Eva was having dinner in the hospital cafeteria when she was joined by Dr. Meyer, an attending physician from Neurology.

"Dr. Okori," said Meyer, scooting up close. "I'm wondering if you can help me out."

Eva gave him a stiff, polite smile. "Sure."

"You remember a no-name patient from a few nights back? I'm told you ID'd him and handled the discharge."

Here it comes, Eva thought. She straightened herself, trying to prepare for the fallout. "That sounds familiar," she said, faking an upward eye roll of recollection.

"Caucasian male, midtwenties?" he prompted.

"Sure, sure," she said, "I remember."

"Great. You happen to know his whereabouts?"

Eve slowly shook her head. Meyer frowned, obviously disappointed. He looked around the cafeteria, then back at Eva.

"You have a few minutes?" he said, lowering his voice. "I want to show you something."

They stood together in the darkness of the neuroimaging lair. On the monitor were a series of black-and-white tomographic images showing the pale border of Coop's skull, filled with an interior of prunish gray.

"Imaging never sent these over, I checked," said Meyer. "So don't worry, you guys in Psych are off the hook."

With a finger he indicated tiny white blemishes in the brain scan. They looked like marks of deterioration in old film.

"One or two of these I'd chalk up to motion artifacts, but look at them all: three, four, five, maybe this one here . . ." he said, his fingers skipping across the screen.

Eva studied the images. It was a relief to be in the darkness of this underground bunker, surrounded by quietly humming computers. So much easier to gain clinical distance.

"This trauma," she said, "could it have caused the patient's hallucinations? From what I understand, the tox screen was inconclusive."

Meyer shook his head. "This looks older to me. The patient, he's maybe a boxer or something? Or a drinker, been in lots of car accidents?"

"I don't know much about his history," said Eva. "But with an addict, there could be any number of lifestyle factors . . ."

"Of course," said Meyer. He was still studying the screen. Nervous about something, Eva thought.

"So what would be your instinct, prognosis-wise?" she asked.

"Look, first thing is, we need to get the guy back for more tests," said Meyer. "MRI, some angiography at minimum. My real worry is that he'll sustain another trauma. Because the thing is, this guy gets hit again, starts experiencing complications? Well, we've got real potential for a malpractice claim. I mean, he never should have been discharged with this kind of brain damage."

Eva nodded vigorously. "I understand."

"So you think you might be able to find him? Get him to come back? I know it's a hell of an ask. But if someone else catches this, advises him of his rights? Puts a bull's-eye right on my department."

"I'll do what I can," said Eva.

"Great," said Meyer. "Listen, don't have him come in through the ER or anything. Have him contact my office directly."

A few minutes later Eva was upstairs in one of the hospital's bathroom stalls, hyperventilating. Gripping the handicap bar she thought: *How do I get Coop back here without explaining why I discharged him in the first place? Especially once it turns out he's not a junkie from Next Start but a soldier going back to Afghanistan?* Suddenly Eva felt a stabbing resentment for Katherine, the dead wife, a coworker she had barely known. This is *your* problem, she thought, *you* should be the one taking care of him.

Okay, she told herself. *Close your eyes. Deep breaths.* Out of her bag Eva fished the bottle of cough syrup, labeled in its mysterious characters. She took a spoonful of the syrup. Then another. Sat on the toilet and waited. Gently came the drunken sparkles of light behind her eyelids. Little glimmerings, not dissimilar in shape to those white-hot holes burned into Coop's brain.

The frozen streets seemed to glide past as she left the hospital, feeling loose and happy. The crisis with Coop and Dr. Meyer was a faraway concern. The miracle of the syrup; everything seeming to drip into place.

She made her way home through the city's snow-strewn wilderness, the blizzard lit from within by strings of yellow lights, and on the walk back she realized she was actually looking forward to seeing Coop, her patient. It was nice to have someone in the apartment.

Except when she got there the living room was empty. Coop's bedding was neatly folded on her couch, but the pills and medical supplies she'd left for him were gone. Eva stumbled around the apartment. Turning on lights. Turning them

off again. There was nothing else missing, though she was surprised to see one of her grandfather's old books on the coffee
table.

Eva sat down on her bed, the gloom of the empty apartment impeding upon her fog of bodily bliss. Her patient was
gone.

CHAPTER THIRTY-FIVE

Theo's workplace was a Warren Street high-rise in downtown Manhattan, the entrance surrounded by a complex network of blue scaffolding. Guarding the mouth of this geodesic cave was an enormous rat. It was about ten feet tall, an inflatable monster with red eyes and fearsome teeth, attended by a half dozen protesting construction workers. The men were handing out flyers to passing pedestrians:

TELL BELLANTE/VANCETTI TO BARGAIN IN GOOD
FAITH WITH 9/11 WORKERS!

Coop stood on the sidewalk, trying to make sense of this. Adding to the surreal moment was the floating, ethereal voice of an opera singer, which drifted up from the Fulton Street subway entrance. Coop had first heard her when he got off the 4 train, and now he felt propelled by her voice as he pushed through the crowd toward Theo's building.

Just a few hours ago Coop had been sleeping on the couch in Eva's apartment when he suddenly came awake, gulping for air, as if the memory had pounced on his chest. He remembered a crouched shadow, long fingers pushing a rag down his throat. Then screaming, and as Coop tried to escape the basement he was grabbed again, fighting the shadow, both of them toppling through a window . . . the man's face thin and seized in rage. He hadn't been wearing his mask. Something had stirred in the back of Coop's brain, and he realized he'd seen the face before: the furtive messenger he'd chased across the churchyard during Kay's funeral. At one point the man had looked back, just a glance before he vaulted the ironwork, and the more Coop had thought about it, the more he felt sure it was the same man. Which meant the people who attacked him had also delivered something to Kay's family. A message Theo hadn't wanted to share.

Coop passed through a revolving glass prism and into a crowded marble lobby. He explained to the receptionist that he was hoping to see Mr. Theo Bellante. The receptionist told him he would need a visitor's pass. On top of her computer monitor was a digital camera, and she angled the pod in Coop's direction, telling him to smile, then printed out a bar-coded temporary badge.

"Fifteenth floor," she said, already ushering the next person in line.

Coop rode the elevator up to a smaller lobby, where he encountered another receptionist. This woman was younger, about his age, wearing a black dress suit and rectangular metal glasses. Behind her was a high wall of frosted glass with the embossed logo of Bellante/Vancetti.

"I'm sorry," the receptionist said, after Coop had explained who he was looking for. "Mr. Bellante is currently on leave."

"I see," said Coop. "Listen, it's pretty urgent. Is there a way I can reach him?"

The receptionist raised a skeptical eyebrow. "What exactly is this concerning?" she asked.

Coop sucked air through his nostrils and summoned every ounce of indignity available to him. He placed his hands on the desk and leaned forward, trying to squeeze out vapors of condescension through his mismatched military gear and second-hand hospital clothes, through the battered colors of his face; even through his eye patch.

"It's a family matter," he growled.

Indecision danced in the receptionist's eyes. "Excuse me," she said, and pivoted out of her chair, disappearing through a door in the glass.

Coop leaned on the desk. He felt much improved after taking a few more painkillers and washing them down with coffee, but he was still weak. A few minutes passed and the receptionist still hadn't returned. Coop peeked over the wall of her desk. There were papers and envelopes stacked in upright metal files, including a bin for outgoing mail. Glancing around to make sure he was truly alone, Coop began sifting, and there amid the letters and glossy mailers and padded manila packages he found a rubber-banded stack of envelopes bearing Theo's name. Coop saw that each piece of mail had been stamped with a forwarding address. Stuffing one of the letters into his coat, he limped back to the elevator and punched the button for the lobby.

CHAPTER THIRTY-SIX

Theo's forwarding address was just ten blocks from his office, a glass-fronted apartment complex with a doorman standing on the sidewalk. Coop walked past, scoping the entrance, then circled back. He decided to wait. Gusts of cold wind blew down the narrow streets and he could feel his bones clattering with hypothermic pain.

The cold is just a state of mind, Coop told himself. *You don't need to shiver.* Shivering is how the body fights against the cold, when the trick is to accept it: I am cold, this is how I feel right now. I can live with that. *There are homeless people sleeping in this weather,* he reminded himself. *You're a United States Paratrooper, and if the hobos can hang, so can you.*

In an effort to distract himself, Coop looked at his map again, wondering where the ruins of Ground Zero were located. He had been expecting something obvious and totemic, as in the photos Kay had obsessed over during the crazy months following the attacks. Pointing at images on her laptop screen: graveyard jags breathing smoke, broken stalks of rebar, a monster footprint.

"This is my city," she would say. "I used to live here."

That day had begun for Coop in the predawn hours, his whole unit piled into cattle trucks to go searching for a lost pistol. Some cherry lieutenant had dropped his weapon during a night jump, and all of Fort Bragg would remain on lockdown until the handgun was located. Coop remembered drifting back asleep with his head against the window, purple light just starting to show over the trees. They drove to DZ Bastogne, a miles-long field used for airborne training. Coop and the rest of his unit formed up into a long one-man column, each grunt standing at arm's length from the next, and they began marching with their heads down across the field. An enterprising NCO had suggested they might clean up while they were out there, so each soldier had been issued a small clear trash bag, which each of them was expected to fill by the time he arrived at the other end of the drop zone. Every few feet someone would stop to pick up litter from past training missions: a glowstick, a shell casing, a tube of camouflage, a shred of plastic from an MRE bag. Like everyone else, Coop griped about these bullshit details. But he was also privately awed by the effect, all this manpower casually deployed to hunt through a few dozen acres of raw North Carolina scrub. It was a thing you could only do with soldiers, felons, or slaves.

As the sun rose and the search continued, Coop gradually became aware of a disturbance within the ranks. He heard distant, raised voices, and for a bright moment Coop thought someone had found the missing weapon. But then, in a shocking display of mutiny, the line began to dissolve. Soldiers were coming together in clumps, talking excitedly.

The first thing Coop heard was "Planes are falling out of the sky." *A weird thing to hear spoken in an Airborne unit,* Coop remembered thinking. An inversion of the natural order. *The planes don't fall,* he thought. *We do.* Just last week Coop had jumped into the sky over this very drop zone, twisting under the belly of a C-17 Globemaster, unreal in its whale-like enormity, Coop floating suspended in an underwater silence as the planes grew smaller toward the horizon, leaving rows of bobbing white jellyfish in their wake, each carrying a soldier toward the ground. And now these soldiers came together to trade rumors on the field. A few minutes later the trucks began honking and they rushed back to the parking lot, loaded up, and hung on, piling out at the barracks to fetch their go-bags and sprint to Company, where they would be briefed on the terrorist attacks, then ordered to draw weapons and paint their faces in camouflage, all in preparation for a no-shit, honest-to-God airborne invasion of *somewhere.*

It wasn't until later in the afternoon that Coop had gotten a chance to call Kay.

"The buildings just keep falling down," she had said to him. "I'm watching the TV and they just keep falling, and people I know are definitely inside those buildings, Coop, do you understand? Everything is going to change."

Coop did his best to comfort her, but privately he felt that everything had already changed. He shared nothing in common with the person he'd been that morning—a purposeless half soldier, picking up trash after fake battles—and the Coop of now. And even though his unit didn't get deployed that morning, or that month, even though it took *two years* for him to finally get orders, Coop knew he was already different. They both were.

Before the attacks, Kay had been fixated on the global land mine problem. In a year and a half Coop would finish his enlistment, and Kay's plan had been for them to start a nonprofit together. The idea was that they could work in Vieques, or Vietnam, or some other exotic locale strewn with munitions. She would handle the organizational development side of things, Coop would bring the technical expertise. It was one of Kay's habits that had driven him to private fury, before the attacks, how she always talked about his military service in terms of what he might *do* with it, as if she couldn't believe his years in the Army might possess stand-alone value. Then, in a single morning, Kay's view of the world had been sliced open with a box cutter. And deep in the ugly recesses of his heart, Coop had been glad. *Finally,* he thought, watching the black fires over New York. *Finally the world is worthy of my rage.*

Afternoon came to lower Manhattan. It was cold despite the sun, but still Coop waited, hoping to catch Theo. His mind tricks had failed and now he shivered freely. *Eva would not approve,* he thought, as he walked up and down the block to keep the blood moving, never letting his eyes off the entrance.

Then through a vented cloud of steam across the street Coop spotted a familiar figure. Detective Melody, holding a walkie-talkie up to his mouth while he fixed his stare on Coop. While Coop tried to make sense of this, Melody limped out into the street, raising one hand to halt an oncoming taxi so he could cross. He came up onto the sidewalk and stood in front of Coop, stuffing the walkie-talkie into his coat pocket. He looked Coop up and down.

"Fuck," Melody finally said. "What happened to you?"

"How did you know I was here?" said Coop.

"One of these bystanders reported your suspicious ass, and I heard the call about a potential lurker. Seeing as I was already in the neighborhood I told patrol I'd check it out."

Melody's face went flat, no trace of his usual bullshit smirk. "What are you doing here, Coop?"

Before Coop could answer, Melody leaned in closer, dropping his voice. "You know what, don't say anything yet, just come with me."

Without another word, Melody crossed the street toward the massive glass building. Coop lingered for a moment. Down the street he saw an NYPD patrol car turn onto the block and start drifting through traffic in his direction.

"Hey," said Melody, talking back over his shoulder. "You want to come upstairs, or stand out here in the friggin' cold? Either way is fine by me."

CHAPTER THIRTY-SEVEN

Melody fixed his tie in the polished steel door of the elevator while a counter ticked through the floors: 22, 23, 24 . . . Coop's stomach lurched as they rushed up through the innards of Theo's building. Melody had hit 34, the highest button on the panel. Coop was starting to feel like he'd made a mistake, following Melody with no idea what might be waiting for him on the top floor.

"What did you say on the radio?" said Coop.

"I informed the patrolmen you were just another confused vagrant, and that I successfully moved you along with the courtesy and professionalism for which the NYPD is legendary."

As the elevator passed 30 they began to slow. Melody used both hands to tuck his shirttails into his pants, and when he lifted his jacket Coop caught sight of a small black revolver holstered in his waistband.

"What is it?" said Melody.

"Am I in some kind of trouble?" said Coop.

Melody met Coop's eyes in the reflective steel.

"You tell me, Coop."

The elevator eased to a stop and the doors slid open on a dimly lit, unfinished hallway. One of the brick walls had been torn open to reveal ancient plumbing, and the walls and floors were covered in plastic tarps. Melody led Coop down the hallway toward a big pair of industrial fire doors. He stopped just short of the doors and put a big hand on Coop's shoulder.

"I want you to listen to me for a second. There are things you don't know, and in my opinion it's not right you don't know them. Which is why I'm bringing you in on this. But doing that means I'm putting my ass in the wind, you understand? So when we get in there, you need to be straight with us."

Coop tried to keep his face blank. His mind raced to make sense of what Melody was telling him. "I don't know what you mean, Detective," he said.

"See, that, that's exactly what I mean. Don't do that. And please, spare me the 'detective' shit. Right now it's just Melody."

Melody yanked open one of the big fire doors and they stepped into an enormous open loft. Factory windows filled the apartment with the red light of dusk. Arranged near the windows were a tufted leather sofa, a bar cart, and two gnarled blocks of wood, each of which had been roughly hollowed out to make a seat. Theo Bellante sat on the sofa facing the sunset.

The doors clanked shut behind Coop, and in response came a sudden high-pitched yapping, followed by an explosion of black fur across the floor.

"Goddamn," said Melody, dancing to avoid a little dog as it scrabbled past them, barking in alarm.

"Chaplin, sit," said Theo.

The dog ignored him, snatched up a stray slipper from the doorway and thrashed its little head, shaking the slipper like a dead rat.

"Bad dog!" yelled Theo. He scooped a chunk of ice from his drink and threw it at the dog. Chaplin abandoned the slipper and chased the skittering cube to the other end of the loft.

"Wait till he gets bigger," said Melody. The detective had gone straight for the bar cart and was pouring himself a whiskey. "I told you, you put down these nice wood floors, that dog's gonna tear them up."

"That's as big as he'll get," said Theo, his eyes still tracking the dog.

Coop followed all of this with a dazed sense of unreality. His brain was still returning to him through a long and cold tunnel.

He realized Theo was looking at him.

"What?" said Coop.

"I said, how are you liking New York?" Theo wore a tight smile, but there was a wild glimmer behind his eyes.

"Let's sit down, for fuck's sake," said Melody. He squeezed himself into one of the wooden cubes while Coop perched on the other block, still wearing his coat. Under his patch Coop's eye was throbbing. He felt aware of all the bandages on his face.

"Okay, gentlemen, I think we ought to start this meeting of the minds by putting some shit on the table. Coop, we get the sense you've been busy since you got to New York, am I right?"

Coop stared silently back.

"Because here's the thing," Melody continued, "we've been pursuing what you might call a parallel course of inquiry. Which is why we have some sense of what you've been up to."

Melody was running the show, but Coop noticed that he kept glancing toward Theo, like he was checking to make sure he had permission to keep talking.

"So here we are this very night, myself and the young master Bellante, preparing to close out this chapter, when you show up outside. And we thought, here's an opportunity for all of us to get on the same page, so we're not stepping on each other's dicks."

"Great," said Coop. "Why don't you two start?"

"That seems fair," said Melody. He cleared his throat. "So lemme begin with some background. Several days back, Mr. Bellante here was approached with an offer."

"At the funeral," said Coop, picking up the thread even as he spoke the words. "The guy with the envelope."

Theo gave a reluctant nod. "That's right."

"So who was he?" said Coop.

"Guy's an immigrant from Albania," said Melody. "Part of a crew. Small, but we're talking serious players. Connected back to the Balkan syndicates, from what I gather."

"You said they had an offer. What offer?"

"These Albanians claim to have information about the person responsible for Katherine's death. Further, they claim to be in possession of said person."

"Possession," Coop repeated. His words sounded far away.

Theo finished his drink and set the glass down hard. "A fucking junkie," he said. "Someone she was working with."

Coop chewed it over. Things began to take shape, connections flashing from deep in the caverns of his confusion.

"This junkie," said Coop. "His name Sean Hudson?"

Melody's eyebrows went up.

Theo stared at Coop. "How do you know that?"

"These Albanians," said Coop. "What do they want?"

"What does anyone want?" said Melody.

"I don't think we should be going into much greater detail," said Theo. "The important thing for you to know is things are being handled."

Coop tilted his head back, looking at the bare steel beams that ran across the ceiling. The loft had been stripped down to its bones, then polished to a clean finish. The illusion of exposure. He stood up.

"I think you two are full of shit," he said.

"C'mon," said Melody.

"So what, you two got worried I was getting close, figuring out this deal of yours? Thought you'd bring me up here, spoon-feed me just enough so I'd stand down?"

"Yeah, that's pretty much exactly what we're saying," said Theo, his voice rising. Melody shot him a look but he didn't notice. "We are very, very close to ending this. And we don't want you fucking it up."

"Easy, easy," said Melody.

But Theo was on his feet now too. His drink sloshed as he pointed the glass toward Coop. "This guy just shows up at Katherine's funeral, doesn't even tell us he's coming. Two days later he appears on my aunt's doorstep, asks for Katherine's old phone, and just walks off with it. Just steals it from my aunt, a grieving mother."

"Okay, sure, but maybe now we hear it from his side," offered Melody. "That's why we're here, right? Exchanging what we know."

"He doesn't know anything. Look at him." Theo stalked back over to the window, putting his back to Melody and Coop. "He's a liability," he muttered.

"Whoa," said Melody, patting the air with his hands. "Let's try and settle, okay? Maybe remember we're all here for the same reason?"

"Actually, why *are* you here?" said Coop. "I don't get it. You're a fucking cop."

"Me? I'm keeping the peace," said Melody. He jabbed at his chest. "That's what *I'm* doing."

"Don't forget getting paid," murmured Theo.

"You know what, Theo, you're right," said Coop. "I'm one of those people, in the military we call it having a bias for action. I'd rather have information. Orders. Something to go on. But somebody out there killed my wife. And Theo, you don't need to like it that Kay and I were married. What you do need to accept is that I will keep taking action until I understand what happened."

The room fell into a hostile silence. Through the windows Coop watched the sun as it fell across Warren Street, lighting the harbor in a fierce orange glow.

"Man says he needs orders," said Melody, watching Kay's cousin.

"Fine," said Theo. "Let's see where it goes." He went to the bar cart, poured himself another drink, and returned to the couch.

"So what happens after these Albanians give you Sean?"

Melody was starting on his third drink. "It's sort of an old-school proposition. These Albanians, let me tell you: they take the whole 'blood debt' thing very seriously."

"So do we," said Theo.

"The Albanians want two hundred fifty thousand dollars. Cash. The money, it gets us . . ." Melody trailed off, choosing his words.

"Proof," said Theo. "It gets us proof."

"Of what?"

"Of the motherfucker who killed Katherine being dead."

From somewhere came the sound of ice being crushed by little teeth. Coop drummed with his fingers on the wooden armrest of his seat. He put his hands together.

"You know for sure it was this Sean guy?"

Melody dug a cellphone from the pocket of his jacket, fiddled with it a few seconds, then handed the phone to Coop.

"Take a look at these."

Coop scrolled through grainy digital photographs of a demolished car.

"Albanians told me where to find the vehicle. It was abandoned in the Port Morris tunnels. Old Volvo, registered to our man, Mr. Sean Hudson."

Coop kept scrolling through the close-ups. One shot showed where the Volvo's hood had been violently dented. The camera flash revealed a faint spattering of red grime.

"What happens if you don't pay?" said Coop. His eyes stayed locked on the photograph.

"Probably they let the guy walk," said Melody.

Coop handed back the phone. "How does the exchange work?"

Theo gave a strained and abundantly condescending smile. "Any advice you want to pass on?"

Coop leaned forward, folding his arms across his knees. "Watch yourself," he said.

"They kicked your ass pretty good, huh?" said Melody.

Coop nodded. "Broke a few ribs. Knocked out some teeth. I almost lost this eye," said Coop, readjusting his patch. It was an exaggeration, but Coop was running on the instinct that he needed to scare them if they were going to fully bring him in on this.

"Well, we appreciate—" Theo began.

"Plus they injected me with something," said Coop. "Some kind of drug. I woke up in the hospital. Apparently I'd been running all night in the cold, getting frostbite, pneumonia . . . I don't even remember it. Doctors said I'm lucky to be alive."

"Those Albanians," said Melody, speaking quietly, as if to himself. "Let me tell you."

Coop stared at his boots. When he looked up, Melody and Theo were once again exchanging glances.

Melody cocked his head toward the far wall, where plastic tarps sectioned off another area within the huge loft. "Coop, maybe you can give us a minute?"

Left alone, Coop wandered along the bank of windows,

surveying the darkened streets. He had the sudden dizzy feeling he used to get on jumps; that helpless momentum when the light above the door flashed amber to green and you shuffled forward, the wire above you singing from the drag of static lines. All of you advancing toward the breach in the dark wall of the plane, that gap of roaring light.

After a few minutes he heard the crinkle of plastic. Melody came out alone.

"The man's making some calls," said the detective.

They both looked for a while at the city below.

"This deal," said Melody.

"Yeah?" said Coop.

"I'm wondering, how would you like to be a little more involved?"

Coop turned to the detective. As if in answer came the low, throaty snarl of the hiding dog.

CHAPTER THIRTY-EIGHT

Sean shuffled through the orange gloom of the van. It was dark out, and the only light came from a radiant heat fan, which Kosta had wired to a generator, the generator going *chug-chug-chug* outside in the snow. Sean tried to move with deliberation in the cramped quarters, but his body was numb and he was further hobbled by the cuff around his left ankle, which chained him to a U-bolt in the floor. Leaning against the wall, Sean examined the stencil he'd made from a flattened shopping bag perforated with a paperclip. Satisfied, he gently opened his hand, where he held a black palmful of dirt. He'd spent the afternoon exploring every recess of the cargo hold, using his fingers to scrape grime from the panel cavities, then spread this paste of collected filth across the crumblicked wrapper of an energy bar. After several hours drying under the space heater, the muck had dried into a fine powder. Now, moving with great care, Sean formed his hand into a boat, fingers aimed toward the stencil. He put his lips together and gently puffed out, dusting the perforated bag in soot.

After long days of silence there had suddenly come pandemonium. Knocking, thumping, screams, the crashing of glass, and then a long, low moan that had thrust Sean from his stupor and left him cowering in the corner of his cave. Finally it had gone silent again, Sean had heard footsteps in the hall. A clicking at the lock to his cave. When the door had opened Sean thought: *This is it.*

Kosta had smelled strongly of soap. He was shirtless, his torso scrubbed pink and raw, and as he came closer, Sean saw a pistol tucked into his belt.

"No, wait," Sean had begged, scooting himself against the opposite wall. "Please."

Kosta had crouched, staring at Sean with a black-eyed intensity. Then he thrust out a fistful of pills.

When Sean woke again he'd found the van in motion. He was still chained, still lying on the same thin mattress, but now through darkened windows he could see the passing shadows of tree branches, and underneath him the hum of an engine and the rumble of gravel in his spine. Even the air tasted different: sharper, cold, mingled with gasoline.

After several hours they had come to a stop. Behind him the wall opened with a metal creak and Sean blinked against the early morning light. Kosta was standing in the van's doorway, dressed in an enormous, fur-lined black coat that gave him the look of a Mongol warrior. Behind him was a barren, snow-covered parking lot, and farther back, a dense treeline.

Kosta had thrown a black plastic bodega bag into Sean's lap. Inside were three energy bars, a bottle of water, baby wipes, and several disposable heat packs.

"Eat, clean yourself," said Kosta. Then he closed the doors again.

It soon grew cold inside the vehicle. Groping around, Sean had found an assortment of blankets and sleeping bags and nestled himself into the mound of bedding. He broke open the heat packs and held them to keep his fingers from freezing. Gradually, the passing of light revealed the details of his new enclosure, and Sean had realized he was in a passenger shuttle, one of those vans designed to ferry the elderly and handi-capped. The seats had been ripped out, but there were still grab handles along the vinyl wall, and near the door, the ex-posed gears of a wheelchair lift.

Huddled in the back of the vehicle, Sean had found himself thinking of Kay and their time together in his tenement hide-out. A wretched apartment, but with Kay he'd never been em-barrassed. She always acted impressed by the squalor; all part of the staging, he thought, each of them knowing their roles in this ghetto drama. There were other times, though, that felt genuine, unstaged, like when he'd be holding her and she'd bite on his clavicle, and Sean would feel her teeth and imagine their skeletons were touching. Connection, that was Kay's thing. She believed all people were linked in an interdependent knot, whereas when Sean thought of humanity, all he could imagine was moon bunkers. The image came from one of Gem's oversized art books, a history of imagined utopias, and there was a diagram of these glass domes spread across a lunar surface, biohabitats, the whole setup floating in an unlivable abyss. That was the kind of connection Sean could appreciate. With art being like radio signals shot between the bases.

Sean watched as the plastic bag template crinkled and fell away. He'd gotten the rough outline, a gestural impression of shadow. In a bottle cap he stirred up an emulsion of soot, water, and gasoline, and into this primitive ink Sean dipped a thumbnail and came toward the wall again, cocking his head, examining the transfer from multiple angles. Circling like a predator, choosing where to cut in. Finally he reached out with a black-stained thumb.

He started with her eye.

CHAPTER THIRTY-NINE

12/7/2003

I'm thrilled to report Sean's progress, which has been HUGE in the last few weeks. In group sessions, particularly, he's gone from being a wallflower to a total star (especially with the female clients, I've noticed . . .). Where was this guy before? To be fair, Sean always had a quiet kind of charisma—the few times he spoke up in group, the others would listen. But in past sessions he'd mostly just sit there drawing in his notebook, never wanting to show the rest of us what he was working on. So it's amazing to see him come into his own, these last few weeks. I'm proud of him.

Coop felt acid rise in his throat. He stared at the page but no longer saw the notes, his mind crowded instead with Melody's photographs. The underground tunnels, Sean's abandoned car with its dented hood. The rusty spatters of blood. Coop checked his watch. Melody had been gone an hour. The detective had dropped him here, at the Crotona, saying he'd be back soon with further instructions, and Coop had gone upstairs to find his room still in a state of wreckage from the Albanians. His equipment was scattered amid the Next Start paperwork in a chaos of desert gear and patient files. First he straightened the bed and plucked up his equipment—bundles of camouflage fabric, extra pairs of boots, Ziploc packs of tightly folded underwear and socks—and crammed it all down into his duffel bag. Then he began to sweep up the paperwork, trying to match the files to the way he'd found them. The way Kay had done it. He had found Sean's file under the bed. Coop sat down with it, feeling an uncanny sense of dislocation, and had begun to read. Now he finished the entry:

> *I'm not sure how much credit I can take for the emergence of "New Sean," but I think it has something to do with our last one-on-one. I tried explaining how much it could help the others to hear about his experiences, and this seemed to resonate. By framing his participation as a gift to the others—instead of a therapeutic necessity— Sean gets to skip the self-pity. It takes the focus off him and expands it out to the world, and this works because at his very core, Sean is a person of great compassion . . .*

Coop slapped the file closed.

"Stupid," he said. Speaking to the empty room.

Coop lifted himself up and paced to the window, his thoughts beating against the glass and the empty cold beyond. The moon lit a sheen of ice across the telephone wires, and in the distance he could just make out Manhattan: a half-formed darkness, silent and gnawing.

Melody came upstairs hauling a black utility bag in one meaty hand. He looked even more disheveled than usual, his paisley tie half yanked from the collar. The missing buttons showed a sweaty, blood-flushed neck.

"Where can I put this thing?" said the detective as soon as Coop let him into the room.

Coop nodded toward the bed.

"All right, some quick things we gotta go over." Melody unzipped a side pocket and pulled out a device the size of a small cellphone, encased in survival orange rubber.

"You ever use one of these GPS devices before?"

Coop looked it over. He nodded. "In the Army we call them pluggers."

"Good," said Melody, "very good. Our Albanian friend wants to use it for arranging the meet-up."

From his pocket Melody produced a yellow notebook, the front page covered in scrawled instructions, and squinting, he began to fiddle with the GPS, glancing between his notes and the screen. Coop observed these preparations distantly. Normally this was where his mission brain would take over, when his mind would flex itself outward to envelop the manifold details and checklists, chugging along to the rhythm of imminent action. Instead, he found himself going inward, pulled by the persistent tug of doubt.

"Let me ask you something," said Coop, as Melody configured the device.

"Yeah?"

"This guy, Sean. How did you say he was connected to these Albanians?"

"Dealing for them," said Melody, matter-of-factly. He hit a few more buttons and the GPS made a chirping noise. "Okay, there it goes. Should be all set to receive coordinates. The Albanian, he'll have the other device. Got it? So the next thing . . ."

But Coop had drifted to the other side of the bed.

"Hey," said Melody. "You following this? What you got there?"

Coop picked up the manila folder from his bedside table and tossed it toward Melody.

"Sean's file," said Coop. "Tell me, does this guy sound like a killer?"

He watched Melody go rapidly through the notes, giving each page a cursory flick.

"Who wrote this?"

"Kay."

Melody glanced up. He dropped the folder flat on the bed. "Listen," he said. "From what I gather, Next Start wasn't too stringent when it came to employee qualifications. And no disrespect, but it's not like your wife had much experience with this social element."

Coop stared at Melody and flexed his jaw. He'd wanted the cop to have a better answer. But instead Coop was just getting a sly, buddy-buddy grin. *Kay wasn't stupid,* Coop thought. The words arrived with a chill of sudden conviction. *My wife wasn't stupid.*

"I don't know," said Coop.

"Hey, I get it," said Melody. "After what those Albanians did to you? You're thinking: Why trust them? But listen to me, Coop. I got thirty years on the force, seeing how things go down. You want the most plausible story of who did this thing? It's right here."

Melody stabbed his finger at the photograph of Sean.

"All you're doing is meeting someone. You give him the money. The Albanian, he takes care of Sean. You don't have to watch. Though if I was you, I'd sure as hell *want* to . . ."

Coop was silent. Melody leaned in a little closer, lowering his voice.

"You know how many people lose someone, never get a chance like this? You want this, Coop. We *all* want this."

Coop nodded. "Yeah," he said. "You're right."

He saw the conversation with Melody going nowhere—the detective had all the evidence he'd ever need. But Coop's own thoughts raced down a new tunnel, gaining momentum.

"Okay," said Melody, "last piece, and this one's fucking crucial."

Next from the bag came a heavy-duty aluminum case. Packed inside were a dozen bricks of rectangular black plastic. Melody lifted one of these packages and used his thumb to pry away the corner, revealing a thick stack of hundred-dollar bills.

"Quarter million in there," he said, staring meaningfully at Coop. "I probably don't need to elaborate on the consequences, right? I mean, if this doesn't arrive where it's supposed to."

Coop shook his head. "Not going to be a problem."

Melody stared at him for a long, long time.

"I need us to understand each other," he said. "This is not the Army. You're not protected, Coop. These people, if you fuck with them . . ."

Coop stared back.

"So what happens next?" he said.

"I call the Albanian, tell him it's on for tonight. I mean, if you're a hundred percent ready."

Coop nodded. "Sure. But I have another question."

"Shoot."

"The Albanian," said Coop, speaking tentatively at first. "When's he going to kill Sean?"

A slight duck of Melody's head at the word *kill* like it made him embarrassed.

"Why's it matter?"

"Tell him I want Sean alive when I get there."

"Why?" said Melody. The detective crossed his arms. Paying attention, now, to Coop's line of inquiry.

"Because you're right," said Coop, his voice coming faster than his thoughts. "I'm lucky to have this chance. So tell the Albanian I want to do it. I want to be the one."

CHAPTER FORTY

"**M**ilitary Legal Assistance. This is Jackie."

"Hi," said Coop. "Do I have to use that stupid code word?"

"Fancy Dancer, I presume?"

"It's Coop. Specialist Cooper."

There was a pause on the other end. He heard Jackie clicking.

"So, Specialist Cooper," she said, as if trying out the name. "Last time we spoke, you were absent from service. Is that still the case?"

"Yeah."

Coop stood up from the bed, unspooling the phone cord. He had to step carefully around the room. His duffel and rucksack were laid out inspection-style on the carpet, with the contents of each bag arranged neatly on top. Next to this gear was the money case and GPS given to him by Melody, along with several shopping bags from a local hardware store.

"But that's not what I wanted to talk about," said Coop.

"Okay," said Jackie, "what can I do for you?"

"There's something I want added to my file. On the record."

"Great, shoot."

Coop cleared his throat. He began to talk but heard a wobble in his voice. He sat down on the bed. Took a deep breath and started again.

"The date was October twelfth," said Coop. "I was part of a convoy element traveling west from Forward Operating Base Snakebite." Coop put his fingers to his sinuses. A heavy chemical odor drifted from the bathroom, and he was beginning to get a headache.

He heard Jackie's fingers striking the keyboard. "October twelfth of this year?" she asked.

"Correct," said Coop. "At approximately 0300 Zulu time, our convoy was ambushed . . ."

While he talked he removed his purchases from the shopping bag: a bulb syringe, a pack of three road flares, two boxes of waterproof matches, a rubber toilet flapper with a four-inch chain, and a refillable pressurized spray can. Using his knife, Coop carefully removed each item from its packaging, being sure to get all the tags and labels. It was easier to tell the story while doing something with his hands, but still Coop felt his throat closing up when he got to the part about finding the boy in the temple. He closed his eyes and went quickly through the rest. Then listened in the silence while Jackie typed. A slow, methodical clacking.

He opened his eyes and took a deep breath through his nose. Jackie was still typing, and while he waited, Coop pulled the final item from his bag. The hardware store hadn't sold kitchen timers. Instead, the owner had pointed Coop toward a heavy mechanical switch called a Shabbat clock.

Jackie cleared her throat. "Specialist Cooper, I just want to make sure you understand . . ."

"Yes?" Coop noticed her voice had assumed a more formal tone.

"We don't normally collect evidence *against* soldiers."

"I know," said Coop. "I just wanted someone to write it down. Thank you."

Jackie was silent again. Coop got up, still holding the

phone, and went to the bathroom. He opened the door, wincing from the fumes. In the bathtub was a one-liter plastic bucket, and in the bucket, several chunks of styrofoam floated in a slurry of liquid soap and butane, slowly dissolving.

"So . . ." said Jackie. "Is there anything else you'd like to discuss about your current legal situation?"

"No thanks," said Coop, kneeling at the edge of the tub. With a toilet plunger he carefully stirred the mixture. "I think I'm set."

CHAPTER FORTY-ONE

K osta steered the van down a dark, wooded road. He came to a stop in the middle of the two-lane, cranked the wheel, and turned sharply toward a break in the trees, branches slapping the windshield as they rolled down an unmarked access trail and into the wilderness of Pelham Bay Park. It was the largest protected woodland in all of New York, encompassing three times more acreage than Central Park—this according to the guidebook Luzhim had given Kosta when he first arrived in the city. Even during the hotter months there were few visitors, and in winter the park became a frozen wasteland. Over the last few years Kosta had familiarized himself with the overgrown terrain. It was an excellent place to conduct business. Now he followed a familiar route, the trail intersecting with an old bridle path that veered south toward the iced-over pond. It was the same way he'd taken Dr. Presser; now he carried a new passenger.

Kosta couldn't see Sean but he heard him, mumbling from somewhere in the mud-smeared shadows. He sensed the kid was fading. Earlier that day he'd been surprised to find the crude drawings on the wall of the van, but more unnerving was the ashy color of Sean's skin, the way his clothes hung about him like a cloak. And Kosta and begun to smell the reek of death on him, these last few days in the van, waiting for the phone call.

Now, finally, the call had come.

Up ahead there was an opening in the trees, where Kosta sighted a dark shape of rubble. He eased the van over, the chain-wrapped tires crunching through the snow, and pulled up next to the ruined brick building. According to his travel guide, this had once been a train station connecting the mainland Bronx with City Island, but the track had been abandoned for nearly a century. Dunes of snow were swept high against the brick walls, and the roof had fallen away to reveal blackened timber posts.

From under his seat Kosta retrieved a bundle of blankets, tightly wrapped in tape. Inside was his rifle, a short-barreled Kel-Tec with a folding stock, a night vision hunting scope, and a noise suppressor made out of an oil filter.

Kosta locked Sean inside the van, then followed the trail south, the rifle slung from his back. He pulled his big fur-lined coat around himself. The temperature was dropping fast. Kosta followed the path about a hundred meters as it bent around a rocky embankment, then veered off to the left, trudging upslope. The trees were thick and he grabbed at small branches to pull himself along. After a few minutes of climbing he arrived at a rocky bluff crowned in a thicket of pine. On the southwest side was a deadfall, and here Kosta took a knee, his breath coming hard in his throat. With one glove he brushed snow from the log and propped up the rifle, scoping the terrain below. The night vision optics reduced the world to a depthless green field. Kosta could make out the bright curving trail and the pond, a black abyss, and far off, the dim emerald haze of the city.

Satisfied with his position, Kosta pulled out his GPS unit. He waited for the satellites to acquire his location, then ordered the machine to share these coordinates through a channel he'd given to the Bellantes' representative. It made him nervous, broadcasting his position, but he hadn't been able to devise a better way of arranging the meet. Directions would be too unreliable in the frozen wilderness, and after all, he didn't want the bagman to get lost. Kosta was still fooling with the GPS when he heard the nearby crack of a branch.

He looked up and listened. Something moving, out in the wind-still forest.

Kosta brought the scope to his eye. Nothing but trees. Then came another gentle snap. Turning toward the sound, he spotted a figure in the undergrowth: a small deer, profiled between the crosshairs. The animal was no more than thirty yards away, stepping carefully through the hardened snow on the far side of the trail. Kosta watched the deer raise its head to sniff at a frost-heavy branch. It was an opportunity, he realized, to test the rifle. He hoped he wouldn't need the weapon, but one never knew. Kosta held his breath.

The deer bent to sniff at the snow. When it straightened, Kosta applied gentle pressure to the trigger.

The deer lurched, a dark cherry bursting on its neck, and fell off at a stagger. Kosta tracked its fleeing haunches until it vanished among the trees. He was pleased with the silencer. There had been the clinky echo of the rifle's action, but no gunshot.

From his pocket came a ringing chirp, foreign in the massive darkness. Kosta checked his GPS and saw that a second dot had appeared on the screen. The bagman, approaching from the southern tip of the park. He settled back into his sniper's nest and watched the screen. One blip inching toward the other.

CHAPTER FORTY-TWO

Coop made his way through knee-deep snow. All around him were dense trees and dark night. The cold was getting to him, despite his winter gear: the Gore-Tex camo jacket, long thermal underwear, and the Christmas sweater, which he wore for good luck. He was sweating heavily, and every time he stopped, the sweat began to freeze and he felt a lancing pain in his feet and fingers. Eva would not approve.

He paused to readjust his rucksack, yanking on his shoulder straps to center the weight on his back. He checked the GPS that Melody had given him. The screen showed a God's-eye view of the park, fourteen kliks of green spread across the northeastern Bronx. Coop's position was marked with a small dot, and a trail of pixels showed the ground he'd already covered. A brighter pathway connected him to a second dot, the other GPS, still three kliks northeast. Coop was concerned about his progress. At this rate he estimated he could cover a half klik every hour, and he wasn't sure how long he could keep up that pace.

Coop tried to move faster, grunting with pain. The trees thinned ahead and he was surprised to see dim constellations, tiny breaches of light in the smog that hung above the city. Coop felt his heart stammer with primal exhilaration. It was the same feeling he got on missions, that nervous, hollow buzzing of his senses. In one breath he thought about land navigation, the next, a whispered cadence rose up in his mind, something from Eva's book—*one day he will make restitution for blood*—and then his attention was back on the march—low temperature, uneven terrain, lots of jostling. He worried about the effect these conditions might have on the bomb in his rucksack. Coop didn't have a particular plan for the device. He knew he was entering an environment saturated in falsehood and misinformation, and there was no procedure for such a situation, just principles, such as the plaque on his commander's wall: BE POLITE. BE PROFESSIONAL. BUT HAVE A PLAN TO KILL EVERYONE YOU MEET.

CHAPTER FORTY-THREE

Coop smelled the deer before he saw it, a sudden odor of hot blood. Coming over a frozen stream he saw the animal capsized in a dark patch of snow, and Coop halted for a moment, listening. He crossed the stream and knelt beside the corpse. A dark puncture in the deer's neck indicated where it had been hit, and Coop found a larger, ragged opening in the shoulder where the bullet had exited. He put a hand on the deer's flank. The body was still warm.

The wind went down Coop's neck. He turned and looked around at the woods. The forest was cold and shadowed, with no movement in the trees. Coop checked the plugger and saw he was less than a half klik from the designated meet site. The deer was freshly shot and he hadn't heard a thing. *So that's how it is,* thought Coop. He wondered how many of them were hidden out here. Three he'd seen in the basement, four including Sean. Maybe Sean and the Albanians were working together. *They screw over Theo, kill me, and walk away with the money. Okay,* Coop reminded himself, *but you have something they want. The money.* It would be a mistake to go up there with the case. Better to hide it. Coop looked around where he stood. Trees and snow and no prints other than his own and the slurred bloody track of the fallen deer. He wanted to stash the case someplace he'd be able to find it again. Coop looked at the deer, steaming in the night. He took his Strider from his pocket and opened the blade.

A few minutes later he was crawling up toward the bridle path. Coop heard his own breathing coming raggedly and tried to stifle his breaths as the numbing wet snow crept closer around him in the darkness. He crested the trail. The moon lent pale streaks through the forest canopy and by this light he saw the half-buried architecture of a railway station. Parked nearby, a white van.

Coop considered his options, sifting through the frozen slush of his brain for a formal plan. He moved on his elbows and knees through the dead branches, keeping to the shadows.

Kosta watched through his scope as a snow-covered man appeared at the eastern edge of the trail. He brought his face from the scope to check the GPS: the two glowing dots coincided. Kosta held his breath, pressed one eye to the scope and leaned forward from his position behind the deadfall.

The figure low-crawled farther from the shadow of the trees. Kosta saw the bagman's face illuminated within the green glow of the scope and was surprised to recognize the soldier. The one they'd questioned in his basement, who'd stabbed Buqa in the neck with those poisoned needles. Who'd made her go insane.

Instinctively Kosta's thumb depressed the safety catch. He let his breath escape his mouth, halting the silent exhalation as the scope's crosshairs bobbed toward the center of the soldier's frame. His finger paused on the trigger. The bagman wasn't carrying a bag.

A flutter of panic. Kosta took his eyes from the scope. He puzzled over the new information. *Why send the soldier?* he wondered. Were the Bellantes trying to betray him?

Kosta turned back to the scope and found the soldier paused at the tree line. The thing to do would be to hit him in the leg. Let him cry out, see if there were any others, and if he was alone, Kosta could go down and talk to him. Find out what was going on. This new plan was just taking shape when the soldier vanished, moving backward on all fours the way he'd come.

Kosta swore.

He waited for a second, watching the tree line. Listening. Then, moving very slowly, Kosta eased himself up from his cover and followed the soldier down the hill.

CHAPTER FORTY-FOUR

Coop backtracked from the trail, crouching to keep a low profile. Every few steps he stopped to listen. The forest had assumed a new stillness and he was conscious of his aching, clumsy body as he struggled down the slope. His prints led him back to the killed deer. Coop took a knee amid the snow and the spilled guts and tried to get his thoughts in order. The trail was too exposed. If he were to walk out there, it would be easy for the Albanian to kill him from concealment. What Coop wanted to do was reverse that position.

He'd noticed an outcropping of rock up the near crest. If he could place himself there, out of sight, it was just a matter of luring the Albanian down. Coop looked around at the churned-up snow. His footprints would be a problem. *I can backtrack farther,* he thought, *back toward the rails. Then range around and settle among the rocks.* He took out the GPS unit, knelt, and wedged it under the deer's body. The Albanian will get impatient. He'll come looking for the money, and when he finds it, I'll be watching.

Coop had rigged the explosive in the money case with a two-phase ignition system. Undoing the latches would cause the can to empty itself, filling the case with a payload of flammable jelly, and opening the lid would spark the detonator. The result would be a spectacular fireball—assuming the device worked. The possibilities for malfunction were endless. His hike through the woods might have shaken the components from their proper alignment, or maybe the man in the store had sold him faulty hardware. In his apprehension of these many variables, Coop was struck with a sudden insight into the mind of his country's enemies. What faith it required, or what desperation. To take up your mission, your very life, and endow all this to the fragile clockwork of a handmade bomb.

He was still kneeling in front of the deer when Coop heard a rustle of snow. The sound came from behind him. His thoughts fell away in a panic, but instead of turning he stared straight ahead, willing the noise to breeze past him and reveal itself as something innocuous, a rabbit, perhaps, or maybe a scavenging bird. Again came the rustle.

Coop turned and found himself facing a hooded man.

He wore a massive cloak of fur and snow. The rifle in his hands was pointed at Coop's chest.

"Ssshhh," said Kosta.

Moving slowly, Coop pulled his gloves out from under the deer. The knife was in his coat pocket and his hand floated in that direction, his fingers moving as if independent of the rest of him. *Just a few steps away,* Coop thought, his eyes fixed on the rifle. *Maybe he's alone, you can surprise him. Don't think, do it now.*

Something stung Coop's face. He fell sideways into the snow, covering his head with one arm while the other hand fumbled for the knife. A hot sticky pain was growing against his cheek.

When his eyes came open Coop saw the Albanian perched calmly over him. A small wisp of smoke escaped the canister-shaped silencer. There was a new bullet wound in the deer. *A warning shot,* Coop realized. He'd been struck in the cheek by a fragment from the animal's corpse.

Now Kosta gestured with the rifle.

"The money," he said. "Where is it?"

Coop couldn't speak, lying on his back in the snow. He was still processing that he hadn't been shot.

Kosta took a knee and peered into the bloody cavity of the deer. He clucked his tongue.

"You put the money in *there*?"

Coop managed a nod.

Kosta stood up, frowning. With his eyes he followed the crooked path of footsteps leading up toward the trail. He looked around at the trees and the churned-up snow.

"You go up the hill," he said. "You see the meeting site, but then you come back down here." Kosta turned his face back to Coop. "What's the deal, playboy? You don't trust me?"

Coop stared back. He had nothing to say.

Slowly Kosta turned his attention back toward the deer. With the barrel of the rifle he lifted the flap of the deer's belly.

With Kosta's eyes elsewhere, Coop felt his courage return. *You still have the knife,* he told himself. But he couldn't translate intention into movement. Lying in the puddling cold, Coop felt a fuming, helpless anger expanding inside him, a twitching in his jaw and spine, something sick and hateful. The fury so strong he could smell it.

Then he noticed Kosta sniffing at the air. The Albanian showed his teeth.

An acrid vapor curled up from the deer's mouth. From under the animal's fur came bubbles of movement, like some witchy transformation. *The bomb,* Coop thought, *he punctured it.* Incendiary fuel was leaking into the carcass.

Kosta blinked, uncomprehending.

"The money's burning," said Coop, and he kicked himself backward, scuttling over the snow to get away.

Kosta lunged for the strap and pulled, but only succeeding in tugging the deer toward him. Now the animal was smoking furiously, black vapors pouring from the belly and mouth, the deer jerking in a miasma of seizures. Kosta circled the strap around his hand and put a boot on the twitching flank. He strained.

A burst of guts as the case came free, and with it the burning payload, a tail of liquid fire whipping across Kosta's arm.

Coop rolled, turning in the snow, and he patted himself frantically, searching for any spots of heat. The jelly solution he'd made in the hotel was a crude form of napalm; even a small droplet could burn you to the bone. When he looked up, Coop saw Kosta absorbed in a strange performance. He swung the bag in a bright whirlwind, the hot coil winding snakelike around his arm. Kosta fell and punched his arm into the snow, where it hissed for a second before he yanked the limb back, screaming in fear and confusion as the blistering jelly fire climbed across his shoulder and neck. Then he began to run, howling, toward the black glimmer of the pond, as if speed could keep the fire behind him. He broke from the tree line and collapsed onto the frozen surface, crawling forward to pound his fist against the black ice. But his own reflection stood against him, warped and unyielding, while the fire spread across his back and into his hair.

Coop stepped out onto the pond and for a moment the Albanian looked up at him, his face a dripping snarl. He still clutched the case of money under one arm. Fire drew toward the blistering hole in the case, trembling momentarily as it made contact with the payload.

And then, like a magic trick: a burst of white-hot light.

Coop reclined in the darkness, his back against the ice. He heard the forest breathe in gusts across the pond. When he opened his eyes he saw stars. Coop lay there for a while, trying to remember how his lungs worked. He could feel the force from the blast still lodged in his sinuses, a bubble of dizzying pressure, as if the explosion had crawled into his head and gotten stuck there, or found itself a home. As he watched, the stars crackled and came apart, little lights drifting and falling toward the earth in loopy spirals. Not stars, Coop realized. It was Theo's money. Thousands of bills, burning and twisting in the night air.

CHAPTER FORTY-FIVE

Back in Maine there was an inlet behind Coop's house, and every winter it would freeze. The trapped ocean never hardened entirely, but for a few bitter days it would seem as if the coastline had expanded, the water changing into a new landscape of jagged islands. Every year Coop would stand on his family's old fishing pier and survey these continents of ice, and every year he'd swear that if he was fast enough he could run straight across the cove, leaping from one bobbing island to the next as each capsized or submerged beneath his feet. He'd imagined it so many times—darting across the frozen sea, leaving a trail of broken ice in his wake—and now he played the vision over and over, a kind of prayer as he stumbled through a kingdom of mysterious streets: Ampere, Lucerne, Throgmorton, Griswold. His chest felt full of broken glass, and at the corner of Marmion, Coop stopped to gag, leaving spatters of black in the snow. The sky was still dark. It was early on a Saturday morning.

After a few more blocks he noticed his left leg dragging. The foot was soaked in a needly dullness and Coop thought about little pieces of shrapnel, how deep they can go. Fill your body with blood before you even know you're hurt. He wasn't sure why he was walking, or what toward. The world was bits and pieces, fragments floating in his head.

Sunlight appeared over the rooftops and the city came awake with sirens. Two old men came out from a tobacco shop to have a look as a dozen SUVs went screaming past, vehicles brandishing the emblems of Police, Fire, and Homeland Security.

Up the street Coop saw a group of uniformed officers setting up steel barricades. It took a few moments for him to comprehend the scale of this mobilization, and to realize, *Jesus Christ, they're looking for me.* Overhead came the *chop-chop-chop* of a helicopter and Coop shrank down inside himself as he staggered down the road. *Of course they are,* he thought. *You're a killer.*

As he limped down the street Coop waited for hands to fall on his shoulder, the riot of uniformed bodies that would push him to the ground. Zip-tie and hood him like an Afghan villager. *It's all right,* Coop told himself, *it doesn't matter if they catch you.* He was ready to give himself up, and wildly he scanned the block, hunting for a way to avail himself of this conviction.

He spotted two cops setting up barricades and staggered in their direction. The cops looked up at him, and then at each other. Coop's throat felt too dry to speak. He hoped the soot on his clothes and his burned eyelashes would be enough of a confession.

"No luck, buddy," said one of the cops. "Street's closed off."

Coop stood there blinking. He thought, *I'm the one you're looking for.*

The other cop came over. "Look chief, I know it's cold out here, but you see this? This here's a police line. You cross it, all you'll get is a ticket, you understand? We're not putting you in a cell."

"So move along," said the first cop, waving him away. "Just keep it moving."

Coop managed a nod before continuing down the road. *Goddamn,* he thought. It was getting harder to walk.

He saw a crowd gathered at the next corner. People unloading from passenger vans, the transports logoed with KING OF PEACE TABERNACLE. Mostly older-looking black folks, guided by kids carrying placards, folded reams of cloth, and bundles of sticks. Coop headed toward them, drawn by the collection of bodies. More people were arriving, many of them in like-colored assemblies, wearing sweatshirts and hats with the same letters and numbers, like military units. One of the groups carried a banner saying WRONG WAR. Coop puzzled over this for a few seconds before comprehending. The police hadn't come for him after all.

Probably no one had even heard an explosion, Coop realized. The clap of Kosta's death would have been just another noise, lost in the city's innumerable commotions. Looking upward to the sky, Coop felt himself reduced within the multitude. His efforts were little more than feeble sparks of rage. Everything was light, even the new, raw truth he carried of Kay, freshly scooped from his heart.

Back on the lake, Coop had taken a long time to lift himself up from the ice. Of Kosta there had been nothing left except a watery crater and bad-smelling smoke. Coop wandered back to the site of the deer, where he fetched Kosta's rifle from the snow before hiking up to the old rail station. He came low toward the van, circling the vehicle with the rifle raised in front of him. Peeking through the driver's side window he saw the keys had been left in the ignition. Taking these, he went to the rear of the van. Unlocking the door, he found Sean, a thin shadow chained to the floor, and above him, a portrait rendered in wild strokes of grime. Instantly Coop recognized Kay smiling down on him from the foul-smelling cave of the van, and in that moment, standing in the open door, Coop finally felt as if he understood the situation.

When Coop opened his eyes he saw the crowd was moving.

There were drumbeats now and it seemed there was no end to the people joining the march. Coop found himself following despite his exhaustion. He didn't want to be left alone.

Off in the distance someone was making a speech, but the static echo was lost to the racket, a hundred discordant chants, the music from drum brigades, gutter punks playing kazoos, the jingling bell of a Buddhist monk in gray robes. Then came a river of flag-draped coffins. Dancing over the coffins were giant skeleton puppets dressed raggedly in the manner of Afghans and Iraqis, American soldiers, pin-striped bankers and politicians, all carried by women wearing black masks. Around the protesters were police and more police, riding on motorcycles, bicycles, horses, armored vans, manning the mazes of steel barriers, heads angled to better catch radio chatter.

The protesters chanted and yowled. *This is where Kay would be,* thought Coop. *If there's any place she would be, this is it.* The thought made him smile. Of everything that had happened since he'd come to New York, joining this mad procession was the first thing he'd done that would have made her happy. *No, the second thing,* he reminded himself. Extricating Sean, of that Kay would have approved. Not that it had been a conscious idea, setting down the rifle against the van's rear fender and passing Sean the keys. Coop had barely looked at him when he did it, and the two of them never said a word to each other. Coop couldn't be sure how long he had stood there before turning away and retreating into the snow. All he knew was this: if Kay had ever belonged to him, however briefly, that time was long over. In truth she had been gone before she died.

"Welcome home, brother," said a voice nearby. Coop swiveled his head, registering that he was being addressed.

The man was tall and skinny and obviously homeless, almost as if one of the skeleton puppets from the protest had detached itself and come to life. Angular and scraggle-faced, he wore a baseball cap and a green jacket that Coop realized was a faded Army uniform with sergeant stripes. A row of multi-colored ribbons were pinned to his chest.

"You just get back?" said the man.

Coop blinked. The man reached out and put a finger on Coop's chest, where his dog tags had fallen out of his coat. Coop felt the twitch of drill reflexes, the hobo sergeant activating Coop's grunt brain, and he felt cold tingles of pain in the straightening of his spine as he slipped his arms behind his back, assuming the position of parade rest.

"Roger, Sergeant," said Coop.

The man grinned. "C'mon, we're over here," he said, loping off into the crowd. Coop followed.

The sun rose higher as more and more protesters filled the streets. Coop and the old sergeant zigzagged through the thickening crowd, the distant speech and the chants growing to a static roar. Along the edges of the avenue, orange-vested parade marshals waved the onlookers back, dividing the multitude into separate formations. The old sergeant led Coop to the front of the march, where they joined a white-haired crowd of old hippies in camouflage.

"I'm Red," said a geezer in a boonie cap. He pointed at Coop. "Your eyes look funny."

There's blood leaking in my brain, Coop wanted to say. Instead he nodded and gave a thumbs-up.

"Hobbes," said the tall sergeant, "lemme borrow your wheelchair."

Coop tried to decline but his protests were waved away.

"Hobbes don't need it," said Red, "bastard just *lazy*. Get up, Hobbes!"

Then the parade marshals swooped in, forming a chain of orange vests between marchers and the sidewalk audience. Coop had been locked in with the contingent of old vets. The avenue was clear ahead, exposing the bridge and the dim city, and farther out, the hard glitter of the distant sea. Now the crowd's shouting grew louder. A brass band jumped noisily to life.

"C'mon, men," said the giant, and a flag was put in Coop's hands. They wanted to push him in the wheelchair. The marshals parted and Coop was staring down a long and empty bridge flanked by flashing sirens, orange cones, bodies pushing against the barricades. There was no New York, just the protest, and as they pushed forward Coop gave himself to the lift and swell. For a moment everyone waited, a stillness of quiet bobbing. Then came a chant, a seagull shriek of rage, and seemingly from nowhere Coop was lifted and tossed forward, high among the shouts and picket signs, and all around people marching and screaming and banging on their instruments. Crowds of onlookers stood on either side of the bridge. Some were crying, others saluted. As the group of veterans neared them, these spectators broke into applause, their hands coming together, matching the beat of helicopters against the sky.

A chill passed through Coop's back, up his leg and into his damaged lungs, across every beating inch of his body. *They're clapping for me.*

Tears ran down his nose and fell from his trembling jaw. The wind came over the water and iced the streams on his face. He felt a great heat at his back. Coop closed his eyes and saw glowing coals; red rocks, the sun flashing on sand. The parade staggered over the bridge, a grim jangle, and Coop smiled as he felt himself come apart.

CHAPTER FORTY-SIX

The television showed a woman skiing through Times Square. She glided across the empty plaza, heels snapping rhythmically with every stride, while all around big electric screens glowed hot against the blizzard. The camera zoomed back to better frame the shot, a wilderness of neon and gently drifting snow.

Eva watched the news with a dozen of her colleagues, all of them crammed inside a tiny call room. They'd been stranded together ever since the storm began. Anticipating a surge of patients, St. Barbara's had activated the emergency staffing plan, but so far, the hospital had been relatively quiet. Apparently no one was making it through the snow.

"Diya, can you hear us?"

Now the television cut to a reporter on the street, dressed in an oversized parka. Fat snowflakes fell all around her, some sticking to her hair and face. The reporter gestured around herself, speaking with exaggerated facial expressions, but there was no sound.

"Nope, not getting anything from her."

Back to the newsroom, where the correspondent wore a look of good-humored concern.

"Seems to be a problem with her mic. Well, folks, I think these images speak for themselves . . ."

A lone car fishtailed across the freeway. Then a shot of the tarmac at JFK, cluttered with planes. In the next clip, soldiers from the National Guard canvassed a dark neighborhood, searching for people trapped in their homes.

Eva rubbed at her shoulder. She got up to stretch, feeling the eyes of Dr. Adjaye on her. He sat on the nearby couch, squeezed in among the other white coats. Without looking Eva could perfectly imagine his expression in the glow of the television, a kind of hopeful attentiveness.

"Now for other top stories . . ."

The mayor was announcing the creation of a new task force to address the heroin crisis in New York. Meanwhile, in national news, Condoleezza Rice was being asked if the weekend's global protests against the planned invasion of Iraq had shaken the administration's resolve.

"Nothing could be further from the truth," said Rice.

Eva left the call room and fetched a cup of burnt coffee from the cafeteria. She paced the floors. The wind howled outside. Maintenance teams patrolled the hallways, cleaning up leaks of brackish water that had sprouted from the walls.

Eva didn't realize she'd been heading toward Three East until she arrived in the derelict wing. The lights were off but the hallway was illuminated by a polar glow. Eva came close to the windows. She felt a shiver of cold through the glass, the storm reaching for her.

Out of her coat pocket came the cough syrup. The bottle was nearly empty, just a thin coating on the bottom. She tipped it back. Then an electric bell sounded at the other end of the hallway, followed by a figure emerging from the elevator. Dark face, bleach-white coat. *Adjaye,* thought Eva. He must have followed her.

The doctor turned his head, saw her, and smiled. He paced in her direction, carrying two steaming coffees.

"Hello," said Adjaye.

Eva smiled politely and raised her cup to indicate she had her own.

"That's okay," he said. "I'm tired enough to drink them both."

He looked out the window. They stood there for a while surveying the city, lost beneath a desert of white-crested waves.

"Your friend, he's back in the hospital."

Just two days ago, Adjaye had spoken those few words to Eva. It had been intended as a friendly heads-up between colleagues, something quick as they passed each other in the hallway. But the comment had stopped Eva as if she'd been slapped. Immediately she had gone to speak with an admissions clerk. The clerk had sent her to several departments before Eva found a chief resident who remembered Coop. He had arrived at the ER earlier that morning, wheeled in by a gang of old hollering vets. Protesters, it seemed like, some of them still carrying banners and signs.

Yes, Eva had interrupted, *but where is he now?*

The chief told her where she could see him.

Coop was lying on a cot with his eyes closed. He hadn't been prepared yet and was still dressed for surgery. The light overhead caught the pale display of his hand sticking out from under the sheet. The mortuary wasn't busy that night, and Eva was able to stay awhile with the body.

Afterward there were a number of phone calls to the hospital. The first was from a detective. Then came calls from an Army commander, an attorney representing the Bellante family, a young law student from Berkeley. Then more detectives. One of the interns had asked Eva if she wanted to speak to any of them. She shook her head. It was too much.

Now, up in Three East, Eva looked out over the white city.

Out in the snow, a single soldier sat in a booth at the entrance to the parking lot. There had been a small detachment of New York National Guard deployed to the hospital to assist with snow removal and emergency transportation, and this man was posted, Eva supposed, in case any patients arrived from the cold. She watched the helmeted silhouette as the wind and snow battered his small enclosure.

Eva finished her coffee, reached over and took the extra cup from Adjaye's hand. They went back to watching the snow.

"Beautiful, isn't it?" said Adjaye.

"Beautiful," Eva replied, speaking barely above a murmur.

"Like a big blank sheet of paper," Adjaye continued. "I like to imagine someone could go out there and write whatever they liked."

What a nice thing to imagine, thought Eva. If only you could do it. Just forget about the past, shed it like a coat. Go traipsing across the whole bare world, mindless of all that lay buried beneath your feet.

ACKNOWLEDGMENTS

I would like to thank my agent, Nathaniel Jacks; my editors, Samuel Nicholson and Alexis Washam; and the incredible team at Random House.

To the many teachers, mentors, and guides who have schooled me over the years: Bill Gavin, Daniel Burland, Judith Reppy, Mike Phelan, Chuck Wachtel, Kate Bronfenbrenner, Darrin Strauss, David Lipsky, and most of all the late E. L. Doctorow.

Endless gratitude to Roy Scranton, Jacob Siegel, Matt Gallagher, Phil Klay, and other alumni of the NYU Veteran Writers Program. Thank you also to Deborah Landau, Major Jackson, and Ben Fountain.

To my family and friends for their love, support, and inspiration: Yunhee, Josh, Taemin, Yuna, Taz, Sean, Trosha, Grandmother, and especially to my parents, Annie and O.B., for being my first readers. And to Jim Bentley, Andrew Woods, David Donnelly, Rory O'Toole, Josh Cousins, Nathaniel Adams, Matt Crepeau, and Tom Gagne.

Finally, to Hannah Jean, who read the book after one date. Thank you for everything.

ABOUT THE AUTHOR

PERRY O'BRIEN served in Afghanistan as a medic with the 82nd Airborne Division. He was honorably discharged from the Army as a conscientious objector. His fiction has been featured in the war anthology *Fire and Forget,* and his nonfiction has been published by *The New York Times* and the *San Francisco Chronicle.* He currently lives in New York City.

ABOUT THE TYPE

This book was set in Sabon, a typeface designed by the well-known German typographer Jan Tschichold (1902–74). Sabon's design is based upon the original letterforms of sixteenth-century French type designer Claude Garamond and was created specifically to be used for three sources: foundry type for hand composition, Linotype, and Monotype. Tschichold named his typeface for the famous Frankfurt typefounder Jacques Sabon (c. 1520–80).